FAT CAT

ALSO BY ROBIN BRANDE

Evolution, Me & Other Freaks of Nature

ROBIN BRANDE

EMBER

Text copyright © 2009 by Robin Brande, LLC
Cover and title page photographs copyright © 2011 by Shutterstock & Alfred A. Knopf

All rights reserved. Published in the United States by Ember, an imprint of Random House Children's Books, a division of Random House, Inc., New York. Originally published in hardcover in the United States by Alfred A. Knopf, an imprint of Random House Children's Books, New York, in 2009.

Ember and the colophon are trademarks of Random House, Inc.

Visit us on the Web! www.randomhouse.com/teens

Educators and librarians, for a variety of teaching tools, visit us at www.randomhouse.com/teachers

The Library of Congress has cataloged the hardcover edition of this work as follows:
Brande, Robin.
Fat Cat / Robin Brande. — 1st ed.
p. cm.
Summary: Overweight teenager Catherine embarks on a high school science project in which she must emulate the ways of hominins, the earliest ancestors of human beings, by eating an all-natural diet and forgoing technology.
ISBN 978-0-375-84449-2 (trade) — ISBN 978-0-375-94449-9 (lib. bdg.) —
ISBN 978-0-375-89357-5 (ebook)
[1. Science—Experiments—Fiction. 2. Overweight persons—Fiction.
3. Interpersonal relationships—Fiction. 4. Self-perception—Fiction. 5. Friendship—Fiction.
6. High schools—Fiction. 7. Schools—Fiction.] I. Title.
PZ7.B73598Fat 2009
[Fic]—dc22
2008050619

ISBN 978-0-440-24033-4 (pbk.)

RL: 7.5

Printed in the United States of America

10 9 8 7 6 5 4 3 2 1

First Ember Edition 2011

Random House Children's Books supports the First Amendment and celebrates the right to read.

For the real Matthew and Amanda,
For John, source of all my favorite boyfriend lines,
And for Carolyn, a better best friend than any I could invent
in a novel.

1

"**Y**ou're all good little machines," Mr. Fizer told us. He sat there this afternoon in his tweed jacket and his white shirt and plaid bow tie and glared at us over the top of his half-glasses. Which was a seriously scary sight.

"You know how to take tests," he said. "You know how to memorize facts and mimic everything your teachers have taught you—but do any of you really know how to *think*? We're about to find out."

I know I should have been concentrating. I should have kept my eyes locked on Mr. Fizer, practically reading his lips to make sure I caught every word. His class is going to be the hardest thing I've ever taken in my life.

But sometimes my body parts have a mind of their own. And there my eyes were, straying off to the right, seeking out that one particular face in the crowd the way they always do, no matter how many times I've told them to stop. And since this was a crowd of only nine, he was way too easy to find.

Unfortunately, right at that moment Matt McKinney was looking back at me, and our eyes met for just that one split second, and even though I instantly looked away, it was too late. I had to see that subtle little smirk of his, and it made me wish more than anything I had something sharp and heavy to throw at his head.

"Here are the rules," Mr. Fizer said.

As if he needed to tell us. Every one of us understood the deal long before today—Fizer's Special Topics in Research Science class is legendary, not the least because every few years someone has to run out of there on the first day and vomit because of the stress.

I had a light lunch.

"When I call your name," Mr. Fizer said, "you will come up, close your eyes, and choose a picture. You will then have one hour in which to devise your topic. You may not use the Internet or any other resources. You may not discuss it with your classmates. You will have only your own creativity to rely upon.

"We do it this way," he continued, "because true scientific progress comes through innovative thinking, not merely reciting what other scientists have taught us. Albert Einstein believed that imagination is more important than knowledge, and I agree. We must always push ourselves to discover more. Understood?"

No one bothered answering. We were all too busy staring at the folder he'd just opened on his desk, revealing this year's Stack.

The Stack. It's your whole future resting on a pick of the cards. Only in Mr. Fizer's case, the deck of cards is actually a stack of pictures he's gathered throughout the year—pages torn out of magazines like *National Geographic* and *Nature* and *Science*.

If you luck out, you can end up with a picture that applies to a field you're already interested in—like for me, insects and their co-evolution with plants. It's what I spent the whole summer helping research in one of the biology labs at the university. I figured if I ended up with a picture even remotely dealing with either plants or bugs, I'd be able to use everything I just learned about fig wasps.

On the other hand, you can also end up with something completely outside your subject field, which is why people like George Garmine had to flee the room last year to puke.

Because if you bomb, you might as well plan a career as a drone in some laboratory at some obscure college in a town nobody's heard of, because you're never going to get the premium offers. But if you do well—I mean really well—you can not only get Mr. Fizer's recommendation for college applications, but you might also win your category at the science fair and then go on to internationals. Some of Mr. Fizer's students have done just that. And then you have a great shot at winning scholarships and impressing college recruiters, so that even people like me can end up at places like MIT or Duke or Harvard or wherever. So yeah, it's a big deal.

We all just wanted to get on with it already, but Mr. Fizer still had one more rule to tell us about.

"This is not a time for teamwork," he said. "This is a competition. This is your chance to show bold thinking and a true commitment to your science. For the next seven months you will work independently and in secret. I am the only person you will share any details with until it is time to reveal your project at the science fair in March. Is that clear? Good. Miss Chang, we will begin with you."

Lindsay wiped her palms against her pants and walked so slowly to the front of the room it was like she'd just been told to come up there and drink poison. She stood in front of Mr. Fizer's desk, did the palm swipe one more time, then reached into the Stack.

You could tell Mr. Fizer was watching to make sure she kept her eyes closed. Lindsay pulled out a picture, pressed it against her chest, and went back to her seat without even looking at what she'd chosen. That seemed like a good strategy—no point in freaking out in front of everyone if it turned out to be really bad.

Next he called up Farah, Alexandra, Margo, and Nick. Then me.

I eased between the lab tables and walked to the front, and that's when I started to think about my butt. And about how Matt McKinney was no doubt looking at it right at that moment and noticing how much larger it was than the last time he saw it. Seven more pounds over the summer, thank you very much. When you're working in a lab as intense as the one where I was, all you really have time for every day is the vending machines and the Dairy Queen on the corner. Everyone at that lab was a pudgeball.

So I stood in front of Mr. Fizer's desk, my hand shaking, thinking about my future and how it was about to change, but really thinking more about my thighs and gigabutt and trying to pull my shirt down a little lower to cover them, and finally I closed my eyes and reached into the Stack. That's when I heard Matt clear his throat, which sounded like he was suppressing a laugh, and my hand jerked from where it was, and I suppose that makes it fate that I chose the picture I did.

I couldn't look. I clutched the paper against my chest and went back to my seat and did my best to control my breathing.

Matt was next. Mr. Cocky. Mr. Casual. Mr. I've-Won-More-Science-Fairs-Than-Any-of-You. He pulled out his picture, looked at it, and actually smiled. *Smiled.* Not a good sign.

Which caused me to peek at my own picture, and OH HOLY CRIPE. No way. I slapped it facedown on the table and heard my pulse pounding in my ears.

Because Matt McKinney *cannot* beat me this year. Please—there has to be a law. I've only beaten him once, and that was probably the worst night of my life. It would be nice to win for once and actually get to enjoy it for more than five minutes.

Kiona and Alyssa went last, and they both looked about as sick as I felt. Then it was time.

"Go find a corner," Mr. Fizer told us. "Your hour begins"—he checked his watch—"now."

Everyone scattered to find some private space to work. I chose a little nook between the wall and a file cabinet and scrunched myself down onto the floor. Then I turned the paper over and faced the reality of my situation.

The picture was worse than I thought.

Naked Neanderthals.

No, I take it back. Not Neanderthals, but something even more ancient—*Homo erectus*, to be exact. Early hominins from 1.8 million years ago, the caption said. Great. Highly relevant to my own life, not to mention my fig wasps.

Whereas Matt, I'm guessing from the smug little smile I saw on his face, must have chosen something that plays directly into his field—astronomy. Probably a picture taken by the Hubble telescope, or something from the Mars expedition, or maybe a computer simulation of a black hole. Something easy and perfect and effortless, because that's how it always is for Matt.

But I couldn't worry about him—I had to worry about me. I went back to staring at my picture.

It was an artist's rendering of how these early humans might have lived. There were three men and a woman out in a meadow of some sort. They were all lean and muscular and tan—and did I mention naked?

They were gathered around a dead deer, guarding it from a pack of saber-toothed hyenas who were trying to move in and snatch it.

One of the men was shouting. The woman had the only weapon—a rock—and she stood there poised to pitch it at the hyenas. It was a great action scene if you're into that sort of thing—the whole anthro-paleo field of studies where you care more about the dead than the living. But it's not going to be my thing now or ever.

Naked hominins and hyenas. Great. This was going to be my life for the next seven months, I thought. Chalk up another win for Matt and another failure for me.

But that was before I understood just how perfect this whole thing is going to be.

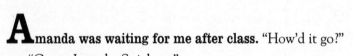

2

Amanda was waiting for me after class. "How'd it go?"

"Great. I need a Snickers."

"Oh, yeah?" she said, perking up. "Does that mean the diet is over?"

"Um, pretty much." Although I knew the real answer was going to shock her.

"Thank goodness," Amanda said. "No offense, Kit Cat, but you have been seriously cranky these past few days. I think some people just need their sugar and carbs."

Matt came out of class just then and gave us both a nod. "Hey, Amanda. See ya, Cat."

Neither of us answered, of course. Usually Matt's only that friendly when Amanda's boyfriend, Jordan, is around. They're on the swim team together, and Jordan is always telling us how "solid" and "quality" Matt is, whatever that's supposed to mean. What it really means is Matt continues to fool most people into thinking he's this sweet, charming guy who happens to be a brilliant scientist on top of it.

But Amanda and I know the truth. And unfortunately, it's not something we can share with Jordan or anyone else. So people go right on believing what they want to about Matt.

"He is looking slightly better than normal," Amanda said, watching him disappear down the hall. "I think he's discovered the comb."

"Can we talk about something else, please?"

"Sure," she said. "I wrote a new poem last period. Want to hear it?"

She recited it for me as we headed toward the vending machines. It was another in her series of poems exploring the secret thoughts of inanimate objects. This one was about a blender.

Don't laugh. Or do. The poems are supposed to be funny, but they're also sweet and sometimes a little sad in their own way. The blender, so the poem goes, can touch food but never actually taste it. By the time it swirls everything around into a liquid form it can ingest, someone pours it out and takes it away.

"Ever chewing," Amanda concluded, "never satisfied."

We both nodded in silent appreciation.

"I really love it," I told her. "It's almost as good as the one about the La-Z-Boy."

"Yeah," Amanda agreed, "that was a classic."

We hit the vending machines, and I bought not only a Snickers, but also a Butterfinger and some peanut M&M's.

"Wow," Amanda said. "You weren't kidding."

I bit off about half of the Snickers and said with my mouth full, "You'll understand in a minute."

I made her wait until we were safely in her car, since I couldn't let Mr. Fizer or anyone else see me showing her the picture. His secrecy rule is fine—in fact, I'm grateful for it, since it means no one will know what I'm doing until I unveil the whole thing next March—but there was no way I was going to keep it secret from Amanda.

As soon as we were settled, I pulled the picture out of my backpack.

"Oh," Amanda said.

"Right," I said.

Amanda pointed to the guy closest to the dead deer. "He's sort of hot."

"Are you kidding me?"

"What?" she said. "Nice butt, nice legs—I'd go for it."

"Good to know."

"Don't tell Jordan."

I finished my Snickers, started in on the Butterfinger, and explained to Amanda how the whole thing came about—how with time running out, my brain finally came to understand exactly what I should do.

People always want to know how scientific discoveries are made.

They like the stories about the apple falling on Newton's head (myth) or Archimedes leaping out of the bathtub and running naked through the streets shouting "Eureka!" ("I found it!") (True.) (Unfortunately for the neighbors.)

For me, it was the hominin's killer butt.

Not the guy's, like Amanda noticed, but the woman's.

"Ten minutes," Mr. Fizer had called out. I was in full-on, meltdown panic. I didn't have a single idea in my head.

Meanwhile everyone else was furiously scribbling away in their notebooks. Everyone except for Matt, of course, who was already done and just sat there reading what he'd written.

I squeezed my eyes shut. This was horrible. Silently I pleaded with my new naked friends to give me inspiration—any sort of inspiration at all.

When I opened my eyes again, there was the woman's butt. And the rest of the woman. And for some reason, it occurred to me in that moment that she was actually kind of cool in her prehistoric way—strong, determined-looking, ready to haul off and hurl that rock while the guys just shouted and looked concerned.

And she was thin. Not emaciated, fashion-model thin, but that good muscular thin like you see on women athletes. She looked like she could run and hunt and fight just as well as the men—maybe even better.

And that's when I realized: I wanted to be her.

Not her in the sense that I wish I had to fight saber-toothed hyenas just to get a decent meal, but her in looks. I want—and I know this sounds incredibly shallow, but science requires the truth—I wouldn't mind for once in my life seeing what it's like to actually look . . . good. Or at least better than I do right now. Maybe even pretty, if that's possible.

It's not that I'm hideous, but I'm also not stupid. I know how people see me. I might spend an hour every day straightening my hair and getting my makeup just right and picking out clothes that camouflage at least some of my rolls, but the truth is I'm still fat and everyone knows it. When I wake up in the morning it's like I'm wearing this giant fat suit, and if only I could find the zipper I could step out of it and finally go start living my real life.

And that was my *eureka*.

Because seeing the hominin woman, just out there in all her glory, naked boobs and butt and stomach and everything, and noticing how lean and fit and strong she looked made me realize something.

When anthropologists or forensic paleontologists find a skeleton, they bring it back to the lab and build a clay model over it to see what the person might have looked like. They have to decide how much muscle and flesh to give the person to make it look like a real body, but here's the thing: they never *ever* make the person fat.

Because obviously each person's skeleton is made to hold a specific amount of weight, right? A small skeleton gets a little bit of weight, a big one gets a lot more.

And that made me think about what some scientist would do with my bones if she found them thousands of years from now. She'd build a body that looked normal for my skeleton, and she'd think that's what I looked like. But she'd be wrong. Because she wouldn't have factored in all the pizza and ice cream and chocolate and everything else I've been using as materials over the years to sculpt this particular version of me.

That's when I knew what I should do. I knew if I made this my project, I'd really have to take it seriously. I couldn't back out. I couldn't cheat. This would be for a grade and for the science fair, so I'd have to do it for real. Once I committed to it—once I wrote my idea on a piece of paper this afternoon and turned it in alongside everyone else's research topics—I'd have no choice but to take it all the way.

Mr. Fizer said he wants big ideas. He wants us to be creative and to really push ourselves. He wants us to throw ourselves into our projects, mind and body and soul.

Well, you can't get more committed than this.

"I'm going to do it," I told Amanda. "I'm going to become prehistoric."

3

"**S**o . . . **what exactly does that mean?**" Amanda asked.

"No more candy, for one thing," I said, polishing off my Butterfinger. I stuffed the M&M's in my backpack for later. "No modern food of any kind—only natural foods they could have found back then, like nuts, berries—"

"You're only going to eat nuts and berries for seven months?" Amanda said. "Are you insane?"

"I'm sure they had other things," I said. "There was that dead deer."

Amanda made a face. "Awesome."

"And probably vegetables and a bunch of really healthy stuff."

"So what you're telling me," Amanda said, "is you're going on another diet."

"No! It's not that at all. I mean . . . not entirely. This is going to be an actual science experiment. On myself. It's not just the food—I'm going to give up everything modern. Computer, telephone, car, TV—"

"And this is supposed to prove what?" Amanda broke in. "Other than that you're crazy?"

"That we've screwed ourselves up," I said. "That somewhere along the way all of our modern advances have gone too far and we've let ourselves get lazy and soft."

"Excuse me," Amanda said, "but I happen to think my iPod is a brilliant piece of evolution."

"No, but look at our bodies." By which I really meant look at mine. "We have all these modern problems like obesity and diabetes and cancer and heart disease—"

"That's because nobody used to live long enough to get those," Amanda pointed out. "They were all getting chomped by wild beasts."

"Yeah, but I think if we just went back to living a simpler life, we'd all be a lot better off."

"I'm sorry," Amanda said, "but I think it's my job to tell you that you've finally gone too far."

But I just smiled. Because the more we talked about it, the more radical it sounded, and that's exactly what I need. Nothing ordinary is going to impress Mr. Fizer or the science fair judges—especially not with Matt in the game. I really need to bring it.

"Besides," Amanda said, starting up her ancient yellow Mazda, "you can't just give up everything. Some of our advances are actually pretty important."

"Like what?" I said.

"Like running water, hello? Electricity? Soap? Are you just going to sit in the dark at night and rub yourself with dirt? And do you get to sleep in a bed anymore or do you have to sleep on the floor? Is carpeting allowed?"

"This is good," I said, fishing for my notebook as Amanda pulled out of the parking lot. "I need to make a list. Keep going." I had approximately forty-seven hours until my next class with Mr. Fizer. We were supposed to use that time to do as much preliminary research as possible before turning in our formal research proposals. I had a lot of work to do.

"Okay," Amanda said, getting into it now. "You said no car—but they had the wheel back then, right? Can't you improvise? Maybe you could ride your bike."

"Right, and let Mr. Fizer catch me? 'I wasn't aware *Homo erectus* had the bicycle, Miss Locke.' Forget it—I'm going to have to walk everywhere."

"Everywhere?" Amanda said. "What if it's dark out? Or it's like twenty miles away and it's raining and lightning outside? You can't put yourself in danger."

"Okay, good point. Maybe I need to make a few safety exceptions."

"Yeah, like your cell phone," she said. "I can see not talking on it in general, but you have to have it for emergencies, right?"

"Right," I said, jotting that down. "Hold on." The ideas were really flowing now. The whole thing was a lot more complicated than I thought—issues of safety, practicality, unavoidable conveniences like showers—

"So when does all this insanity begin?" Amanda asked. "This eating of leaves and berries and such?"

"I don't know, Wednesday night. Maybe Thursday." *Soap, shampoo, toothpaste—* "I want to make sure Mr. Fizer approves my proposal first."

"Great," Amanda said, "because Jordan and I were just talking about you last class."

She said it in a really cheery, innocent voice, and normally that would have been a clue if I weren't so distracted. I knew she and

Jordan had Creative Writing together while I was in Mr. Fizer's, so I didn't really think anything of it.

"So . . . what are you doing tomorrow night?" Amanda asked.

Cell phone, darkness, weather— "Working my face off on this project. Why?" *Refrigeration, soft bed, clothing, shoes—*

"I was just thinking you could take a break," she said. "You know, like for an hour or so. Maybe for dinner."

Finally some innate sense of self-preservation kicked in and I noticed what was happening. Amanda's voice was about half an octave higher than normal—always a bad sign. The fact is my best friend is a really terrible liar. I put down my pen and gave her my full attention.

"Okay, what's going on?"

"Nothing," she said, a little too innocently. She squinted at the traffic ahead of her as if it were suddenly the most important thing in the world. "It's just that tomorrow's Jordan's and my anniversary."

We'd only talked about it a dozen times in the past few days—she knew very well that I knew. "Yeah . . . and?"

"And so we're going out to dinner tomorrow night, and we thought you might want to come along."

"Um, don't you think that would be a little weird?" I said. "Jordan would probably rather be alone with you on your anniversary. Just guessing."

"Actually, it was Jordan's idea." Amanda glanced at me nervously. "Really. He likes you."

"Yeah, I like him, too, but I still say you two should be alone."

She made the left turn. "Oh, we will be—we're ditching you right after dinner. We just thought . . ."

Amanda glanced at me again and saw I wasn't buying it. She

sighed and gave it up. "Okay, fine. Look, here's the thing. Jordan has this friend—"

"No. Stop right there."

Instead she just talked faster. "He said he's a really nice guy—he's on the swim team with him—and Jordan thinks the two of you will really hit it off—"

"No," I said. "No, no, no."

"Come on, Cat! Just this once?"

Amanda has this delusion that guys might actually like me—that somebody out there is seriously wishing he knew some fat girl he could date. But rather than get into that debate again, I went with the easier excuse. "Have you not been listening? I have tons of work to do. This proposal is huge—it has to be perfect."

"It will be! Come on, Kitty Cat, it's just for an hour or two—"

"I can't," I said. "This whole semester is going to be a nightmare if I don't stay on top of it. I've got Fizer's, AP Calc, AP Chemistry—"

"I know," Amanda said, "but that's why I worry about you. When are you ever going to have time to do anything but go to school, go to your job, and do homework?"

"I'm very organized."

"Yes, I think I know that," she said, "but there's this other matter you seem to keep forgetting about—it's called a social life."

"I don't care about that."

"That's what worries me," she said. "Don't you know how happy I am with Jordan?"

"Yes, and I'm very happy for you. He's a great guy."

"There are other great guys," she said, pulling up to the side of the hospital. "I'm sorry, but I have this fear that someday you're going to wake up a dried-out, bitter old hag with plenty of science awards but no personal life whatsoever. And you'll sit there at night and sob about how you've wasted your life."

"Thank you," I said. "That's a really horrible story."

"Good. I'm calling it 'She Didn't Listen to Her Friend.' "

I thanked Amanda for the ride and got out. But she wasn't through with me yet. As I walked up the steps she rolled down the window and called out, "Will you at least think about it?"

"No."

"But how will our babies grow up next to each other if you don't ever go out on a date? Cat?"

I waved to her over my shoulder and escaped.

Amanda has this fantasy that we'll both go to the same college, we'll both meet our husbands there ("Jordan can apply for the position if he wants to," Amanda told me, "I'm not ruling him out"), and then we'll move to the same city, both have fabulous jobs—me as either a research scientist or a doctor if I decide to go that route, her as either a poet/novelist or an English professor—and we'll have at least two children apiece, and we'll all live happily ever after next door to each other, our kids playing together, our husbands taking turns barbecuing while Amanda and I sneak off to the kitchen to bake fabulous desserts and talk all night.

There are definitely parts of that I like. It's fun to sit back and listen to Amanda spinning her tales about what our lives might be like in the future. I kind of like the person she imagines me to be. Except when the story involves me being a dried-up old hag.

So I suppose it's not the worst thing in the world that she—and now Jordan, apparently—wants to find someone for me. But even if I wanted that, which I don't, they're both ignoring an obvious fact: there has never been a single guy who has ever liked me. I mean, there have been guys who have been nice to me—friend guys—but never, ever one who thought of me romantically.

Maybe Amanda and Jordan have gotten so used to me, they just don't see me the way other people do anymore. I guess I should take that as a compliment. But I think it also doesn't occur to them that it's just easier for me not to ever go down that road and end up disappointed. Or worse, really hurt.

Only one heartbreak per customer, thank you.

4

Before I headed down to the basement, I stopped by the hospital cafeteria and picked us up a few things. Everyone likes a little after-school treat.

My mother's eyebrows lifted as I came in carrying my load. I told her the same thing I'd told Amanda: "You'll understand in a minute."

But just then the phone rang and my mother had to take it, and her co-worker Nancy was already on another call, so I just handed them each a bag of Doritos and a few Rolos and settled down to my own snack and work.

My mom is one of the pharmacists who work for the Poison Control Center—the people you call when you find out the kid you're babysitting just ate some dog food, or you're wondering if that rash might be because you sprayed self-tanning lotion on top of your acne cream, that sort of thing. They'll also tell you what to do if you've been bitten by a rattlesnake, stung by a scorpion, attacked by killer bees—apparently there are a lot of disasters out there. It's good to know you can call someone and scream, "Help! My face looks like a beach ball!" and a voice will calmly tell you what to do.

Right then Nancy was calmly telling someone to immediately go to the hospital. My mom was calmly telling someone that no, despite what the caller had read on a website, rinsing her hair with grapefruit juice would not make it grow faster. Proving my mother's point that I should never automatically believe what I read on the Internet.

As soon as they both hung up, we all relaxed. I went over and gave my mom a hug.

"Hi, sweetie. How was school?"

"Good." The phone rang again and my mother took it.

"Cute outfit," Nancy said. "Is that new?"

"Yeah."

"Very slimming."

"Thanks." Nancy and I both know there's no amount of black in the world to make me look slim, but it was nice of her to say.

The phone rang nonstop for about the next half hour. I spent the time opening and sorting the mail and taking care of some of the filing.

Finally there was a little lull in the phone calls. It's funny how disasters seem to come in waves.

"So," Nancy said, "any first-day gossip to report?"

"Nah, not really."

"No stabbings or breakups or fashion crimes?"

"Nope."

"Who's in your classes?" my mom asked.

"The usual."

"Matt?" Nancy wanted to know.

"Of course." It's one of the features of being on the AP/Honors track that you always end up taking classes with the same people.

There are almost two thousand kids at my school, but I probably only know about thirty of them. And still hang out with only two.

I helped myself to the last of my mother's chips.

"I need to meet that boy someday," Nancy said. "I keep picturing him with horns and a hunchback."

"Close," I said.

"Cat, stop it," my mom said. "I don't know why you're so mean to him—you used to be such good friends."

"Yeah, I'm the one who's mean."

"He always seemed perfectly nice to me."

"I'm sure he did."

And then both phones rang, and we were all back to work.

It's not the first time my mother's taken me to task for dissing Matt. I never told her what he did—Amanda's the only one who knows, and that's just because she was there. So it's hard for my mom to understand what changed. All she knows is suddenly Matt was out and Amanda was in, and it's been that way ever since. And believe me, I'm grateful—Amanda is a far better friend than Matt could ever be.

I couldn't wait any longer. As soon as there was a break, I took out my picture and showed them. And I told them my idea.

My mother and Nancy exchanged a glance.

"What?" I said.

"Are you sure?" my mother asked. "Maybe you should pick something easier."

"What are you talking about?" I said. "It's a great project! I thought you'd be excited. And besides, it's too late—I already told Mr. Fizer this is what I'm doing. I'll start just as soon as he approves my proposal."

"Well, we'll have to talk about it some more," she said.

"No offense," Nancy said, "but I doubt you'll last a week."

"Why?" I asked.

"The body isn't meant to take that kind of abuse."

"It's not abuse," I said. "It's the opposite. I'm going back to the way we're supposed to live."

She pointed to my can of Diet Coke. "How many of those do you drink a day?"

"I don't know, four or five."

Nancy whistled.

My mother shook her head. "That's going to be awfully hard, honey."

"Why?"

"I tried to give up coffee a few years ago," Nancy said. She lifted her mug in salute. "You see how well that stuck."

"The withdrawal symptoms can be a little rough," my mom agreed.

"Rough?" Nancy scoffed. "My husband finally threatened to move into a hotel if I didn't get in the car with him immediately and go to Starbucks. And I hate to say it, Cat, but it's going to be even worse for you."

"How come?"

"Those things are full of artificial sweeteners—that's a whole separate drug. People really have a hard time getting off it. Are you sure you're ready?"

Yeah, now that they'd boosted my confidence like that?

"I have to," I said, my mouth suddenly dry. "That's my project."

"Well," Nancy said with a shrug, "guess all I can say is good luck."

"We'll talk about it," my mother said. Then both phones rang at once. Thank goodness for other people's crises.

And sure enough, when we got off work, my mother spent the

whole ride home peppering me with questions just like Amanda had—what about this? What about that? And even though I didn't have all the answers yet, I knew once I finally sat down and started doing the research tonight, it would all fall into place.

That was the plan, at least.

Except instead it all fell apart.

5

It's funny how you can be so stupid and not realize it until you've already gone too far.

Actually, not funny at all.

I've now spent the last several hours researching this, and there's just no way around it: I have made a monumental mistake.

Because what did *Homo erectus* eat? Was it tasty fruits and vegetables and nuts and berries?

Um, no.

They ate carrion. Also known as dead and putrefying flesh.

That picture? It doesn't show the hominins defending their food from the hyenas, it shows them trying to *steal* it. Because apparently *Homo erectus* didn't quite have the whole hunting thing worked out. They mostly lived off of roots and tubers and other plants, and whatever leftover meat they could steal after the predators were done with it. Which usually meant by the time they got to it the meat was nice and ripe and maggoty.

Oh, they ate fresh stuff, too—insects, baby birds they stole out of nests, the occasional rabbit they managed to trap and beat to death with a stick—but mostly they were just skulking around, trying to steal food from other, more successful creatures.

And—AND!—they didn't have fire yet. No fire! Raw meat! Sweet! I'm going to die!

"Well, you just have to quit," Amanda said when I called her.

"I can't quit!"

"So what are you going to do—start Dumpster-diving for leftover scraps? Come on, Cat—sometimes you just have to walk away."

It wasn't the thought of rancid meat that was making me feel so sick to my stomach. I've never ever dropped a class, and I'm certainly not backing away from this one.

"There has to be a way," I said.

"Yeah, if you're willing to end up in the emergency room," Amanda said. "Face it—this isn't going to happen."

"I have to do more research," I told her. "Bye."

There has to be a way.

Matt does not get to win by default.

6

"**W**hoa, haven't seen that in a while." Amanda pointed to the mass of hair I'd jumbled into a ponytail. Thanks to getting only four hours of sleep last night, I woke up too late to do the full blow-dry and straightening this morning.

"Get used to it," I said. My voice was hoarse from lack of sleep. "Hominins didn't have product."

"So you're still going through with it?"

"I don't know," I said. "I still have to figure it out. Right now I don't even have a brain."

"Here." Amanda handed me one of the two Diet Cokes she was holding. "Thought you might need it."

"Bless you." I took a long, deep gulp of it. I needed all the caffeine I could get. My first class on Tuesdays is AP American History with Mr. Allen, the world's only living zombie teacher. Amanda managed to avoid him this year because he didn't fit into her schedule. Lucky.

"So what are you going to do?" Amanda asked. "If you can't figure it out?"

"I don't know. Beg. Cry. Fail."

The bell rang and we downed the last of our caffeine.

"See you in English," Amanda said, then she gently took me by the shoulders, turned me around, and pushed me in the direction of Mr. Zombie's room. I sat in his class for over an hour, and I have no memory of a single thing he said. I think he was talking about toast.

At least the class after that is always going to be good—Amanda and Jordan are in there. So is Matt, unfortunately, but there's nothing I can do about that.

Amanda and Jordan were definitely the superstars in English today. Both of them have already been published—Amanda in some poetry journals and a contest in *Seventeen*, Jordan in a few snowboarding and swimming magazines—so our teacher, Ms. Sweeney, asked them to make short presentations about how they got published and what it's like.

The thing I appreciate about both of them—actually, there are tons of things I appreciate about both of them, but we'll start with this one—is that neither Jordan nor Amanda is the least bit conceited about their accomplishments. I'm sure if Matt McKinney had been published in a national magazine, we'd never hear the end of it. But it took Ms. Sweeney more than a little coaxing to get the two of them to talk about their experiences, and then they were both incredibly humble about what had happened.

Matt made this big show of going up to Jordan after class and giving him one of those fist-bumping handshakes guys use and telling him congratulations. He looked like he wanted to say something to Amanda, too, but she just froze him out. My girl always has my back.

As we left class, Amanda signed to me, *"See you in Sign Language."*

I nodded my fist, "*Yes,*" and headed for Homeroom.

I was halfway down the hall before I realized Matt was following me.

"So," he said, "you ready with your proposal?"

"No." Of course he had to rub it in. Knowing him, he probably finished his last night and still had time to read a book and watch TV. I tried to ignore him as I kept on weaving through the crowd.

He stayed right with me. "Do you like the picture you chose?"

"No." As if it were any of his business. And I could tell he wanted me to ask if he liked his picture, but I wasn't going to give him the satisfaction.

"Okay," he said, "see ya," and I didn't say anything back. I swear, it's been like that since junior high. He knows I don't want to talk to him, but he keeps on bothering me. I think it gives him some kind of sick pleasure just to get on my nerves.

But then for some reason it clicked: Jordan and Matt talking after class, Matt pretending to be all friendly just now, Amanda saying Jordan wanted to fix me up with someone from the swim team.

I would have texted Amanda right that second if I could, but our cells are off-limits on campus. So I had to sit through Homeroom, Lunch, and Piano before I could finally get to the bottom of it. Who cares about arpeggios when your best friend's boyfriend has just betrayed you to the enemy?

The rule in Sign Language is that the minute you cross the threshold of the classroom, you have to sign everything you say— even if you're just talking to your friend. Amanda was already in there. My hands started flying right away.

"*Jordan try make me go Matt?*" That's what my hands said while my lips formed the full sentence, "Is Jordan trying to make me go out with Matt?"

Amanda wrinkled her brows and scratched her index finger down the palm of her other hand. *"What?"*

"You said," I began, then paused. I had to think about how to phrase it, based on the words I know how to sign. The two of us only started taking American Sign Language last year, so my vocabulary isn't terribly huge. Amanda, on the other hand, was obviously born with some kind of language chip in her brain, because she picks this stuff up so easily it's shocking. After just a semester of freshman Spanish, they booted her up to advanced. This year she's taking AP Spanish with the seniors in addition to our second-year Sign Language class.

I went with, *"Jordan ask Matt eat tonight?"*

"No," she answered. *"Why?"* She keeps her sentences easy for me so I can understand them. It's only when I see her signing with our teacher that I get a true flavor for how exceptional Amanda's skills really are.

"Not friend you said?" I finger-spelled, *"Date?"*

Amanda's eyes widened. Then she laughed. Her hand gave an emphatic, *"No!"*

"Okay." I wiped imaginary sweat off my brow. Ms. Wilch likes us to be a little dramatic to help get our meaning across.

"You're crazy," Amanda signed, dancing two crooked fingers across her face.

I nodded my fist once, then made a small circle with it on my chest. *"Yes. Sorry."*

Once class started, Ms. Wilch had us break into groups of three to practice telling each other what we did over the summer. The combination of trying to figure out how to express yourself while having to move your hands and remember to mouth the words at the same time can be really exhausting. Almost as mentally challenging as calculus, in its way.

After class Amanda handed me a Tootsie Pop and unwrapped one for herself. I ate like it was the last morsel on earth.

"You sure you want to give these up?" Amanda looked around to make sure no one was listening. "Cave Girl?"

"Right now a cave sounds great," I said. "I just want to crawl into a dark hole and sleep."

"Now you know why I always have to nap after school."

It's true—Amanda is fiercely devoted to her naps.

I actually dozed for a few minutes while she drove me to work. But then that nagging issue woke me up. I didn't really want to ask, but I was too curious to let it pass.

"So who was the guy supposed to be tonight?" I asked. "I mean, if it wasn't Matt?"

"Oh. Greg something-or-other. I've never met him."

"Excuse me? You're not pre-screening these people?"

"Kit Cat, if I thought there was even the slightest chance you'd go on a date, I would have run a full FBI check on the guy—you know that. All you have to do is say the word."

"Some other time," I said.

"You swear?"

"No."

I almost left it at that, but I needed to make absolutely sure that we understood each other. "You . . . never told Jordan anything, right? About Matt?"

"Of course not. It's in the vault."

"And if he ever even suggested that Matt and I—"

"Not to worry," she said. "Matt McKinney will never get within twenty paces of you if I have anything to do with it. I'll defend you to the death, even against my boyfriend, no matter how irresistible he is."

"Thank you."

"My pleasure."

She pulled up to the hospital. I dragged my sleepy self out of her car.

"Sure you don't want to come out to dinner tonight?" Amanda asked. "It'll just be the three of us—I promise."

"Thanks," I said, "but I'm in deep, deep trouble here. I have no idea what I'm going to do about Fizer's."

"Poor little Kitty Cat," she said. "I'm so sorry. I mean, I still think the project is insane, but you know you're going to pull it off, right? You always do. Have some faith."

I gave her a feeble smile. "Thanks."

"And you're going to kick Matt McKinney's sorry little behind, aren't you?"

I shrugged. "Hope so."

But that was this afternoon. And what a difference nine hours of fear and frustration and incessant research can make. It's after midnight, and it's possible I've found the answer I need, but I just don't know. And that's led to a craving like I haven't had in such a long time.

It's not a craving for ice cream—I've already had two bowls. Not for chips and salsa, either—already had those, too. Not even for sleep, even though right now that sounds sweeter than anything.

I understand the point of Mr. Fizer's secrecy rule—we're supposed to prove that we can think for ourselves and not depend on anyone else's opinions or help. I get that.

But I swear if I had just one wish in the world right now, it would be that things were different and I could just pick up the phone and talk to him. Ask him what he thinks. Tell him I've been having a hard time, and hear him say it's going to be all right—that I'm a great scientist and I'll be able to figure this out. Because Matt McKinney is still the smartest person I've ever known, and it's nights like this when I miss my former best friend the most.

But things aren't different, and that's just how it is. Matt showed me who he is, and I can't forget that.

But I still wish it weren't true.

7

Catherine Locke
Special Topics in Research Science

**CAN MODERN HUMANS BENEFIT FROM
RETURNING TO THE EATING AND LIFESTYLE
HABITS OF THE EARLY HOMININS?**

PROPOSAL: Over the course of seven months
(207 days), researcher will act as own test
subject and attempt to duplicate as closely
as possible the living conditions of early
hominins.

METHODS:
A. *Rules:*
1. Subject may eat only foods that would

have been available to early hominins. This means nothing processed, manufactured, chemically altered, or preserved;

2. Subject must refrain from using any modern conveniences wherever possible. These include motorized transportation, appliances, and electronic equipment.

B. *Exceptions:*

1. Where safety is involved (subject may use motorized transportation after dark or for great distances, may carry cell phone in case of emergency, etc.);

2. Where hygiene is involved (subject may use toothpaste, soap, shampoo, etc.);

3. Where technology is necessary for school or employment (can use computer for school and job only);

4. Where there is no reasonable alternative to the modern method or equipment (can use running water, stove, and oven but not microwave to duplicate cooking over fire, etc.);

5. Where someone else would be adversely affected by the above rules (may drive someone to hospital, answer emergency call on telephone, etc.).

ANTICIPATED RESULT: Returning to the simple diet and lifestyle habits of our early ancestors will result in better health for the subject and will return body to its "natural state."

ANTICIPATED RISKS: Altering diet and other habits may be physically and psychologically difficult.

8

I added my proposal to the stack of others on Mr. Fizer's desk. As soon as the bell rang, he scooped up the papers and began flipping through them while we all waited, silent and on edge.

Finally he spoke. "Farah Halaby, acceptable."

Farah looked like a doctor had just told her she was going to live.

"Nick Langan, see me. Matthew McKinney, acceptable. Catherine Locke, see me. Alyssa Thompson—"

I didn't hear anything else. *See me.* That was it. It was over. I was going to have to walk out of there, a failure before I'd even begun. Matt would get the scholarships, Matt would get the glory, Matt would know he was always the superior scientist and I was nothing.

And there my eyeballs were again, moving to the right against my will. Why do they have to do that? Who's in charge here? I fought them as hard as I could, but they wouldn't be satisfied until they locked onto Matt's face and saw for themselves what he thought about the whole situation—was he laughing? Was he sorry for us? Did he even care?

All I knew was that he was looking at me. I caught that flash of brown iris and then got my eyeballs out of there as fast as I could.

Meanwhile Mr. Fizer had finished reading his verdicts. He told the acceptable people to begin work—at the computers, in the research files, wherever they chose—while the unacceptables (just Nick and me) should come up when called.

"Mr. Langan?" He took Nick outside. Not good. They were out in the hall for at least ten minutes, and when Nick came back he looked even paler than a blond guy with blond eyebrows can normally look. Really not good.

"Miss Locke?" Mr. Fizer called from the doorway.

I took the long walk across the room. Managed not to look at Matt along the way, even though he was sitting at one of the computers near the door.

There was nothing to say. I just stood there in the hall and prepared to take it.

"Have your parents agreed to this?" Mr. Fizer asked.

That wasn't what I was expecting. "Um, yes, sir." Which wasn't technically true—my parents knew about it, but so far they hadn't exactly endorsed the plan.

"An interesting idea," he said. "And ambitious."

Ambitious sounded good. I think. Still, little beads of sweat broke out on my nose.

"However, I do question a few of your items. 'Rule number one,'" he read from my paper. "'Subject may eat only foods that would have been available to early hominins.'" He studied me over the top of his glasses. "Are you certain you want to take that position?"

"Um . . . I think so."

"Interesting. I assume by now you've researched what they ate?"

"Yes, sir." Sweat was starting to bubble all over my skin. I had the feeling this could go very, very badly.

"And what do you believe they subsisted on?" he asked. "Primarily?"

I swallowed. There was no point in lying—he could look it up as well as I could. "Rotten meat and tubers."

"I see. How do you propose duplicating their diet?" He held out his hand to stop me from answering yet. "In a way your parents will approve of?"

"Oh. Well, I wasn't really going to eat bad meat—I don't even like meat all that much. I was mostly going to stick with the plant foods they ate—you know, potatoes for tubers, lettuce instead of grass . . . vegetables . . . berries . . . stuff like that. . . ."

I sounded like I hadn't thought it through for even five minutes. This wasn't going well.

"I think you need to reconsider that first requirement," Mr. Fizer told me. "Live with it for a few days. Poor parameters make for poor science."

Not going well at all. "Yes, sir."

He referred to my proposal again. "Now, for the second half of that rule: No processed, manufactured, chemically altered, or preserved foods. That seems more attainable, doesn't it?"

Finally, something he liked. "Yes, sir." But I was wrong.

"I think you'll actually find it quite difficult to attain," he said. "There's an astonishing amount of chemical adulteration in our food supply. You'll be surprised once you begin investigating it. But I'll leave that to you to research more fully."

"Yes, sir." I didn't even want to listen anymore. Clearly Mr. Fizer hated my project. I was starting to think I might hate it, too.

"Next item," he continued. "Exception number four, giving you the use of a stove and oven to duplicate fire—"

"Oh, okay," I interrupted before he could say any more. "Then I guess I could just use our outdoor grill, or maybe build a fire pit—"

"The problem is more basic than that," Mr. Fizer said. "You seem to think *Homo erectus* cooked his food. Are you aware many scientists would disagree with you?"

"Yes, sir."

And right there my heart sort of lifted. Because I was actually prepared for this conversation. This was the piece of the puzzle I discovered last night—the part that makes the whole thing workable.

"I know a lot of people think we didn't have fire until about 500,000 years ago—"

"Less than that," Mr. Fizer said. "Some say it's very new—only 250,000 years. But in any case, certainly not 1.8 million years ago."

I took a deep breath. I needed to make my case.

"There's a group of biologists," I said. "They just came out with this theory a few years ago, and even though a lot of scientists think they're wrong, I think what they're saying makes sense."

"Do you?" I couldn't tell if he was being sarcastic or if he was genuinely interested in my opinion. But I just forged ahead.

"They noticed that there was this big change in anatomy by the time *Homo erectus* came along—suddenly their jaws were smaller, their teeth were smaller—even their rib cages weren't so distended, so their bellies must have been smaller, too."

"Which means?" he asked.

"It means they didn't have to work so hard to chew their food. Or to digest it. There must have been some big dramatic change that allowed their bodies to adapt in a short period of time—to go from having teeth and jaws like apes' to having ones more like humans'. So I think the biologists are right. I think the difference was . . . fire."

Mr. Fizer was silent for a moment. He gazed at the poster across the hall announcing that the new lunch cards were on sale. Then he looked at me over the top of his half-glasses and said, "Very good, Miss Locke. I'm aware of that research."

Score! "And so if I can cook," I told him, "that means I can make my own food out of whatever ingredients they had back then, and that way I can keep it all as pure as possible."

He nodded thoughtfully. "Interesting."

I almost started to relax. But he wasn't done with me yet.

"I do have one last concern," Mr. Fizer said.

It felt like we'd already been out there an hour. "Yes, sir?"

"Your project seems . . . monocentric."

"Mono—"

"You're relying exclusively on one source of data—personal experimentation. I think the judges would prefer to see a broader range of information—perhaps an analysis of the various diets and lifestyles throughout time and across cultures. Show us how our choices have impacted the human form."

Actually, that sounded like a really good idea. "Okay, I can do that."

"Good," Mr. Fizer said. "Then proceed."

And that was it. *Proceed.*

When we walked back in the classroom, I was so happy and relieved I could barely keep a straight face. I'd survived. Not only that, Mr. Fizer actually seemed to think my project might be a good idea. *Ambitious.* I'll take ambitious.

Before class was over Mr. Fizer handed me a few forms my parents have to sign. Since I'm using a human subject—me—I need their permission before I can do any experiments. But that shouldn't be a problem—especially once I tell my parents how enthusiastic Mr. Fizer is about my idea. Well, maybe not enthusiastic, but at least he approved it. That has to count for a lot.

So now I can begin. This is going to be the most radical experiment I've ever done in my life. It's better than the fig wasps, better than any of my other science fair projects—and better than whatever Matt thinks he's trotting out for the judges. I'm going to win this time *and* get Mr. Fizer's college recommendation. Everyone's going to know what I can do once I put my heart and mind into something.

I can't wait to get started.

And I'm not the only one who's excited.

9

I gave Amanda the thumbs-up as I left the classroom.

She grinned and hopped in place. "Told you!"

Then Matt came out, and we had to play it cool. But once he was gone, I escorted Amanda to the vending machines and bought us both one last round of chocolate in celebration. "Today's the last day I can get a ride," I told her. "The whole thing starts tomorrow."

As we drove to work, I filled her in on everything that had happened, including some of the nuances of my plan.

"I'm going to have to start making everything from scratch," I told her. "I can't just eat stuff from the store anymore. So I'm probably going to have to—ow!"

It's a good thing we were at a stoplight, or we might have gotten into an accident. Because Amanda had taken both hands off the steering wheel to dig her pointy little fingers into my arm. "Do NOT tease me," she said. "Are you saying what I think you're saying? Are you actually going back to cooking? Oh, PLEASE say yes!"

I laughed. "Yes. I have to."

Amanda did a little dance in her seat despite the fact that the light had changed and she was holding up traffic. "Yes! She's back! Chef Cat, Chef Cat, where have you been—"

Before she could launch into a new poem, the guy behind us honked and made her drive on.

"I'll have to be careful about the ingredients," I said. "Nothing modern—it all has to be as natural as possible. Only foods they would have been able to find back then."

"I think I saw on the Discovery Channel that cavemen used to make sopapillas," Amanda said. "And cheesecake—lots of cheesecake. With cherries on top."

"Oh, really."

"Mm, and chocolate chip cookies," Amanda said. "You can make those, right? You make them from scratch."

"Yeah, but I can't use chocolate or processed sugar. Those weren't available. It has to be real food."

"Oh. Well, how about banana bread? Bananas are real."

"Yeah," I said, "but there's still sugar in it. And butter."

"You can't use butter?"

"They didn't have cows back then—there weren't any kind of domestic animals. So no milk or cheese or butter."

"Well, this has the potential to suck," Amanda said. "I want the café to start back up. I'm telling you, Cat, that was possibly the best food I've ever had in my life. I would quit my job at the restaurant right now if you tell me you're starting back up—except we have to charge more this time so I can actually afford gas. Come on—let's do it!"

Our café. It was how I consoled myself the summer between seventh and eighth. I burned through my library card checking out piles of cookbooks, and every week I'd have a new theme: Italian, Asian, Tropical, Greek, French—I used ingredients I'd never even heard of before.

Amanda came over three or four times a week to help me run the café. She'd bring supplies from home or make do with whatever she could find around my house, and decorate the dining room to match what I was cooking that night. She'd download pictures of Rome or Paris or the Parthenon, then tape those all over the place to help set the mood. She'd go through all our CDs to find the right music to play in the background. She made these great centerpieces out of fruits and flowers and candles—the whole thing was just beautiful. Then she'd hand-letter these fancy menus, and we'd relax and wait for the guests.

Which were just my parents and little brother. Everyone got into the act and took it very seriously. I was really a chef, Amanda was really a hostess and server, and my family were the paying customers. It cracks me up to think that I actually charged my parents for dinner, even though they had obviously paid for all the groceries.

Then after Amanda and I cleaned up for the night, we split the proceeds—not bad for a summer job. Especially since it was one of the funnest things I've ever done—which is saying a lot considering how brokenhearted I was at the time.

"When do you start cooking?" Amanda asked. "When can I show up for my first meal?"

"Probably not till this weekend. I have to get ingredients and figure out what I can actually make."

"What are you going to eat until then?"

"What do you think? Nuts and berries."

10

My last bag of Cheetos.

My last ice cream sandwich.

My last snack pack of Oreos.

All washed down with a Diet Coke.

My mother looked sort of horrified when I laid it all out on my desk, but then I handed her the permission form. "He said yes." I hoisted my Diet Coke. "Cheers."

Nancy chuckled and shook her head. "You're a brave girl, Cat."

"I can do it," I said. "I'm motivated." I tore open the wrapper to the ice cream sandwich. "And it's just seven months."

"I could have three litters of puppies in seven months," Nancy said. "It's longer than you think."

"I don't care, I'm excited," I told her. "It's going to be great."

I decided to give my body a good send-off tonight. I talked my mom into ordering deep-dish sausage and onion pizza. I'm not proud to say I ate five slices—I was like a condemned girl savoring her last meal. And then I followed it up with my last bowl of ice cream and hot fudge topping. I was so incredibly overstuffed afterward I could barely move or breathe. But I kind of felt content, too—like I'd given my stomach a little party.

One last thing to do before I went to bed. I unplugged everything in my room but my computer and printer. I stowed most of the electronics in my closet, then wheeled my TV and DVD cart into my little brother's room.

"Want these for a few months?"

Peter looked at me like he was afraid to seem too excited. For an eleven-year-old, he can be awfully suspicious. "Why?"

"It's an experiment. Want to borrow my iPod and CD player, too?"

I could see he was skeptical.

"It's okay," I assured him. "No trick. I just want to focus on homework this year."

That sounded more like me. "Okay," he said, "I guess, if you want." Like he was doing me a big favor.

I also unplugged my alarm clock, which is going to make it hard to get up tomorrow morning—especially since I have to make sure I'm up early enough to walk to school. But I figure I'll gain the time I normally spend straightening my hair. This is a time for serious sacrifices, and I'm afraid decent-looking hair is going to have to be the first thing to go. But that's what ponytails are for.

I just realized I can ask my mom to wake me up—there's no reason she can't use an alarm clock. And tonight both my parents seemed surprisingly supportive of the whole project—especially once I emphasized all the health benefits of giving up junk food for seven months. My dad even said he might try that. I'll believe it when I see him eating fruit after work instead of barbecue chips and a beer.

The one thing my mom did say is that she's making an appointment for me next week with a registered dietician friend of hers from the hospital. She wants to make sure I'm still going to get all my calcium and everything, even without all the ice cream. Ha.

The one favor I asked them is that they not tell Peter what I'm doing. The last thing I need is him blabbing to any of his little friends who have older siblings that go to my school. People probably already think I'm weird enough—I don't need to give them another reason to think so.

Time to do some homework and get to sleep. Then tomorrow is it. Clean slate. Start over and keep it real and keep it pure.

And watch the transformation unfold.

11

RESEARCH NOTEBOOK, CATHERINE LOCKE

Day 1, Thursday, August 21

Breakfast: Glass of water, apple, banana.

Technology avoided: Opened curtains instead of turning on bedroom lights. Had to use bathroom light—no windows. Cell phone and computer off since last night. No music. No TV. No blow-dryer. No wristwatch. Walked to school.

We're supposed to record everything in our research notebooks so Mr. Fizer can take a look at them every week and make sure we stay on track. We also have to bring our notebooks to the science fair in case any of the judges want to check our work. But I figure not everything is everyone's business. Some facts are just for me.

Like the fact that I looked so ugly when it was time to leave the house this morning, I almost backed out of the whole deal.

I never really thought I was vain, but now I understand that's a huge lie. Because looking at my face in the mirror this morning—my unadorned face with its squinty eyes and big red zits and fat cheeks and nothing lips—and knowing I'm not going to be able to wear makeup to fix any of that for the next seven months—well, it sort of threw me into despair.

And my hair—what an unbelievable fright. It's one thing to have to occasionally pile it up with a scrunchy just to get by, but the fact that it's going to look like this giant bird's nest for the next seven months? Somehow that seems almost too much to sacrifice for science. It's bad enough that my fatness is out there for anyone to see. Now I can't even try to distract people with a little eyeliner and hair gel.

All I kept thinking about was Matt. And how he was going to take one look at me and think I was even uglier than I used to be in junior high. I really almost called off the whole thing right there.

And then there was this second moment I almost faltered, when my dad asked, "Are you sure you don't want a ride?" And I thought, Who's going to know? I could have had him just drop me off a few blocks from school and walked the rest of the way. But I would know. I want to do this whole thing honestly. And I really do want to lose weight—which means exercise is part of it.

So even though I looked the way I did and wished I could put a bag over my head, I forced myself to leave the house. I gave myself a whole hour to get to school, but as I got closer, I saw about six empty buses go past and knew I'd miscalculated. I had to sprint the last block and a half. I came skidding into the building, all sweaty and heaving for breath, just as the first bell rang. Great way to start the day.

And the worst thing? I couldn't grab a Diet Coke.

Which meant enduring AP American History with Mr. Zombie Man without a drop of caffeine in my system. TORTURE.

And then I had the humiliation of walking into English the next period and letting Amanda and Jordan and Matt see me that way. Amanda was too nice to say anything, of course, and Jordan was busy talking to Matt and didn't even see me, but Matt looked up as I moved to my chair and I could tell he was shocked by what he saw. I kept my head down the rest of the class and just wished I were out there in the wilderness with my hominin pals, fighting off a pack of hyenas. At least that would have been easy.

> **Lunch:** Orange, another apple, another banana, bag of sunflower seeds, box of raisins, water. That's all I could find in the cafeteria that qualified as prehistoric food. I'll need to start figuring it out the night before and pack something. NO DIET COKE. DYING FOR DIET COKE. And a cookie. How I would love a cookie.
>
> Walked to work. Took a lot longer than I thought. Exhausted. And late.

> **Afternoon snack at work:** Another apple (already hate apples), water, bag of salt-free almonds. NO DIET COKE. No chocolate. Torture.

I could barely concentrate at work. I had to call around to a bunch of hospitals in the state to make sure they have enough antivenin to last for the next few months. A lot of places in Arizona stay hot until the end of October, which means rattlesnakes have a longer season here. But after about three of those calls, all I wanted to do was put my head down on my desk and go to sleep.

"Honey, do you want a ride home?"

I nodded. I'd told my mom earlier that I was going to walk home, but forget it. I had no strength. And it's possible I was seriously depressed. A big fat Snickers and a slice of pizza would have made everything so much better.

So much for feeling strong and powerful and cave-woman-like. Today I would have just let the hyenas eat me.

But tomorrow will be better. It has to be. Today it was all new. I'll get used to it. I'll learn how to feed myself, how to avoid mirrors, how to survive this project for the next seven months. I can make it work. I just have to try harder.

Tomorrow will definitely be better.

12

Day 2, Friday, August 22

OH.
MY.
EXPLODING.
HEAD.

When I woke up this morning, I thought maybe I had died. Or maybe I just wished I had died. Because the pain was like nothing I've ever felt.

It started at the base of my neck, and then swept forward and crushed my entire skull like someone had parked a car on top of my face, and then swirled down through my stomach so I felt like maybe I'd like to vomit if only heaving like that wouldn't make my head hurt even worse.

Couldn't eat a thing for breakfast. Part of me felt like I was starving, but the thought of food made me sick.

As did the light coming in through the windows. And the sound of my feet hitting the carpeting. And my parents' and little brother's shrill voices—I'm sure they were just talking normally, but to my oversensitive nervous system, it felt like they were screaming.

I knew it would take me even longer to walk to school in that condition, so I just started out and got it over with. An hour and a half later, I shuffled into the loud, bright, overstimulating zoo that is my high school and commenced suffering on a whole new level.

I kept my eyes squinted for most of the day. In part to keep the light down to a minimum, and in part because somehow it seemed to protect me from the noise.

With block scheduling, on Fridays we have every one of our classes, but for a shorter time. Which means not only did I have to start the day with American History—which, I realized, wasn't so bad since Mr. Zombie's monotone can actually be kind of soothing—but I also had to go to Piano, and even though they're all electric and we listen through headphones and I had mine on mute, I could still hear everyone else pounding their keys. It was like listening to an army tap-dance on top of a quilt.

The only bright spot of the day was having lunch with Amanda and Jordan. My stomach was still too iffy for me to risk eating anything, but Amanda made me at least sip some water.

"Here," she whispered, looking around warily before she slipped something into my hand. "Ibu."

I understood why she was being so secretive. Even giving someone ibuprofen can constitute a violation of our school's anti-drug policy.

"Can't," I said, giving them back.

"Why?"

"*Homo erectus* didn't have it."

"You did not just say that."

"I'll be okay," I said, hoping to convince us both.

"You're not okay. You look like even your hair hurts." Amanda put the pills back in my hand. "*Take* them."

I shook my head and immediately wished I hadn't. "Owwww . . ."

Jordan whispered something to Amanda, she whispered back, and the next thing I knew there were two massive hands gripping the back of my neck and pushing deep into where the pain was. I nearly screamed with relief.

I closed my eyes while Jordan gave me one of the harshest, meanest, most necessary neck massages I've ever had. His thumbs felt strong enough to push straight through a wall. He dug them into the base of my skull and down the tight, throbbing nerves of my neck, finishing with the knots on top of my shoulders.

It was better than chocolate, better than Cheetos, better than anything I could ever imagine. I didn't want him to stop.

At one point Amanda had to warn me to be a little quieter. "You're moaning. People are looking."

But when you're in the midst of bliss like that, who cares what anyone thinks?

Lunch was over far too soon. The minute Jordan took his thumbs away, the pain came rushing back in. But at least I knew where to push from then on.

"I think I love him," I whispered to Amanda.

"Der."

All was going as well as it could, under the circumstances—which means terribly—until I got to Mr. Fizer's class. I was sitting at my lab table, eyes closed, kneading the back of my neck, when suddenly I heard his voice.

"What happened?"

I squinted up at him. "Nothing happened."

"Why do you look like they just pulled you out of the morgue?"

"Oh, thank you, Matt," I said with fake sweetness. "You always know just what to say."

"'S'what I'm here for."

I groaned. "Would you please go away?"

"Give me your hand first."

"What?"

"Cat, just give me your hand."

I felt too weak to resist. Matt picked up my hand and pinched it hard on the webbing between my thumb and index finger. "Here," he said, "you do it." He moved my other hand to where his was and showed me where to squeeze. "It's a pressure point. It takes away headaches."

He let go of my hand and walked away.

I didn't want to, but I muttered, "Thanks," because it seemed like the polite thing to do. I don't think he heard me, which is just as well. The less conversation with him, the better.

For about ten minutes I concentrated on keeping pressure on that point. And then I sort of got distracted, and I don't know when I stopped pressing, but when I thought about it again the pain was gone.

He was right. Again.

It almost would have been worth having the headache back just to prove him wrong.

13

After school I walked to work. And I'm shocked to say it actually felt good. The fresh air, the quiet, the sun beating down on me—it all made my head feel a lot better. By the time I got there I was bone-tired, but I almost wished I could have kept on walking. As soon as I stopped, the headache came rushing back.

I hobbled down the stairs (no more elevators for this hominin), made it to Poison Control, and then slumped into a chair.

"You look terrible," Nancy said.

"Oh, honey," my mom agreed.

"Is it possible to die of reverse poisoning?" I asked them.

"Only two ways to handle it," Nancy said. "Either go back on caffeine and the chemicals or ride it out."

"I don't have a choice," I said. "I have to do this."

My mother typed something into her computer, and read what she found. "'Symptoms of caffeine withdrawal are most acute within the first twelve to twenty-four hours.' How long has it been?"

"I can't do math right now."

She read on. "'Symptoms may include headache, muscle aches—'"

"Yep."

"'—nausea—'"

"Oh, yeah."

"'—and a general feeling of malaise.'"

"Does that mean wanting to die?" I asked.

"'Symptoms may last two to nine days.'" She typed something more. "Let's see what it says about withdrawal from artificial sweeteners."

"Mom, this isn't helping."

"Oh, sorry. Want some aspirin?"

"Can't." If one more person offered me that, I was going to cry.

I wasn't much use to them today, both my hands being occupied most of the time (damn Matt—that pressure-point thing really does work). The most I did was put postage on a few brochures. My mother offered to go get me some soup or something from the cafeteria, but I couldn't be sure it would pass my rule of being made of only hominin food, so I had to decline. I went up there to look around for myself.

I brought back a banana, an apple, a plum, and a bag of nuts.

Nancy took one look and said, "That ought to make some interesting bowels."

No point in acting embarrassed—nothing is off-limits to talk about in a hospital.

"What do you mean?" I asked.

"You'll see. You ought to have an interesting few days adjusting to all that. When I gave up coffee, I was constipated the whole time. But with all the fruit you're eating—not to mention the nuts—hmm, should be interesting."

"You keep saying 'interesting.'"

"No better way to describe it," she said. "You'll see."

My bowels were the least of my worries this afternoon. I had zero energy. I felt like death. I was finally hungry, but I didn't feel like eating what I could eat, and couldn't eat what I wanted to (like that nice big cinnamon roll I saw up in the cafeteria).

I took one bite of banana, then put it aside.

"Honey," my mom said, "are you sure about this?"

I put my head down on the desk and moaned, "No."

Day 2 (cont.)

Total food intake: One bite banana, one slice dry toast (bread processed and full of preservatives, but safety exception, since subject appears to be dying).

14

Day 3, Saturday, August 23

A little more human. Barely.

I opened one eye, testing the situation.

Head? Still attached. Still achy, but not nearly as bad as yesterday.

Stomach? Still a little queasy, but also so empty I could eat a whole boatload of bananas.

Mood? Hmm . . . hard to tell. It might take some interaction with my little brother to really test that out. Last night he got on my last nerve by asking me, "You sure I can keep your TV? You're not kidding? You swear?"

"YES!" And then I cradled my poor head in my hands because some unthinking person had just shouted.

I think I fell asleep around seven-thirty last night. One minute I was reading about the Abolitionists and the next it was morning. That combo of starvation and caffeine deprivation must do wonders for insomniacs.

But now it was morning and it was time to test my legs. I swung them over the edge of the bed and stood. Tried to stand, I mean. My head got all squirrelly, and I had to collapse back onto the pillows or I would have pitched straight down to the floor. I lay on my back for a few minutes and waited for everything to stop feeling like a bad carnival ride.

And that's when I knew I can't keep living like this. Either I have to give up and go back to my modern ways—Diet Coke (bless you!) and all—or I need to figure out a way to get through the next seven months without suffering every day. Otherwise there's no way I'll make it.

The fact was I needed food. A LOT of it, and NOW. Fruit and water for breakfast just weren't going to cut it. I was truly dying.

What would Hominin Woman have done? Saturday morning, 1.8 million years ago. She'd been scavenging all week, running with the men, maybe supervising a kid or two, but this particular morning she decided to kick back and do a little cooking.

Was it going to be nuts and berries again? No way. They could have that any day. No, I think today she woke up starving, and she decided to make something special.

Like maybe an early version of pancakes—without the butter and syrup, of course. Or how about some bread? They did have this kind of wild-growing grain called goat grass back then, even though it's not exactly like what we have right now. But I can adapt.

The closest I could find to a natural grain in our kitchen was a box of plain oatmeal. So I treated myself to two bowls of it—just oats and water—with sliced bananas and walnuts and raisins on top. BLISS.

But it wasn't enough. I'd been almost entirely without bread of any kind for two days already (except for the emergency toast), and there was a hole in my stomach the size of a loaf.

Which led me to my first big ethical question: Am I allowed to make bread or not? Even if my cave woman had grain, it's a separate step to say she figured out how to mill it into flour. And then another step to say she knew how to combine it with other ingredients to make some sort of bread. Not to mention figuring out how to bake it.

But I do know how to do that, right? If I were transported back there in a time machine, I'd know to gather up grains and start smashing them into a powder. I'd know to add some water, mix in a little honey (they had bees back then—I checked), maybe add a stolen bird egg or two, and then cook the thing on top of a hot rock. I would be the most popular cave girl in the region.

So that's what I decided: I'm not going to penalize myself for my skills, I'm going to take advantage of them.

I mean, what's the point of knowing how to cook if you can't actually save your life with it? Cooking is just chemistry. You take a little of this, a little of that, you keep tasting it and adding a little more, and pretty soon you're feeding your entire cave family a nice, nutritious meal of fried insects and leftover rabbit and a soft slab of bread. Right? It's just science.

Not that I'm going to start cooking insects and rabbit. The point is I can do this. I, more than anyone I know, should be able to live for seven months without a food processor, a mixer, a microwave, and normal ingredients like sugar, butter, and premade salsa. Throughout all of history, the great cooks have had to take what they found around them and make the absolute best of it. We've all just gotten lazy since then.

I can do this.

Cave Girl Café, now open for business.

15

"**W**hat if I hadn't stopped by?" Amanda asked, slathering another slice of bread with that forbidden ingredient, butter. "Were you going to tell me?"

"How?" I said. "I can't use the phone."

"We need to work out smoke signals or something," she said. "Two puffs for 'fresh eats.'" She propped her high heels up on the chair next to her and closed her eyes while she savored another mouthful. "I think I'll just skip work and stay here."

She always dresses so elegantly for her job. She's the hostess at the fancy Greek restaurant downtown, and even though the only requirement is that all the workers wear black and white, Amanda always takes it up a notch.

This afternoon it was a knee-length black skirt, high heels, and a crisp white button-down shirt open just enough to show a light pink cami underneath. A long gold chain, a few gold bangles, gold hoop earrings—the whole outfit looked stunning. She'd swept her brown hair up into a loose bun so the tendrils wisped down around her face. And her makeup was just perfect.

The thing is Amanda never busts out that look for school. She's strictly a cargo pants, flip-flops, and T-shirt kind of girl, with very minimal makeup. She and Jordan had already been going out for a month before he stopped by the restaurant and saw that his girlfriend actually looks like a model. If he hadn't noticed the cool poet girl in his class before then, that certainly would have done it.

Every girl needs a friend who really knows about being a girl. Until I met Amanda, I was just a science-geek tomboy hanging out with the boys—well, one boy. She's the one who taught me everything I know about bringing my scary mane of curls under control and highlighting the good features on my face while concealing the bad. Now I may not be any better-looking in my natural state, but at least I know how to hide more of my flaws. When I can use makeup. Which, I have to say, I really, really miss.

Amanda helped herself to a fourth slice of bread. That's the other thing about her—she can eat whatever she wants and never gain an ounce. She's got the metabolism of a wood chipper. If she weren't so nice and completely unconceited, it would be easy to hate her.

"What's for dinner?" Amanda asked, getting up to snoop in the pots.

"Pasta, veggies, and I guess I'll be making another loaf of bread—"

"Cave people had pasta?"

And there it was—my second ethical dilemma.

Because here was the situation: I needed to get groceries this afternoon. There was hardly anything I could eat in the house, and so I needed to stock up. And while I was at it, I thought I could pick up a few ingredients and make dinner for my whole family tonight. Kind of as an apology for what a monster I've been to live with these past few days.

The grocery store is only a few miles from my house. It was daytime. So even though it was furnace-hot outside, I didn't really have an excuse for not walking. I brought my backpack with me to carry the groceries home.

By the time I got to the store, I was hot, tired, and hungry. And even though I really intended to just get fruits and vegetables and some dried beans or something, I got lured away.

Because right next to the dried beans were all these beautiful packages of pasta. Curly ones, flat ones, spinach ones, whole wheat ones—all of them so lightweight and easy to carry home and cook up once I got there.

And some of them were made of just flour and sea salt—no fancy chemicals or preservatives. That was okay, right?

Except it wasn't. Because premade pasta clearly violated rule #1: no manufactured or processed foods.

But I bought it anyway. Even though I know how to make my own pasta—something I learned during Italian Week at Amanda's and my café. But making it from scratch takes a long time, and it doesn't always come out right, and I was tired and hot today and didn't feel like it.

There. That's my reason.

I explained all that to Amanda.

"Whatever," she said. "This whole thing is already crazy. I say anything you can do to dial it back must be right."

"You're not disappointed in me?" I asked.

She scoffed. "Kitty Cat, the only thing you ever do that disappoints me is live the life of a hermit. Other than that, you can do no wrong. And one day, when you actually allow yourself to have a boyfriend, you will have reached perfection as far as I'm concerned." She checked her watch. "Gotta go."

That conversation really made me feel a lot better. But the true test is going to be hearing what Mr. Fizer has to say. He wants to see our research notebooks every Monday. I'll have to give him a full and detailed confession in there and just hope I haven't violated the spirit of the project already before the first week is even over.

Meanwhile, pasta me.

16

"**T**his is good," Peter said as he shoveled in another forkful of my spinach pasta primavera. My dad nodded and kept chewing.

"Excellent, honey," my mom said. "You're hired."

"Gee, thanks."

"I'm serious," she said. "If you'd like to make a little extra money every week, I'd be happy to hire you as our personal chef."

"Great idea," my dad said.

"But—" I didn't want to say anything in front of Peter, but I knew they probably wouldn't want to eat everything I might make. My dad and Peter are pretty partial to their hot dogs and microwave chimichangas.

But then something occurred to me—a way to make my life a little easier.

"Would you do all the grocery shopping?" I asked my mom. "If I gave you a list?"

My mother is no slouch at negotiation. "It depends. How many nights would you cook?"

"How many would I have to?"

She thought about it for a moment. "At least four. That seems to be how many nights we end up ordering takeout."

Then she added the clincher. "And we'll pay you what we save on restaurants."

Considering how paltry my college fund is at the moment, that was too good to pass up.

Besides, I can make a few meals ahead on the weekends and just pop them in the oven when we get home from work. And maybe on the other nights I'll just fix something my father can cook on the grill. A few side dishes and we're there. And now that I'm not watching TV anymore, I actually have the time to cook and still do all my homework.

One more thing. "Do I get to decide what to make?" I asked my mom.

She understood my issue—it had to be something I could legally eat. "Sure."

"Wait," Peter said, "I want pizza."

Whole wheat dough, fresh tomato sauce, veggies, some mozzarella and pepperoni on their half—

"Okay," I said, "I can do that."

"Once a week?" Peter pressed.

My little brother and I shook hands on it. The deal had been struck.

"How come you even stopped cooking anyway?" Peter asked. He took another bite. "You're really good."

"Uh, I just got really busy. With school and stuff."

"But you could have done it in the summers like before."

I got up to start clearing the table, even though I was the only one done eating.

"Yeah," my dad said, "why didn't you? It seemed like you and Amanda had a lot of fun with that."

I took my plate into the kitchen. This conversation would be much easier if I were in another room.

"Well, you know—I had math camp the year after, then chemistry camp, and then last summer I worked in the lab. . . ."

Blah, blah, blah.

They might buy it, but no one who really knew me would. Because the real question, I could have told my little brother, wasn't why I *stopped* cooking after that summer. The real question was why I ever started.

And only Amanda, Matt, and I know the answer to that.

17

It was at the seventh-grade science fair. I had just won—my first time ever. Or since. I was so ecstatic. My parents rushed over to hug me, Amanda was there, and I kept waiting and waiting for Matt to show up. He was in the convention center that night—he'd been competing, too—and I couldn't imagine why my best friend in the whole world hadn't come over to congratulate me the way I'd done all the years when he won.

So I went looking for him. Amanda came, too. I'd just started being friends with her a few months before when she got switched into my English class. I thought she was so funny and nice and talented, and we ended up hanging out a lot during school. All the rest of my free time I still spent with Matt.

So there Amanda and I were, happily walking along, me so excited to share the night with Matt. But then we got closer to his booth, and suddenly my whole life changed.

We didn't mean to eavesdrop. We came around the corner of his booth and I saw Matt talking to this despicable guy named Willie, and I slowed down and backed up and that's when I overheard them.

I still wish I hadn't.

But the truth is the truth. And science deals in truth.

And the truth is what Matt said stabbed me in the heart.

18

I was deep into calculus after dinner tonight when there was a knock at my door.

"Cat?" Peter called. "Can I come in?"

That was kind of odd, but I said, "Sure."

I get along with my little brother just fine, but we don't really have a habit of stopping by each other's rooms to chat. His hair was wet from the shower and he was already wearing his sleep T-shirt and shorts.

He sat on the floor just inside my door, like he was afraid to come all the way in. "Can I ask you something?"

Uh-oh. For a minute I thought he was going to continue grilling me about why I'd hung up my spatula.

But I played it cool. "Sure. I'm ready for a break."

"Um . . . you know the café thing you and Amanda used to do?"

"Yeah."

Peter picked at my carpeting. "Is she . . . gonna come back? You know, and be your waitress?"

"I doubt it," I said. "She has a real job now. And I doubt I could pay her what the restaurant does."

"How much . . . would you pay?" Peter asked, not meeting my eye. So now we were getting to the real issue.

"Why do you ask?" I said, smiling to myself in relief.

Peter had been talking mostly to the floor, but now he lifted his eyes. "Could I be your waiter?"

"Sure—you really want to?"

Peter nodded.

"Okay, you're hired," I said, holding out my hand. I left it there until he pushed off the floor and came all the way over to me.

"How much?" he asked, taking my hand.

I thought about it for a moment. "Three dollars a week?"

Peter obviously learned his negotiating skills from our mother. "Ten?"

I sucked in a breath. "That's pretty steep—Mom and Dad aren't really paying me that much."

"Five?"

We shook on it.

"You'll have to dress up," I added, just for my own amusement. "You have to look like a real waiter."

"Okay," Peter said very seriously. As soon as he left and shut the door, I snorted to myself. What a funny little kid—so weirdly earnest sometimes, like he's already in his forties or something.

I wanted to call Amanda so badly. Or at least send her a quick text: *uv bn rplacd.*

I know it's only been three days, but can I just say how much I miss my phone? And my music and IM'ing and my blow-dryer and makeup and junk food and normal life and everything that goes with it?

Am I really going to do this for 204 more days?

19

Day 5, Monday, August 25

Breakfast: Oatmeal, banana, walnuts, honey.

Technology avoided: Last night I experimented with using candles instead of electric light. It takes five candles to provide sufficient light for homework—only three if I'm using the computer. Used the computer this weekend for homework only. Resisted checking e-mail or playing music or cruising any of my usual Internet sites. In some ways those things feel even harder to give up than chips and candy.

And just on a personal note, I'm beginning to see what Nancy meant about my digestive system—"interesting" is right. Yow. But it actually feels really good—like I'm getting rid of a lot of gunk. I just don't think that's the kind of thing Mr. Fizer or the judges need to know.

I did, however, include in my notebook a full list of everything I've eaten since last Thursday, including the peanut butter and honey sandwich I made myself for lunch today. The peanut butter came from a jar, but the only things in there were peanuts and salt, so I figure I could have duplicated that at home with a bag of peanuts and a hammer.

But rather than just wait and worry about whether or not Mr. Fizer would approve of all these minor modifications, I decided I'd bring it up with him myself this afternoon. He told us last Friday that we can meet with him as often as we want to make sure our projects are progressing the way they should. I don't want to get two months into this and find out I've messed up.

But when I got to class, I saw I wasn't the only one having a problem.

Kiona was already off in a corner with Mr. Fizer, looking all stressed, showing him the picture she had chosen and discussing it in an intense whisper. I tried to read their lips, but Amanda is much better at that than I am. Thanks to our Sign Language classes, she can eavesdrop as far as her eyes can see.

The bell rang, and Mr. Fizer told us all to carry on with our work. Then he and Kiona went back to talking.

After a few more minutes, Mr. Fizer addressed the class. "Let me remind you of something Einstein once said: 'If we knew what we were doing, it wouldn't be called research, would it?'"

That got a chuckle out of some people, but I was too nervous.

"I don't expect you to have all the answers at this point," Mr. Fizer said. "The purpose of this class is to explore an idea and let it take you as far as it will. If you pursue a project believing you already know the outcome, what is there left to discover?"

Kiona looked a little calmer after that. She went off to her lab table, but before I could get to the front, Margo hurried to take Kiona's place. She showed Mr. Fizer her research notebook, they talked for a while, and then before anyone else could snag him, I rushed over.

"You've made a discovery, Miss Locke?"

"Yes, sir." And I explained about the pasta and the peanut butter and some other potential transgressions from the weekend.

"Let me see your proposal again," Mr. Fizer said. He read it over, then instead of talking to just me, he once again addressed the whole class.

"Miss Locke raises an interesting issue."

Great. Clearly my pasta violation was a bigger deal than I thought.

"Einstein also said that 'everything should be made as simple as possible, but not simpler.' Think about that. You might find it applies to several of your projects." He handed me back my notebook. "Including yours, Miss Locke."

What was that supposed to mean? I wandered back to my table wishing I had never gone up there. Not only did he make an example of me, but I didn't even understand the example.

I sat there for almost the whole period, just staring at my proposal. I couldn't see what to do. *Everything should be made as simple as possible, but not simpler?* Okay . . . and?

I was so absorbed I didn't even see him come up. "Making things hard for yourself again, Cat?"

I quickly slapped my notebook closed. "No. Go away."

"So how's it going?" Matt asked.

"Fine. Great." I gazed somewhere off to his left. I'm still not ready for people to see me full-faced, looking the way I do. Especially not Matt.

"I'm serious," Matt whispered. "How's it going?"

"What do you care?" I snapped.

"I just thought—"

"Please go away, all right? I'm busy here."

And I couldn't believe it—he actually looked . . . hurt. Come on! As if he hasn't noticed we're not exactly friends anymore.

Matt stood there a moment longer, then turned and walked away without another word. Good. Go. Thank you.

But then why did I have to spend the next five minutes sitting there feeling guilty?

But I didn't have time to worry about Matt McKinney's supposedly hurt feelings. Mr. Fizer was expecting some brilliant answer by the end of class, and I didn't have it.

And then suddenly I did.

Matt was right. As were Mr. Fizer and Albert Einstein. I'm always making things too complicated. I have the same problem in math, as Matt well knows—I want to take the long way around a problem, when sometimes there's a much shorter, more elegant answer. Sometimes all I have to do is cut out a few extra steps and I'm there.

So I made a few simple adjustments:

A. *Rules:*
1. Subject may eat only the kinds of foods that would have been available to early hominins. This means ~~nothing~~ as few processed, manufactured, chemically altered, or preserved foods as possible.

Once I did that, everything else still fit. I don't have to eat *exactly* what the hominins ate, I just need to stick to foods in the categories that they had back then: fruits, vegetables, grains, beans, nuts, meat. And I can make sure I'm eating modern foods in the simplest, least processed form possible—brown rice instead of white rice, whole wheat flour instead of all-purpose white—that sort of thing.

Plus this way I can make things like pizza for my little brother instead of forcing my family to live off of roots and grubs.

I'm sure I would have seen that eventually. I didn't technically need Matt's stupid comment. It was just a matter of timing. And what was he doing butting in anyway? He doesn't even know what my project is about. He should be worrying about his own project instead of coming over and bothering me.

I took my revised proposal to Mr. Fizer. He reread the whole thing, then nodded. "Proceed."

I caught Matt's eye. And this time he looked away first. Fine with me. If he was expecting me to come over and apologize or thank him for spurring me to a solution, forget it.

I don't care if he thinks he did me the biggest favor in the world today. It's going to take a lot more than that.

20

As soon as I walked into work, my mom sent me right back up-stairs. Her registered-dietician friend, Jackie, had a cancellation and could see me if I came right away.

I wasn't really sure how it was going to go. I sort of stumbled and stammered my way through an explanation of the project, half expecting her at any point to jump in and be just as skeptical as Nancy and my mother had been.

Instead Jackie smiled. "Great. I love it."

"You do?"

"I do."

"Wow."

"I wish more people would decide to ditch the garbage," Jackie said. "All that junk we put into our bodies—we weren't designed to process that kind of food."

And she wasn't even talking about chips and ice cream.

"It's the artificial sweeteners," she said. "They're the worst—so addictive. I've had clients who had actual drug withdrawal symptoms—sweating, shaking, nausea, vomiting, memory problems. They just didn't realize how powerful those chemicals are.

"And then there's all the high-fructose corn syrup in everything," Jackie said. "It's like pouring sugar into your gas tank—the engine stops running after a while."

She also liked that I've given up dairy, even though I confessed how much I miss cheese. And butter. But mainly cheese.

"The payoff is you're going to notice your stomach is a lot happier," Jackie said. "You won't have nearly as many digestive problems. And I wouldn't be surprised if your acne starts clearing up—both the dairy and the sodas have probably made that much worse. We'll monitor it."

"That would be a nice bonus," I said. "So how long do you think it's going to take? I mean before I start feeling any different?"

"You'll notice some of it right away," Jackie said. "Your energy level should really start improving. And the cravings will get less and less every day. Internally, though, it takes longer—about six weeks for your liver to finish processing all the chemicals and sugar that are already in there. But don't worry, everything's going to clean itself up. The body responds well once you give it nutritious food."

I've noticed something weird about people who work at the hospital. Even though you'd think they know better—or at least that they know they should set a good example—there are still plenty of really overweight doctors and nurses. And I always see people in scrubs smoking outside the building.

So even though Jackie looked really healthy and energetic and seemed all pumped up about fruits and vegetables, I still had to wonder if she kept a secret stash of Red Vines in her purse. Nobody's perfect.

So I just asked her. I'm supposed to be doing research, right?

Jackie laughed. "Don't worry, I have my own vices. I'm not sure I could do what you're doing—giving up sugar entirely. That's a little too strict for me."

"It's just for seven months," I told her. But I think I was really trying to reassure myself.

"Well, I think it's a bold experiment," Jackie said. "I can't wait to see how it turns out."

We spent the rest of the time going over some basic meal plans to make sure I'm getting enough protein and carbohydrates and vitamins and minerals. She wants me to take a multivitamin just to be sure. That's fine—safety exception.

She also—and this is the part I hated—had me step on the scale. Everyone knows those scales in doctors' offices weigh you about ten pounds too much. Plus I was wearing very heavy clothes. I didn't want to see the number, but I didn't really have a choice.

It was worse than I thought.

She also used this weird little machine to test my body mass index—the amount of me that's bone and muscle versus the amount that's fat. Also pretty depressing.

But Jackie was cheerful about it. "It's good to face facts," she said. "We shouldn't be afraid of the truth."

Right. Easy for a skinny woman like her to say.

But at least she gave me some hope. "I imagine over the next few months, you're going to see some fairly significant weight loss. Going from a junk food diet to nothing but whole foods and from no exercise to suddenly walking every day—your body is going to love that. I think you'll be pleased with how quickly things change."

So that was good news, and it almost balanced out the horror of the weigh-in. But not really.

We agreed that I'll come back every six weeks or so to check in and see how it's going. That should make my mom happy, too. Plus it's more data for my research notebook, so Mr. Fizer can see how seriously I'm taking this.

Normally after a day like this—the stress of Mr. Fizer's class, my weird conversation with Matt, and then having to face how fat I actually am right now—well, normally that would have called for ice cream. And lots of chocolate. And probably something salty, too, like Doritos. Oh, and maybe a few extra cans of Diet Coke to wash it down.

Yeah. Well.

What did Hominin Woman do when she wanted to sulk—go steal some baby birds out of a nest? Yuck, let's hope not. What did people do before they had junk food to console themselves with? Maybe she knew where there was some special plant that if you sucked on its leaves, you could get a good sugar rush. Or maybe she knew where there was a little patch of salt water somewhere, and she could close her eyes and pretend she lived in the future where we have chips and onion dip.

Here I was thinking she was so cool and strong and capable, when maybe really she was utterly miserable. How can it be a good life if you can't make cookies every now and then?

Grrrr. That's the sound of my saber-toothed cravings. Let's hope Jackie is right and they go away soon, because right now I swear I could lick even a *picture* of a cake.

Maybe I shouldn't be this way, but I'm glad I made Matt suffer a little bit today, if that's really what happened. It doesn't really make me feel better, but at least for once I'm not alone.

I need cookies so badly right now I could scream.

21

Day 17, Saturday, September 6

Dinner: Baked sweet potato fries. Burnt, and I couldn't even use ketchup to cover them up. Very bad.

The first Saturday of every month is Poetry Night at the Karmic Café. It's this vegetarian restaurant down by the university, and it serves perhaps the worst food I've ever tasted. It's not because it's vegetarian—Cave Girl has no problem with that—but it's just totally bland and either over- or undercooked, depending on what you order and whether there's a full moon that night. Kidding. Sort of.

Jordan always gets two veggie burgers with extra onions and pickles so he can hide the taste and pretend they're real hamburgers, and I always order the sweet potato fries. So far that's the only semi-decent thing I've found on the menu.

But it doesn't matter. We're not there for the food. We're there because Jordan and I both love Amanda to death.

And so does the crowd. Ever since she started showing up there last year, Amanda has actually developed a following. People come up to her afterward and want to talk about her poems. I overheard an English professor asking her if she'd decided on a college yet—and trying to persuade her to stay here and join his program.

As usual Amanda takes the whole thing in stride—I don't think she even notices that none of the other poets get even a fraction of the attention she does.

"It's not a competition," she told Jordan when he tried to point that out one night.

"The hell it isn't," Jordan said. "Then why do you keep winning?"

"There aren't any prizes," Amanda said. "We're all just fellow artists. We all have something to say."

"You just say it better," Jordan answered, kissing her on the cheek.

Love him. For her.

Although I have to admit it's times like that when I almost wish I weren't there. I love the two of them together, but sometimes it hurts just a little too much to always be the third wheel.

Tonight Amanda was the last one to go after eight other poets. When the emcee finally called her name, Jordan leaned over and whispered, "Kick some *a*." Amanda rolled her eyes and then glided up to the mike. And proceeded to once again charm everyone in the place.

As applause rang through the café, Jordan looked toward the door and gave someone a nod. I turned to see who it was.

Matt.

"What's he doing here?" I asked Jordan.

Jordan kept clapping. "I don't know, I told him to stop by."

Amanda returned to the table, still glowing from the crowd's reaction. Jordan gave her a hug.

By then Matt had crossed the room. Amanda looked up and her smile quickly faded.

"Hey," Jordan said.

"Hey." Matt stood there, his hands in his pockets. "That was great," he told Amanda.

"Thanks," she said, picking up her glass and taking a sip.

Jordan borrowed a chair from the nearest table and swung it into the space beside me. "Have a seat."

Matt hesitated.

"I have to go to the restroom," I blurted out, standing. Amanda got up, too. I felt stupid, retreating like that, but I didn't know what else to do.

"What's he doing here?" I asked Amanda as we wove through the tables. Strangers nodded and smiled at her. I don't think she noticed.

"I have no idea."

"Jordan didn't tell you?"

"No," Amanda said as we pushed through the bathroom door. "I know they had a swim meet today—they must have talked about it then."

"I wish he'd told you," I said.

"Me too." Amanda ducked into a stall while I stayed at the sinks, surveying myself in the mirror. My skin looked a little better than it did when I first started the project two and a half weeks ago, but that might have been just because of the weak lighting. My hair was its usual wild mess. And even though my jeans were just the slightest bit looser, it's not like I was a beauty queen. I hadn't planned on seeing anyone I cared about tonight.

I mean, other than Amanda and Jordan. And not that I really care about Matt. Anymore.

Amanda came out and washed her hands. "So what are you going to do?"

"I don't know. Ignore him."

"You can't," Amanda said. "Not with Jordan sitting there. You have to act like nothing's wrong—otherwise he's going to ask a lot of questions."

"I hate him. I mean, not Jordan—"

"I know that," Amanda said. "Just pretend."

We returned to the table, and Amanda sat by Jordan. I took my seat beside Matt. But I wasn't going to look at him.

"I was just telling Jordan how much I liked that second poem of yours," Matt said. "What was it called?"

"'Soup Spoon and the Ice Cream Sundae,'" Amanda answered politely.

"Yeah," Matt said. "That was great. I never thought of it that way—'I am concave to your sweetness sliding down a throat—'"

"What time is it?" I asked Amanda.

"Uh . . . almost ten," she answered.

"Wow, I've really gotta go."

"Since when?" Jordan asked. "We're usually here till eleven."

"Yeah, but I've got . . . this thing I have to do with my parents in the morning." I stood up to encourage some movement toward the door.

Jordan leaned back in his chair and laid his arm across Amanda's shoulders. "I can't take her away from her fans. Not yet."

"It's okay," Amanda told him. "I'm actually kind of tired."

Jordan laughed. "What is with you two?"

Matt had watched the whole thing unfold. He's no idiot. He pushed back his chair and stood up.

"Yeah, well, I gotta go," Matt said.

"Hey, you want to take Cat?" Jordan asked. "Looks like she's ready."

I immediately sat back down. "That's okay. I guess I can wait a little longer."

Matt didn't look at me. Or at anyone else. He shoved his hands in his pockets and stared at the empty plates on the table.

"See you later," he said, then turned and headed for the door.

And I actually felt bad. Really bad.

Again.

What's more amazing is that I considered following him out. And saying something. And maybe even apologizing.

Because what is it with me? Even when I'm completely justified, I can't stand to be even a little bit mean to someone. It's so messed up. Matt's the one who should be falling to his knees to beg me for forgiveness, and here I was suffering over the sadness on his face.

It's pathetic.

Jordan gave me a funny look, but then Amanda distracted him by talking about some of the other poets who'd performed, and pretty soon we were back to our regular threesome, me sitting there watching a nice guy treat his girlfriend with respect. Gee, what's that like?

About an hour later we paid our bill and left. We walked the block and a half to Jordan's car, then I slid into the backseat where I belong.

I could see through the divide in the seats that Jordan held Amanda's hand all the way to my house. By the time he pulled up to the curb and let me out, I had a glob in my throat the size of a pumpkin.

"Are you cooking tomorrow?" Amanda asked as I got out.

"Yeah. Stop by if you want." I walked up the driveway to my house. Jordan waited until I'd unlocked and opened my door before he pulled away. I turned to wave, and Amanda waved back.

Then I shut my door just in time for no one to see that first traitorous tear sneaking down my cheek.

22

Day 28, Wednesday, September 17

Found some good research on the
Tarahumara Indian tribe in northern Mexico.
They're this tribe of supersleek, superfast
runners. Until pretty recently they've lived off
of hunting (raccoons?) and a few crops like
corn, beans, and squash, but lately they've
also started eating ramen noodles, potato
chips, and soda. And guess what? Suddenly
diabetes, obesity, heart disease, etc.

Same in some other native cultures I've
been looking into. The older generation—
people who grew up on mostly rice or
potatoes or corn, with lots of veggies on
the side—are much, much healthier than
their children, who grew up eating fast food
and now have all these "modern" problems
like high blood pressure, etc.

Sometimes it feels like I'm not breaking any new ground at all. There have been all sorts of scientists in the last few decades trying to point out that a natural diet—eating whole foods that are actually identifiable as something that comes out of nature instead of a factory or some food company's research lab—is what's good for the body. Everyone seems to agree that junk food is bad.

But it tastes so good. I keep coming back to that. It's not like you're hammering yourself on the head and someone says to you, "Why don't you just stop?" And then you do and it feels so good.

The fact is candy bars taste great. As do chips and pizza and ice cream and everything else that makes up a modern diet.

It wasn't just the caffeine and artificial sweeteners that were hard to come off of. I swear I had just as bad withdrawals from giving up everything else. Sugar feels very, very good. Some days it seems like it's the only thing that can make you happy.

But I'll admit that now that I've been away from it all for almost a month, I am feeling a lot better. I don't get headaches, I'm not so tired all the time, and I definitely don't feel as fat. Don't get me wrong—I have a long way to go. But I have noticed the improvement.

It's just that sometimes having a few carrots doesn't quite do it for me the way a bag of Doritos or a dozen Oreos used to. I think part of it is psychological—eating real food feels so serious, whereas junk food felt fun.

But it's not fun how it looks on you afterward. I guess that's the point I need to focus on. And the fact that I definitely do have a lot more energy now than I ever used to.

But no wonder all those other scientists have had a hard time convincing us to stop eating all the goodies. Nothing says love like a cookie.

23

Day 38, Saturday, September 27

Saturday morning feast for the family:
Omelets with mushrooms, onion, green
pepper, tomatoes, a little basil, a little
oregano. Potatoes and onions sautéed in just
water—that actually works. Fresh-squeezed
orange juice. Homemade bread with honey.
Everyone sufficiently bloated.

Amanda showed up a little before ten.

"Nice tie, Petey," she said, giving it a tug. It's Peter's and my compromise—whenever he's my waiter he can wear a T-shirt and shorts as long as they're clean, but he also has to wear a tie. This morning he had on the one with blue and green frogs all over it. I think I gave that tie to my dad when I was about five.

"So how's my replacement doing?" Amanda asked.

"Excellent," I said. "He doesn't really have your eye for decoration, but he's great at waiting and busing tables. Don't you think so?" I asked Peter.

He shrugged, but I could see he was pleased. He's always a little shy around Amanda—I think he's got a big crush.

As soon as we got to my room, Amanda turned her attention to me. "Okay, Grandma, that's it. I'm here on an intervention. I've taken about all of this I can. Put your shoes on and let's go."

"What are you talking about?"

"We're going shopping."

"No, we're not."

"You don't have a choice," she said. "Get in the car."

I hate shopping possibly more than anything in the world, and Amanda knows it. Nothing ever fits, I always look fat—no, thank you.

But I knew she wouldn't put up with those excuses, so I had to stick to science.

"Hominins didn't have malls."

"Tough," Amanda said. "Let's go."

"They didn't even have clothes," I pointed out.

"They also didn't have nice police officers to arrest them for public indecency."

"Besides," I said, "I think I should keep it real and make my own clothes."

"Cat, the only thing I've ever seen you sew was that purse you made out of a pillowcase in eighth grade. And no offense, but it was really hideous."

"I can learn."

"You can also stop being such a lunatic," Amanda said. "Honestly, I worry about you."

"I'm just trying to play it by the book."

"How about this book?" Amanda said. "How about the book where my best friend, who is a mere seventeen, is starting to remind me of my grandmother, who never bought a new stitch of clothing after she was about . . . oh, twenty-two, and even though at eighty she weighed about half what she did when she was younger, she kept wearing the same pants but just hiked them up to her boobs and double-wrapped her belt and thought she looked fine and dandy. How about that story?"

"I don't care for that story."

"Well, then, we're going to do something about it. Because your clothes are starting to look just as frightening as hers."

I was running out of arguments. "It's daytime," I tried. "I'd have to walk, and I don't really have time today—"

"Distance exception. I swear, Kitty Cat, if you don't start acting reasonably in the next five minutes, I'm going to throw a rope over you and drag you to the mall and dress you in nothing but miniskirts and fishnets. Is that what you want?"

I tried to stare her down, but Amanda always wins at that. I groaned. "Fine."

But I still felt conspicuous driving around where anyone could see me. What if Mr. Fizer decided to go to the mall today? How was I going to explain myself? At least Amanda let me turn the stereo off so I didn't have that technology violation on my conscience.

As we got closer to the mall, I scrunched down in my seat so no one would see me.

Amanda shook her head. "You are really taking this too far."

"I'm just trying to do it right. I shouldn't even be here."

"You just don't like to shop," Amanda said. "Besides, you're the one who makes up all the rules for your project, right? No one's telling you how to do this."

"But it's bigger than that," I said. "I want to *win*. And that means being really, really careful."

"I understand that," Amanda said, negotiating the turn into the parking lot. "I'm just saying you can probably win without completely losing your grip on reality."

I considered that for a moment. I looked up at her from where I was crouched against the door. "Do you really think I'm acting weird?"

"Ha! You mean other than what you're doing right now? How about the fact that you refuse to answer the phone or wear a watch or even look at a text message anymore? And you've given up watching all those science and cooking shows I know you adore, even though no one but you is ever going to check up on what you're doing."

"I have to be honest—"

"And if I'm not mistaken," Amanda continued, "I believe that was olive oil you had smeared all over yourself yesterday instead of lotion—"

"It's more natural—"

"It's a *salad* dressing. Come on, Cat! Why are you torturing yourself like this? Just so you can prove something to Matt? Is it really worth it?"

"That's not why I'm doing it."

"Right. We just met, so I don't know you at all."

Amanda parked the car. I straightened up in my seat, and we both sat there for a minute without talking. Then I had to give in.

"That's not the *only* reason I'm doing it."

"I know." Amanda gave my arm a little poke. "Just promise me you won't stop talking because your people only knew how to grunt. I'm sure they figured out some sort of hand signals." Then she used hand signals of her own. *"You're weird, but I love you."*

I smiled and signed back, *"Thank you."*

"Let's go."

The mall had only just opened, so there wasn't much of a crowd yet. Amanda guided me into American Edge, where the sound system was blasting so loudly I thought my eardrums would melt. Just over a month without music, and it's like my ears have already closed up from disuse.

I shouted above the noise, "I really can't handle this right now."

Amanda, to her credit, didn't complain. She just linked her arm in mine and pulled me to the next store.

Much better. Still music, but at a human level.

"Okay," Amanda said, "here's what I need to see: at least two pairs of pants, maybe a skirt if you're feeling kicky, and three or four decent-looking tops. Think you can handle that?"

"I can't promise."

But Amanda is good. They should give her a black belt in shopping. She's fast, she's efficient, and she's all about the sale rack.

It only took half an hour to accomplish her mission. While I waited in the dressing room, Amanda brought in pants and tops in various sizes, since we really didn't know what size I am anymore.

"I wasn't going to ask," Amanda said, "but just out of curiosity—how much weight have you lost?"

"I don't know. I can't use a scale—technology."

Amanda rolled her eyes.

"Anyway, I decided I'm only going to weigh myself when I'm at Jackie's office."

"Why? Here." She passed me three pairs of the same pants, all different sizes. "I mean, you know you've lost weight, right? Why not enjoy knowing how much?"

"Just a minute." I didn't want to yell it over the top of the dressing room in case anyone was within listening distance, so I waited until I found the right size and pulled the pants on. I opened the door.

"Cute!" Amanda said. "Do you see how cute those are?"

I motioned for her to come closer. "I'm not weighing myself because anytime I've been on a diet, whenever I weigh myself I'm either depressed that I've lost so little—which makes me want to eat—or I'm happy that I've lost so much—which makes me want to eat."

"Oh."

"Right. So I'm trying to work around that particular defect, and avoid it as long as I can."

"Okay, fine," she said. "But would you look at yourself in those pants and tell me you do not look twenty times better?"

I closed myself in the dressing room again and took a good honest look in the mirror.

Wow. Not a huge wow, but a mini one, at least. The pants actually fit—plus they were girl pants. I usually wear men's Levi's.

"Well?" Amanda called.

"Yes."

"Yes, you look great? Yes, I'm a genius? What?"

I opened the door and smiled. "Thank you."

Amanda beamed. "Next time don't fight me so much."

Her cell phone rang. I've missed that sound.

"Hi, sweetie." She listened for a moment. "Aw, really? I'm sorry. We'll come get you. When will you be done?"

She flicked the phone closed. "I know you'd love to stay here and shop all day, but bad news. Jordan's car died on the way to his swim meet. He said he'll be done pretty soon. We need to go pick him up."

"Okay, I'll just walk home." Even though the minute I said it, I realized that would take me hours.

Amanda laughed. "Nice try. You're coming with me."

"It's the swim team," I pointed out. "As in Matt?"

"You're wearing your special new force-field pants now. He won't even be able to see you."

24

I love the smell of a pool. I don't know what it is—the chemicals, the sunscreen, the wet hair, whatever. I know I'm weird. My nose just has this thing for it.

Hardly anybody knows it, but I used to be on the swim team. Matt and me. We both joined the city league when we were eight, and from then on, every summer we'd ride our bikes together to the neighborhood pool for the morning practice, then stay in the water all day racing each other and swimming laps and drills. Matt's specialty was freestyle, mine was butterfly. Both of us were pretty good. I even won some medals over the years. Matt won more.

Somehow I thought maybe I could sneak in there with Amanda today and not have to see him. But he was just at that moment climbing out of the pool, and so of course I had to look.

If he were a nice guy, I suppose I'd think he has a nice body. Big shoulders, good tan, tight stomach, muscular thighs—the kinds of things you don't normally notice under those jeans and plain T-shirts he always wears. Plus when his hair's wet from the pool it looks all dark and spiky and thick, and somehow makes his face seem almost—I hate to say it—handsome. He has these dark eyes and even a little bit of stubble if he goes a couple of days without shaving. I suppose if anyone wanted to look at him separately from his personality—which isn't possible, because he's a pig—they might actually think he's hot.

Jordan spotted us and came over to say hi while he waited for his next heat.

"You're dripping on me!" Amanda complained, which made Jordan give her a big wet bear hug. He started going for me, too, but I put my hands up.

"It's almost over," Jordan said. "Just a few more races."

Amanda and I grabbed a couple of empty plastic chairs.

There weren't that many people there—just a few parents and some boyfriends and girlfriends of the swimmers. I didn't see Matt's parents. No surprise, since they hardly ever came when we were younger.

Next up was the IM—the individual medley. Both Jordan and Matt were competing, along with four other swimmers. I couldn't help it—I was curious. I had to watch.

The IM was my event, too. One lap of each—butter, back, breast, and free. All out, full power, showing what you can do in every stroke. Matt and I used to race each other in that all the time. I even used to beat him when we were little.

I didn't realize until that moment how much I actually miss it—that feeling of freedom and power and strength in the water. I have these big arms and shoulders, and I always loved the way they felt during a good long workout or race. Some girls are made for running, with their skinny little bodies and total lack of boobage, but I always knew I was made for swimming. There has to be an evolutionary reason for these shoulders.

But that was then, this is now. I can't even imagine what I'd look like in a bathing suit anymore. I was already starting to chunk out too much the last time I wore one—I just didn't want to admit it until someone else pointed it out.

The swimmers sprinted the last length of the pool. And Matt won, of course. Jordan came in a close second. Jordan shook Matt's hand and then got out of the pool to go talk to some other guy wearing the team swimsuit.

I saw Jordan point over at us. I figured he was showing off his girlfriend.

Wrong. The two of them came over, and Jordan said, "Cat, this is Greg. Greg, Cat."

Greg leaned over, dripping on me, and shook my hand. I sort of looked away, since he was wearing just his Speedo.

Wait a minute, I thought. Greg?

Amanda realized it, too. She passed me a look. This was the guy Jordan had wanted to invite on that surprise double date back at the start of school.

I could see why he thought Greg might be my type. The guy is *big*. Not entirely muscular big—there's some definite flab going on. Not that I should talk, but I noticed it.

I acted appropriately cool. "Amanda, I really need to get back. I have a lot of homework today."

"Yeah," Greg said, "Jordan says you're a real brain."

I smiled in what I thought was a polite but uninterested way. "Not really. I have to work at it."

Greg folded his big arms over his big chest. "I heard you're really good at math."

"Sort of."

"Come on, Cat," Jordan said. "Stop acting so modest. She's at the top of our class—math, science—"

I noticed Matt out of the corner of my eye, watching us.

"Speaking of math," I said, "I've got about twenty curve sketches to do for Calc. I really have to go."

But that Greg guy couldn't take a hint. "Hey, I heard you used to swim."

I shot Jordan a look. He shrugged innocently. I looked past him to Matt, who was now talking to their coach.

"Bet you were killer," Greg said. "What was your stroke?"

"Butter," I mumbled.

Greg grinned. "Hey, me too. Why'd you stop?"

As if that were any of his business! I cleared my throat and subtly pressed my leg against Amanda's.

She understood perfectly. "Sweetie, we should probably get going," she told Jordan. "I promised Cat I'd get her back."

"Okay, I'm just going to rinse off and change," he said.

Greg felt compelled to shake my hand again—what is it with guys? "It was really nice meeting you."

"Yeah," I lied. "You too." I just wanted him to go away. Matt wasn't staring at us anymore, but the whole thing still made me feel really uncomfortable.

"What's going on?" I demanded as soon as Amanda and I were alone. "Was this a trick to make me meet that guy?"

Amanda held up her hand. "I swear. No tricks." She picked at a loose thread on her sleeve. "But . . . what did you think of him?"

"Not much."

"Not too bad-looking," Amanda said.

"Not interested," I answered firmly.

Matt passed in front of us, still in his Speedo. He didn't look at me, I didn't look at him. He crossed to the far end of the pool and retrieved his towel. Then he passed in front of me again, but this time turned his head just enough to make eye contact.

Which proved I was watching him. Which I instantly fixed by looking away.

I know I was supposed to say, "Good race, Matt," or, "Congratulations," but forget it. I'm sure Matt McKinney is not starving for attention or accolades. He didn't need me to tell him he had just won the race.

"Not bad," Amanda said when Matt was far enough away. "He's filling out nicely. Like the legs."

"Hate the person."

"Well," Amanda agreed, "yeah."

We wandered to the parking lot to wait for Jordan. He and Greg came out together.

For a tense moment, I thought Jordan might try to invite Greg along with us, but to my relief Greg got into his own car and left. But not before saying goodbye to me again.

Goodbye. Now go.

Once we were all safely within Amanda's car, I slumped back against the seat. Then I told Jordan in as nice of a tone as I could muster, "Please don't ever, *ever* do that to me again."

"Do what?"

"You know what."

Jordan sighed. "You know, Cat, someone might like you someday. I mean, someone besides us. Would that be so bad?"

"Yes," I said. "I am a circle of three. No room at the inn."

"What if I told you Greg thinks you're nice?"

"Then I'd say he wasn't paying very close attention."

At least that got a laugh out of both of them.

"I didn't think he was that great," Amanda said, which really surprised me.

But I went with it. "See?"

"What do you mean?" Jordan protested. "He's a solid guy."

"Eh," Amanda said. "Kind of boring."

"He talked to you for about thirty seconds," Jordan said.

"I could tell," Amanda said. "He just didn't strike me as right for our Kit Cat."

I couldn't believe it. Amanda was actually discouraging me from being interested in a guy.

"You're elitist," Jordan said.

"Choosy," Amanda countered. "That's why I'm with you."

The rest of the ride was pretty silent, except for some polite questions about how Jordan's other races had gone. When they dropped me off, they didn't seem all that pleased with each other.

I signed to Amanda, "*Okay?*"

She nodded and answered out loud, "He still loves me."

"Elitist," Jordan muttered, but I saw the edges of a smile.

Amanda reached over and squeezed his wrist. Jordan lifted her hand and kissed it. All was well.

"Thanks," I told Amanda as I retrieved my bags. "For the shopping."

"You're welcome. You look great. Doesn't she look great in those pants?"

"The men were going wild," Jordan said. "Too bad you're so cold-hearted."

"They'll get over it," I said.

"The whole team?" Jordan asked, smiling.

I knew he was kidding, but still. As soon as they drove off, I went inside and did something I promised myself I wouldn't do.

I weighed myself.

Oh, happy day.

25

Day 40, Monday, September 29

Breakfast: Oatmeal with raisins, sliced pears, walnuts.

Lunch: Lentil and barley soup left over from last night (kept it hot in my thermos). (I know hominins didn't have thermoses, but I can't eat that stuff cold. Gag-reflex exception.) Also banana and water.

This morning at breakfast Peter asked me if he could start walking with me to school.

"Okay, I guess, but why?" I asked. "Wouldn't you rather just get a ride with Dad?"

"Nah, I want to walk with you."

How sweet! But it was still my duty to talk him out of it. "I have to leave a lot earlier than you would. You'd get there about half an hour ahead of the bell."

"That's okay," he said. "Can I?"

How could I refuse?

We didn't really say much for the first few blocks—my little brother's not much of a talker. But then I decided I might as well try to make conversation.

"So, how's school?" I asked.

"Good."

"How's soccer?"

"Good."

"How's life as my waiter?"

"Good."

"No complaints?"

"Nope."

"Any suggestions?"

"Nope."

"Should I make pizza tomorrow night?"

"Sure."

Probably not looking at a future as a talk show host, that boy. I decided to delve a little deeper.

"So, tell me the truth—why did you decide to start walking with me all of a sudden?"

Peter acted like he hadn't heard me. He concentrated very hard on the rock he was kicking.

"Hello?" I said. "Speaking to you."

"I dunno," he muttered.

"Well, if you did know, what would it be?"

Peter shrugged. Then he mumbled it so low I could barely hear him. "'Cause I'm fat."

That stopped me cold. "What?"

He shrugged again and kept on kicking his rock.

"Peter, you're not fat. Why would you say that?"

He simply repeated the shrug.

The truth is he isn't fat, exactly, but he does have our dad's build. And mine. And even though the food I've been cooking the past month and a half has definitely dropped a few pounds from everyone, Peter is still pretty stocky.

And it's not like he isn't active—the kid plays soccer twice a week and baseball and football when they're in season—but there's some definite pudge on him, to tell the truth. Not that he isn't still cute, in his way. Plus he's a really nice, considerate kid. There's just nothing wrong with him the way he is.

"You're not fat," I tried again. "You're just big like Dad—we both are."

Peter looked up at me. "No, you're not. You've gotten skinnier."

"Yeah, I guess a little."

"No," he insisted, "a lot. You look better."

"Well, thanks . . . I guess."

We walked in silence for a while, then he added, "I want to look like you."

"Peter—" What was I supposed to say? I stopped and gave his shoulder a little squeeze. "You're very cute—Amanda says so all the time. You'd be cute whether you lost weight or not."

"Trina said I'm fat."

Okay, *now* we were getting somewhere. And that somewhere was a place I was all too familiar with. My voice suddenly got hard. "Who's Trina?"

"Forget it," Peter said. "See ya." Then he took off and ran the last few blocks to his school.

I stood there and stared after him. Such a cute boy—what's some mean, horrible girl doing telling my little brother he's fat? Where does she get off?

I hardly ever have violent thoughts, but right at that moment I could have dished out some serious big-sister whomping. Trina, you little witch. I *hate* kids like that. Mean, snotty, cruel. A kid like that can ruin your whole life.

I ought to know.

26

Today was my second appointment with Jackie. And for once in my life I was actually pretty psyched about the weigh-in.

"Nice work," Jackie said, reading off the number. "How are you feeling these days?"

"Great!" I may have said it a little too enthusiastically. I was just so happy about the scale.

"How are the cravings?"

"Much better," I said. "I mean, I'd still love a Butterfinger every now and then, but it really has gotten easier."

"I'm glad," Jackie said. "And do you see how your skin has cleared up?"

It's true. Almost all my acne is gone. It's really amazing.

We went over what I've been eating lately, and Jackie made a few suggestions, and then our time was up. Since she's seeing me as a favor to my mom, she's just squeezing me in when she can.

I left her office feeling happier than I have in a long time.

Because the best thing isn't even the fact that I'm definitely losing weight—although trust me, that's fantastic.

The best thing is how different I feel. Before I started the project—back in my caffeine and potato chip and sugar days—I'd have these horrible afternoon slumps when I just wanted to lay my head down in class and take a nap. And I just felt . . . squishy. Slow and lumpy and lethargic.

I had no idea that this project would make me feel so much better. It's like I've finally drained off all the sludge in my body, and now I'm all light and energetic.

I can sympathize with Peter. And now that I know the real reason, I don't mind at all if he wants to tag along. If my little brother wants to remake himself and feel better like this, I'm happy to give him some help.

Not—let me be clear—to impress some girl, but for himself. In fact, I hope once he feels better he'll realize this Trina girl is just a little snot and he shouldn't even care what she thinks.

It's finally starting to feel a little bit like fall here. It was cold and windy as Peter and I walked to school this morning. I stopped by the bathroom before my first class and couldn't help noticing how nice my face looked—cheeks rosy from the wind, eyes bright. I think I looked better this morning than I ever have with makeup. Even my lips had some color on them, and it wasn't from gloss.

I don't mean to be vain, but this is a scientific experiment, and I am required to make observations: I look good. Not great, not perfect, but definitely better than six weeks ago.

Thank goodness I ended up with a picture of naked hominins instead of beetles or black holes or something useless like that. Otherwise who knows what my life would be like right now?

27

Amanda was waiting at my house when I got home from work.

"Hey, what are you doing here?"

She wouldn't answer until we were safely in my room.

"Jordan's car is still acting up, so I had to take him to practice today. And Greg was there."

"Yeah, so?"

"So, he was asking about you. I think maybe you should give him a shot."

"Wait a minute—you said he wasn't good enough for me, remember? You said he seemed kind of boring, as I recall."

"Yeah, but I heard him talk a little more today, and maybe he's not so bad."

" 'Not so bad,' huh?" I said. "A really glowing recommendation."

"Anyway, I gave him your phone number."

"Amanda!"

"What? He's entitled to call."

"Since when?"

"Since he said lots of nice things about you, like how pretty he thinks you are."

That sort of brought me up short, but still.

"I do *not* want him calling me," I said. "I won't talk to him."

"I think he might be okay. And Jordan certainly thinks so."

"First of all," I said, "I don't have time for any of this. Do you not understand my course load this semester? Second, I don't even like the guy—"

"You only talked to him for two minutes."

"On purpose," I said. "Third, you already said he isn't right for me, and we both know I have nothing in common with him."

Amanda sighed. "Cat, I just think it's time, you know?"

"Time for what?"

"To test the waters a little. You've got this slinky little bod now—"

I chuffed. "Hardly."

"And you'd better get used to boys noticing."

"I'm not interested," I said.

"He said he's going to call you."

"Too bad—hominins don't use the phone."

28

He did call. He waited a day and then called me last night. I asked my mother to take a message. It didn't matter—he found me at lunch today anyway.

"Hey."

Amanda kicked me under the table. "Hey," she answered Greg.

Jordan shook his hand. I just don't get that. Girls never shake hands.

"Hey, Cat," Greg said.

I gave him a quick nod and pulled out my chemistry notes from this morning. My face felt hot. My pulse decided to skip around.

I never talk to guys. Other than Jordan, I never have to.

"Have a seat," Jordan said, and I shot him a look, but he either didn't notice or didn't care.

"I didn't know you had this lunch," Amanda said.

"I usually go off campus," Greg said. "But now that I know you guys are hanging out . . ."

Amanda kicked me again. I pretended to read my notes.

Greg cleared his throat. "So, Cat, I was wondering. What do you like to do for fun?"

I didn't look up. "Nothing. I don't do fun."

Greg chuckled. "Yeah, right."

"I don't," I insisted, pressing my leg against Amanda's. She pressed back.

"So, Greg," she said, "tell Cat what you were saying about your entrepreneur class." To me she said, "Greg's taking the entrepreneur class."

"I just heard." I kept on trying to read. My skin felt all clammy.

Meanwhile Greg launched into some lengthy discussion about market studies and prototypes and this great idea he has for selling sweet-and-sour snack mix out of the student-run concession stand if he can work out a deal with the supplier, blobbity blah, and all I could think was, Why is he talking to me? What does he want?

"I figure I'll start selling at the games," Greg said, "get a base, then expand to the daily concession."

"Doesn't that sound interesting?" Amanda asked me.

"Hmm," I said, still not looking up.

Another five minutes of that, and finally Greg moved on. I didn't realize my shoulders had been up to my ears until I felt them relax.

Jordan wasn't happy. "A little eye contact would have been good, Cat."

"I told you, I don't want to go out with anyone."

"Good," he said. "You're there. Beecher's a really nice guy. I'm sorry I ever introduced you."

He grumped off, leaving Amanda and me alone.

"You were really rude," she confirmed.

Okay, they'd both succeeded in making me feel like a total pig.

"What was I supposed to do?" I asked Amanda. "I didn't want to encourage him—that seems even ruder."

"Cat, we're just trying to help you out here."

I groaned. "Listen to me once and for all. I honestly, *truly* do not want a boyfriend. It's just not right for me. I appreciate what you're trying to do, but I'm much happier being alone. I swear."

Amanda handed me back my lunch container. "Thank you for the pizza. And the roasted asparagus. I'm going to try not to curse you right now, mainly because you're my friend and I love you and also because you cook such fabulous food and I want more of it. But tell me the truth—and I'm serious here, Cat. Is it even remotely possible that any of this has anything to do with you-know-who?"

"No," I answered quickly. "Absolutely not."

"Are you sure?"

"I'm sure."

Amanda stared at me. I stared back.

"Some boys are nice," she said.

"I know. Look at Jordan."

"Who may never forgive you." Amanda sighed. "So we should just give up on you?"

"Yes, please."

"And you don't care that you're going to end up a bitter—"

"—dried-out old hag? No. I'm looking forward to that."

Amanda slumped in her chair. "I failed you."

"No, failing me would have been trying to force me to go out with someone I have absolutely no interest in."

"I need you to promise me something," Amanda said.

"Maybe."

"I need you to promise that someday—I don't care if it's a year from now or ten years—but *some*day when you meet someone nice, you'll actually give him a chance. Do you think you can do that?"

I mulled it over. "Possibly."

"I mean, you're not saying you're never ever going to fall in love, right? Because if you tell me that, I'm going to stab myself in the heart with this spoon right now."

"No, I'm not saying that."

"Good. And can I tell you that you were really a bitch to Greg just now? I mean, really."

"Sorry. I just wanted to make sure I discouraged him."

"Oh, you did," Amanda said. "I think we can pretty much count on the Greg vote being lost."

Incredibly, she was wrong.

29

"**T**ell him I can't use the phone," I told my mother.

She handed it to me anyway. "You tell him."

"Hi, Cat?"

"Uh-huh?"

"Hi. It's Greg Beecher. From school."

"Right," I said. "I know who you are."

A fine mist sprang up over my lip, like a tiny sweat mustache. If only Amanda were nearby so I could kick her.

"Great," he said. "I, uh . . . wanted to know if . . ."

Oh my gosh, he actually sounded nervous. Which was impossible, because I was nervous enough for everyone in the world.

I needed to put us both out of our misery, fast.

"Look, Greg, I'm not really supposed to talk on the phone—"

"Oh, did I call too late?"

Considering that it was only seven, that was hard to believe.

"No, but I've taken a vow not to use the telephone for about another 165 days. So I have to get off right now—"

"Wait," he said quickly. "I just wanted to know if you want to go out with me sometime."

There. Words I never thought I'd hear. From anyone. By now even the roots of my hair were sweating.

"No," I said, "but thanks. I have to go now—"

"Wait. Are you joking?"

Like he'd never even considered I might refuse? "No, I'm not joking."

"But Jordan said—"

"Jordan was wrong," I told him. And for some reason the following words just sprang out of my mouth: "And besides . . . I've sort of taken this vow of chastity, you know? So I can't really go out—"

"Yeah, sure—"

"I mean, I shouldn't even be around guys—"

"Yeah," Greg said, "but I like you. I think you're cool. I really want to go out."

What was I supposed to say to that?

30

I used the telephone again to call Amanda because it was a certified emergency.

"Oh my gosh, it was horrible."

"What did he say?"

"That he *likes* me."

Amanda squealed. "What did you say?"

"Nothing."

"Did he ask you out?"

"Yes."

Another squeal. "Well?"

I paused, then let out a groan. "I said yes."

You'd have thought from the scream on the other end I'd just told Amanda a publisher wanted to buy all her poems.

"When?" she asked.

"This Saturday. I told him he could come with us to Poetry Night."

"A double date! I get to see everything! We need to go shopping," Amanda rattled off, "and fix your hair, and maybe do your nails—"

"No," I interrupted before she could get too out of control. "I'm not doing any of that. I'm going as is or not at all. I shouldn't have even said yes."

"But you did," Amanda said, "and that calls for clothes. We barely got started shopping last weekend. We need at least three or four more outfits."

"No way," I said. "We're done."

"Come on, Cat, can you at least be a little bit excited? Please? For me?"

Of course she stared me down, even over the phone.

I groaned again. "Why did he even ask me out?"

"Why wouldn't he?" Amanda answered. "You're fabulous!"

There was no getting around it—this was actually going to happen. "Fine. But I'm just doing this for you."

"I accept," Amanda said.

So we made a shopping date for Saturday morning. Today.

Actually, it wasn't so bad. I have to confess it felt pretty good to hear Amanda say, "Look at that size! Cat, you're wasting away!"

I knew all my old clothes were feeling loose—I just didn't know how loose.

Wow. It's really working.

Amanda brought me some more pants and a few more tops. And a skirt.

"No," I said. "No skirts."

"It's time."

"I don't feel like shaving."

"Cat, are you a girl or what? Have I been mistaken all this time? Let me see your armpits."

"I shave those," I said, shrugging her off. "Why do I have to make such a big deal out of this?"

"Because it's your first date EVER. Well, since at least seventh grade."

"Those weren't dates."

"Uh-huh. Boy, girl, ice cream—that's a date." She waved off any further argument. "My point is, it's been a long, long, LONG time, and maybe we should give this the attention to detail it deserves."

"I'm not going to kiss him."

"Who said anything about kissing?" Amanda asked.

"I'm sure you were going to get to that."

"Well, now that you mention it—"

"Forget it."

"If he moves in like this—"

I pushed her away. "Forget it!"

She cocked her head and assessed my new outfit. "You look awfully cute!" she sang. She reached out and pinched my cheek. "A little makeup—"

"No makeup."

"—a little perfume—"

"Hominins didn't wear perfume."

"—and lose about an inch of hair on your legs, and we're talking gorgeous."

"I don't want to be kissed," I said.

"Of course you do."

31

Greg picked me up at six-thirty. I answered the door wearing the outfit Amanda picked out for me this morning—girl jeans, a white cami, and a cranberry-colored top. She fought hard to do my hair and makeup for tonight, but I stood my ground. Greg was going to have to take me in my native state or not at all. And I was secretly hoping for the not at all.

So why did I even agree to go out with him? He caught me off guard when he called the other night, but I could have backed out anytime these last few days. So why didn't I?

I thought about that a lot while I got dressed. And I decided if I had to be strictly scientific about it, it's because of that vanity thing again. I mean, when has a guy ever shown me the slightest bit of interest? And even though Greg isn't exactly my idea of a perfect match, I know there are girls out there who'd be flattered that he asked them out. And so maybe I'm one of them.

"You look great," he said as I stood in the doorway.

"Thanks. You do, too." And it was the truth. Which surprised me. I guess I'd never really looked at him before. I'd purposely averted my eyes when he showed up at lunch the other day, and same thing when he was standing in front of me in his Speedo. But seeing him tonight in khakis and a short-sleeved knit shirt, I sort of got a new appreciation for the guy's build. His biceps are as big as hams. And he must be at least a foot taller than I am.

He opened the car door for me. Points for that. And he was a pretty careful driver, signaling before every turn. Points there, too.

We rode in silence for a few minutes. My palms were so wet I could have soaked through a whole roll of paper towels.

Finally Greg led with, "So, you're a math and science geek, huh?"

I didn't really care for the "geek" part—geeks can call each other that, but we don't really like it when outsiders do—but I just answered, "Yeah, I guess."

"You like science, huh?"

"Yeah."

"I hate it," he said. "I suck at it."

"Oh." I wasn't sure what I was supposed to say.

"You probably already took biology, huh?"

"Yeah," I said, "freshman year."

"Man, that class is killing me!"

"Oh. Sorry."

"Hey, maybe if I take you out to dinner a few times a week, you'll do my homework for me, huh?" He laughed. "Just kidding. But you're probably good at algebra, too, huh? I'd even buy you dessert—just kidding."

Thank goodness the ride was short.

Amanda and Jordan were waiting for us outside the café.

"How's it going?" Amanda whispered while the two guys did their male greeting thing.

"I have no idea what I'm doing," I whispered back.

"You'll be fine."

Jordan clasped Amanda's hand as we entered the café. I stayed far enough away from Greg that he wouldn't get the idea he should do the same.

We grabbed our usual table—the owner, Darlene, keeps it reserved for us on Poetry Night—and sat down, boy-girl, boy-girl. I really wished it were girl-girl so I could keep whispering to Amanda.

The three of us order the same thing every time, so we didn't need menus. Greg had to go back up front to ask for one.

I made good use of his absence. "Jordan, what did he say about this whole thing? I mean, does he think this is like a kissing date?"

Jordan snorted. "A kissing date? What, are we in first grade?"

Amanda elbowed him. "She's nervous. Be nice."

"It's whatever you want it to be," Jordan told me. "Relax. He's not going to jump you—"

"Here he comes," Amanda whispered.

We all straightened up.

Greg took his seat again, and then scowled down at the menu.

"Get the veggie burgers, bro," Jordan told him. "Extra everything."

"What are you having?" Greg asked me. I pointed to the sweet potato fries on the menu. "Wanna share?" he asked. I know this is ridiculous, but that already felt too intimate. But I stammered out a "sure." Amanda gave me a reassuring smile.

In that moment she and I both knew it: I am so not cut out for dating.

While Jordan and Greg handled the small talk for a while, analyzing some of the results from their swim meet this morning, Amanda looked over her poetry notes and I just sat there trying not to panic.

How do people even do this? Why date at all? You have to figure out what to talk about, how to act, what to eat, what to wear, what to do with your hands—the whole thing is just torture.

And then talk about your torture. The first poet stepped up to the mike.

The woman obviously has some issues, and for some reason she decided to inflict them on all of us tonight. We had to sit through three excruciatingly long epic poems about her horrible mother, her rotten ex-husband, and the abusive, sadistic, blankety-blank boss who recently fired her. I wish the woman had just gone to therapy.

"Are they all gonna be like that?" Greg asked me as we applauded the woman finally sitting down.

"Sometimes. But Amanda's are always great."

"Do you mind if I wait in the car until then?"

I wasn't sure if he was serious, but then Greg flashed me a smile. So he actually has a sense of humor. I guess that's something.

The second guy was pretty good. He had a long, sad poem about growing up in Maine and losing his father to the sea. There were some really good lines in there, but all I remember is, *"Roam . . . to the foam . . ."* He repeated that several times. It was very relaxing.

Then he lightened the mood with a few short poems, one involving a girl with yellow eyes and the other about a dog who scooted his butt along the rug every time the poet and his girlfriend tried to make out.

That's what I love about poetry—you just never know what you're going to get.

I kept glancing at Greg to see how he was taking it. He seemed pretty happy in his own little world, tearing his napkin into tiny strips and laying them out on his place mat like logs. Just a few more napkins and he could have built a fort.

There was a break after the second poet. Greg immediately jumped up. "Anyone want anything to drink?" Jordan asked him for a Coke.

As soon as Greg was gone, the three of us leaned forward again for a quick consultation.

"He's totally bored," Amanda said.

"Too bad," I said. "I'm not leaving."

"That first woman sucked," Jordan said.

"Shhh," Amanda answered. "She was fine."

"If he wants to leave, I'll go home with you guys," I offered.

"He's here to be with you," Jordan said. "He's not leaving till he gets some."

Jordan dodged Amanda's punch. "I'm kidding! He's totally cool. Don't worry, Cat."

"You swear?"

"I told him you're like a sister to me. Nothing's happening. Unless you make the move—"

"He's coming—" Amanda said.

We all jerked upright and tried to look casual.

Amanda let out a muffled laugh and leaned forward once more to whisper, "I can't believe we're on a date together. Finally."

I smiled. It actually was starting to feel a little fun. I wasn't expecting that.

We sat through two more sets of two poets each, and then it was Amanda's turn. And I have to admit I felt incredible pride showing her off to someone new.

I leaned toward Greg and whispered, "You're going to love her. She's really great."

Greg reached down and found my hand. He squeezed it and kept holding on. He brought his lips right up against my ear. "I think *you're* really great."

I know Amanda's poems were wonderful tonight. I just didn't hear a single one of them.

32

As we walked out of the café, the four of us together, Greg was still holding my hand. Amanda widened her eyes at me and I couldn't even widen back. It was like I was sleepwalking.

That's exactly what it felt like. I was very, very tired. Like I'd run a marathon and was now relaxing in a tub. My limbs were buzzing and weak. I think I was in shock.

Amanda must have thought so, too, because she managed to pull me aside for a minute while the guys walked on ahead.

"Are you okay?"

I nodded.

"Cat, look at me. What's going on?"

"I think he likes me."

"Der. Do you like him?"

"I have no idea."

"Do you want to ride home with him?"

"Yeah, I guess so," I said.

"Because if you're nervous at all—"

"I'm completely nervous!" I answered. "I have no idea what I'm doing."

"I told Jordan to put the fear of God into him. Right now he's telling Greg if he lays a hand on you—"

"He was holding my hand," I said. "Did you see that?"

"Is that okay?" Amanda asked.

"I have no idea." A sort of hysterical giggle was working its way up my throat.

Ahead of us Jordan gave Greg a stout punch to the arm. That must have been the end of their man talk. *So if you kiss her I'll rip your face off, 'kay, bro?* Whatever he said, Greg seemed to take it well. He punched Jordan back.

"Ready, Cat?" Greg asked, removing his keys from his pocket. We were already at his car. Jordan and Amanda had parked farther on.

Amanda tilted her head and looked at me. "Say the word—"

"It's okay," I whispered. "It's a short drive."

Greg opened the door for me again. I could see Amanda gave him points for that, too.

"I'll come by tomorrow," Amanda promised. I nodded and slipped into the car.

As soon as he started the ignition, Greg reached over and took my hand again. It was just like what I'd seen Jordan do with Amanda after the last Poetry Night. How weird. I never would have guessed that a month later that would be me.

We didn't talk at all on the way home. Greg stroked his thumb across the top of my hand, and that completely rendered me mute. I'm not sure I was even breathing. It felt like I was watching the whole thing from somewhere above my body.

When he pulled up in front of my house, Greg parked the car, turned off the engine, and unclipped his seat belt. I kept mine on and stared straight ahead.

"Cat?"

I didn't want to look at him, because I was pretty sure I knew what was coming next. I've seen enough movies.

"Okay, so see ya," I said, trying to will myself to open the door.

"Cat." This time it was a statement, not a question, and for some reason that's what got me. I turned to him more slowly than I knew I could. Greg reached out and gently cupped my chin in his hand. Then he pulled me toward him and lowered his mouth and kissed me softly on the lips.

It was my first kiss ever.

And it felt exactly the way I was afraid it would feel.

33

Amanda usually sleeps until noon on Sundays. Which is why I wasn't at all prepared to see her at my door at ten.

"Tell me everything."

I wasn't so sure about that. Being a romantic, Amanda probably didn't want to know I was sick to my stomach this morning. And that I made fabulous whole wheat and blueberry waffles for everyone else, but didn't have a bite myself. Or that my family was under strict instructions to tell anyone who called—*anyone*—that I wasn't available today. I didn't add that I would never be available again.

"Well?" Amanda prodded. I made her wait until we could get to my room and shut the door.

"I don't like him."

She looked so disappointed. "Oh."

"He's just not . . . right."

Amanda flopped onto my bed. "What's wrong with him?"

"I don't know."

"Well, let's go down the list. The way he looks?"

"No, that's okay."

"Too boring? Too jockish?"

"No."

"Slimy hands? Stinky breath?"

"No."

"Then what?" Amanda asked.

I shrugged.

"Did he try anything?" Amanda asked.

"Yes."

"He did? Like what?"

I hesitated to tell her, but I knew there was no way I could avoid it. "We kissed a little."

"WHAT?"

"Shhh! We kissed. It wasn't good."

Amanda slid off my bed and sat on the floor. She patted the carpet next to her. "You sit here and tell me absolutely everything, missy. From start to finish. Don't you dare leave anything out."

So I did. From the cupping of the chin to the soft first kiss to the deeper kisses that followed.

"So what was the problem?" Amanda asked. "Is he bad at it?"

"How would I know?"

"Well, was it too . . . tonguey?"

"Ew," I said. "No."

"Then what?"

"I just didn't . . . feel anything, you know? I mean, I felt something, but not . . . you know, fireworks or anything."

Amanda squinted at me. Squinted and stared me down. "Oh, I see."

"What?" I asked.

"I understand."

"Understand what?"

She stood up and brushed off her pants. "Okay, well, that explains a lot."

"What?" I demanded. She can be so exasperating at times.

"I won't bother you again," Amanda said. She didn't seem angry, just . . . resolved.

I followed her out to the kitchen, where she started snooping around all my latest creations. She cut herself a slice of banana bread (I figured out how to make it the hominin way) and slathered it with butter. "So," she said brightly, "what do you want to do today?"

Something was up with her, I just didn't know what. "Come on—out with it. What do you want to say?"

"Nothing," she answered innocently.

"You think I'm going to end up a dried-up old hag."

"No. Probably. It's fine."

I pinched her arm.

"Ow!"

"Say it," I demanded. "Now."

Amanda took a deep breath. "Fine. But you have to listen to me and not argue."

I knew this wasn't going to be good.

"I think a certain someone broke your heart," Amanda began. "And whether you admit it or not, now you feel like you can't ever let yourself like anyone again."

I started to protest, but she held up her hand. "I know what you're going to say, but you're wrong. The Cat and Matt show is still alive and well in your poor little heart, and no guy—even if he's the greatest guy in the world, which I'm not saying Greg is, but just for the sake of argument—no one is going to stand a chance with you until we finally do something about this."

My little brother came in just then, so we immediately changed the subject. Amanda made small talk with Peter for a few minutes— something she's always been so much better at with him than I have. He grabbed some food and went back to watching TV, and Amanda and I returned to my bedroom.

"You're wrong," I said as soon as I closed the door. "That's not it at all."

"It isn't? Then why haven't you liked a single guy *ever* since seventh grade?"

"There just hasn't been anyone."

"Anyone like him, you mean."

"No," I said. "Anyone period. I'm definitely open to the right guy. I just don't think Greg is it."

Amanda kicked off her shoes and sat back on the floor, leaning against my bed. "Are you telling me you have no feelings whatsoever for Matt anymore?"

"None. Except disgust—does that count?" I threw her a pillow off my bed and grabbed one for myself. I sat next to her and cushioned my back, even though hominins sat on the hard dirt. This wasn't a hominin moment.

"You know what they say," Amanda said. "Hatred isn't the opposite of love, it's just another variation of it. They both mean you still have passionate feelings for someone. If you didn't feel anything at all, then I'd say you were free of him."

"I don't feel anything," I said. "I hardly even notice him."

"So if Matt McKinney came here today, and fell on bended knee, and begged your forgiveness—"

"It wouldn't matter. I don't care anymore."

"Hmm," Amanda said, clearly not convinced. "You keep telling yourself that. Meantime, what are you going to do about Greg?"

"I don't know, hide."

132

34

Day 54, Monday, October 13

Lunch: None. Brought some great leftovers. from last night, but a certain someone had to stick his grubby fingers in there, and it wasn't very appetizing after that. Oh, well, I'm probably not going to starve to death just from missing one meal.

   Although I couldn't help wondering what Hominin Woman would have done in my place. Probably speared the guy through the heart with a sharp stick. Just saying.

I know there's some science behind this. I know there must be some perfect biological explanation for why, even when you don't really like a guy, it's almost impossible to be mean to him once you've kissed him.

So I guess I have a boyfriend now.

The data:

He walks with me to all my classes. He drapes his big swimmer arm over my shoulders and leans into me as we walk through the halls, and it's a good thing I have such a sturdy build or I'm sure my legs would collapse from the weight of him.

He eats lunch with me every other day. He sits there like we're a couple, like we're still double-dating with Amanda and Jordan, and he picks food out of my containers with his bare fingers, even though the look on my face should tell him I'm entirely grossed out by that.

But I don't say anything because the whole thing feels like this bizarre experiment or joke or dream or something. I don't even know how to act.

Mostly I just want to put my head down on the table and take a nap. For some reason being around that guy is like a sleeping pill. Amanda says it's because my hormones are on overload. She thinks it's my body's defense mechanism to keep me from throwing myself at guys.

I say it's because I am so clearly not meant for a relationship, my brain is signaling that to me by shutting down whenever Greg is around. It's gotten so bad I'm afraid it's going to affect my test scores.

Today's a perfect example. Greg plopped down next to me at lunch, started picking the pine nuts and cranberries off my wild rice, and meanwhile handed me five sheets of scribbled algebra.

"Hey, babe, would you mind looking at this?"

Amanda and I both mouthed, *"Babe?"*

It was so ridiculous—and he's so incredibly bad at math—I actually sat there and corrected his homework more as a mental exercise than anything else, just to make sure all my synapses were still firing.

If I'd lost my knowledge of algebra, then I'd know I was destined to be alone.

After lunch Greg walked me to Mr. Fizer's class. He's been doing that lately, and to tell the truth, it's the one time I don't mind him hanging on me the way he does. Because of course Matt sees us. He always has this look of utter disgust, like he can't believe some guy— some guy he actually knows—would even like me. Well, Matt, he does. Deal with it.

Greg deposited me at the door and went for the kiss. I turned my head to the side at the last minute so his lips landed on my cheek.

"See ya later, babe." And then Greg made the monumental mistake of slapping me on the behind.

Nobody touches the butt.

My whole body stiffened. My mouth got small and angry. And I saw Matt sitting inside the room, watching.

"Don't ever do that," I told Greg, my voice icier than I've ever heard it in my life.

He chuckled and slapped my butt again.

Big mistake. My arms are really strong.

35

You'd think after pushing a guy so hard he lost his footing and had to stumble backward three or four feet before catching himself, he'd take the hint and go bother some other girl. But not Greg.

"Cat, I'm *so* sorry." He intercepted me as I came out of Mr. Fizer's class and shoved a red rose in my face. "I'm such an idiot."

Only he didn't say "idiot." And what he did say was entirely accurate.

Matt passed behind us and mumbled something. I think it included my name.

"Go away," I told Greg. I started heading toward the doors.

Greg tried again with the rose. "Come on, Cat, *please*."

Where did he get the rose? Did he skip class to run out and get it? Or does he just keep a supply in his locker for times like these?

"Go away," I said again. Suddenly I wasn't sleepy at all.

Greg followed me outside.

"Don't you have swim practice?" I asked.

"I don't care about that. I care about you."

Again with the rose in my face. "I have to go."

But I couldn't lose the guy. I walked as fast as I could, but I was no match for someone with his long legs.

"I was just joking around," Greg said. "I had no idea you'd get so mad. I'm *really* sorry."

"What did you think I meant when I said don't ever do that again?"

"I thought we were just playing around—honest. C'mon, Cat, look at me."

I stopped and faced him. "What?"

Greg took a deep breath. "I really like you. Don't be mad at me. I'm sorry."

And right then all the fight went out of me. I mean, what was I supposed to say? Someone tells you he likes you, and you're just going to answer, "Too bad," and walk away?

The truth is, he's not that horrible of a guy. Yeah, he wouldn't be my first choice, but I'm never going to get my first choice anyway, so what does it matter? I should just get over that once and for all. Greg's a nice enough person. I really don't have a reason not to like him.

Plus there's that mysterious biological law: *Can't be mean once you've kissed him.*

So I knew I was going to forgive him. But I could still make it clear where we stood on the whole touching-body-parts thing.

"Remember I told you I've taken a vow of chastity. You understand what that means, right?"

"Yeah," he said. "You're very generous. I think that's cool."

I didn't quite get his answer, but I didn't want to prolong the conversation. I was suddenly feeling exposed, standing there on the street talking to a guy holding a wilted rose. I'm sure people were staring at us.

"You're going to be late for practice," I said. "I have to get to work."

"But we're okay?" Greg asked.

I sighed. "Yes."

Greg pulled me toward him and gave me the kind of kiss people have no business doing in public. That sleep thing washed over me. It would have felt good to lie down on the sidewalk and take a nap.

"I'll call you tonight," Greg said.

I shook some sense into my head. "No—I'm not supposed to use the phone. I'll just see you tomorrow."

"Man, your parents are crazy strict."

"Yeah." I haven't told him about my project yet and don't know if I ever will.

I was already almost to the hospital before my brain returned to its normal function. That's when it dawned on me what Greg had meant.

"I've taken a vow of chastity. You understand what that means, right?"

"Yeah. You're very generous. I think that's cool."

Um, that's *charity*, Greg, not *chastity*.

He is so not the right guy for me.

Day 58, Friday, October 17

Breakfast: None. Overslept. Again.

Technology avoided: Could have gotten a ride with my dad this morning, but ended up semi-jogging to school instead. Not a pretty sight.

I swear, Greg is playing havoc with my sleep. Just the thought of him is like having mono. Most mornings I can barely get out of bed. What's going on? I've never read about that in *Cosmo* or any of the other women's advice magazines Amanda gets.

Amanda is sticking with her hormone-overload theory. But since I don't actually feel any hormones kicking in around Greg—my lips still feel like wooden blocks every time he kisses them—I know that can't be it. I think I'm allergic to him or something.

At least I know my brain is still functioning—I've corrected his biology and algebra homework all week.

Greg walked me to Mr. Fizer's again today, but this time I didn't have an audience. Matt wasn't there. I saw him in English this morning, so I know he was at school, but I think I know what's going on.

Mr. Fizer told all of us a few weeks ago that as we head deeper into our projects, we might need to spend more time in the field doing experiments and observations. So he's willing to give a pass to anyone who wants more time out of class, rather than just sitting in there like I do conducting research on the Internet and using the computer to write up reports.

Several students have already taken him up on his offer. I know Alyssa is working with one of the labs at the university, because I overheard her saying that to Mr. Fizer. And Farah is using one of the chemistry labs here at school to do her experiments—I saw her last week when I went to the bathroom. So now I guess Matt is out there in the world doing whatever he's doing to try to continue his reign of supremacy at the science fair.

Anyway. Whatever. Having Matt out of the room can only make my life easier. I don't need him scowling every time he sees me, or particularly every time he sees me with Greg.

If I have to get used to having a boyfriend, then so does everybody else.

37

Day 59, Saturday, October 18

Breakfast: Oatmeal with walnuts, cinnamon, and chopped dried dates. Half a grapefruit with honey drizzled over it. Quite gourmet, if I do say so myself.

Amanda and I were taking a break from homework this morning, helping ourselves to some corn bread I made last night, when she leaned against my kitchen counter and surveyed me up and down.

"Hey, do you want to know what the secret of life is?" she asked.

"Yes, as a matter of fact, I do."

"A good bra. And you ain't got one, sistah."

I crossed my arms over my chest. "Then don't look."

"Kind of hard not to, since they're hanging almost to your waist these days."

"They are not."

"Cat, I could fit about four boobs in your bra right now, it's so loose. Would you face the fact that you're getting skinny?"

"I'm not skinny."

Amanda rolled her eyes. "And blind."

It's true—I'm not skinny—but I am getting smaller. Still on the broad side around the hips and butt, but the waist is starting to actually look like a waist—curvy instead of just blocky—and my chest is definitely losing some of its heft. I've been wearing a 40DD bra the past few years (and even that's been a little tight at times), but Amanda's right—there is quite a bit more room in there these days.

"I think we need to visit my friend Joyce," Amanda said. "Let her tell you what to do with the girls."

"We have homework. And it's daytime—I'm not supposed to ride in the car."

"Cave people took Saturdays off," Amanda said. "Look it up."

The last time Amanda and I went bra-shopping together was in eighth grade. I needed one, she didn't. But she got one anyway, even though, as she pointed out today, she could have gotten by with two Band-Aids and a rubber band strung between them.

Joyce and I stood alone in the dressing room. She clicked her tongue. "Very bad."

"I heard." I lifted my breasts (still inside my bra) and let them drop. One of them sneaked out the bottom.

"Oh, very bad," Joyce said.

"Is there anything you can do?" Amanda called from outside the door—ultra-dramatically, like Joyce was my surgeon instead of a lingerie saleswoman.

"Oh, yes," Joyce said firmly. I could tell she takes her job very seriously.

I'm not too fond of showing my naked self to strangers, but Joyce was so clinical it was hard to feel uncomfortable. She measured me, clicked her tongue about fifty more times, brought in bra after bra for me to try on.

Finally we found one that fit. I mean FIT—like someone was just holding them in place for me, no strap pain, no chafe, no underwire cutting into my stomach.

"See?" Joyce said proudly. "38D."

"Wow," Amanda said from outside. "You still beat me by two cup sizes."

"It's not a competition," I pointed out.

"Yeah, but you still made my girls cry."

I bought two new bras—one in black, one beige. While I was at it, I thought I'd also ask Joyce for a sports bra. That little bit of jogging I had to do to get to school yesterday after I overslept showed me I probably need better support.

I explained the problem to Joyce, and she fitted me with this contraption that has about forty clasps all the way up the front.

"Nuclear bomb won't make them jiggle," Joyce claimed. Yowza.

Amanda decided I also needed some new underwear, which Joyce happily measured me for. I felt like she and I should get engaged after all that.

"Don't you feel better?" Amanda asked me as we left the mall. I wore one of my new bras out—Amanda made me turn over the old one to Joyce. "She'll give it to charity," Amanda assured me. "Some kid can use it as a swing."

On the way home, Amanda took the opportunity to quiz me about Greg. "Where are you going tonight?"

"I don't know. To eat somewhere."

"What are you wearing?"

"I don't know, pants and a shirt."

"Wow," Amanda deadpanned, "you sound *so* excited."

I hesitated, but then mustered up the courage to ask her what's been on my mind. "When you first met Jordan, you liked him right away, didn't you?"

"As you may recall," Amanda said, "I wrote four poems about him that night."

"Oh, yeah." They were really good, too—highly romantic, but also providing a vital factual record of his most important features, such as "eyes dark as an abyss" and "a nose sharp as the ridge of a mountain." She had a few things to say about his lips, too: "fleshy and warm and tasting of fig." (She was just guessing on that one, since they didn't actually kiss until the next day.)

I don't usually ask Amanda for a lot of details about her and Jordan—and she hasn't really shared any for a while—because we're all really comfortable hanging out together. And I think Amanda knows I'd have a hard time looking Jordan in the eye if I knew too much. It works much better for me if I can pretend we're all just platonic friends.

But this was different—I needed advice.

"Do you guys kiss . . . a lot?"

"Yeah."

"Do you, like . . . make out?"

Amanda snorted. "Uh, *yeah.*"

"And you . . . like that?"

"Kit Cat, I sense a problem here. Want to tell me?"

I slumped back in the seat. "I just don't feel anything when he kisses me."

"Still? Really?"

"But he's so *nice* to me all the time. He's always thanking me for helping him with his homework, and complimenting me, and giving me flowers and telling me how smart I am—I mean, don't you think I should feel something by now?"

"Jordan never brings me flowers," Amanda said. "And yet I will love him until the day I die."

"Is that true?" I'd never heard her put it so forcefully before.

Amanda shrugged. "It might be true. We'll have to see. But I do love him, and I do think he's incredibly hot. So if you're not feeling the heat—"

"I think there's something wrong with me," I said. "I think I *should* like him, you know?"

"Should?" Amanda said. "What's 'should'? You should eat your Brussels sprouts. You should wipe your feet. 'Should' doesn't go with liking someone—either you do or you don't."

I leaned my head back and closed my eyes. "We're supposed to be celebrating our two-week anniversary tonight."

"Uh, news for you, honey—two weeks is no anniversary."

"What should I tell him? I don't even want to go."

"Tell him you just got a new bra and it's shy around strangers."

38

He took me to Goony Golf and we sat up inside the giant Mondo Head in the dark and he kissed me, which I was prepared for, but then he made an unauthorized reach for the breast. Luckily I was wearing my new special sports bra with all the complicated hardware and about fifteen layers of fabric between me and the outside world, impervious to both nuclear weapons and unauthorized groping, and when I pushed Greg away and said, "What are you doing?" he answered, "Come on, babe, I love you," and—

WHAT??? This guy doesn't even know me. We've been going out for two weeks! He doesn't know the first thing about me. He doesn't know what there is to like about me, let alone love about me.

He doesn't know how well I can cook, or that I can play Beethoven's Fifth blindfolded (okay, just the first few lines), and that I named all my stuffed animals after elements on the periodic table, and I have a photographic memory for phone numbers and addresses and math and chemistry equations, and I learned how to drive in one weekend by taking my mother around to every errand she could think of, and my right pupil is slightly larger than my left, and I used to want to be a trapeze performer, mainly because of the costumes, and I was once in love with the same boy from the time I was eight until I was thirteen—

And mostly Greg doesn't know that I had been saving my first kiss for him. That other boy. Not for Greg. And now Greg's ruined that. Actually, Matt already ruined it. The whole thing is a mess.

But one thing's for sure: Matt McKinney used to know me better than anyone in my life, and he never loved me. So what's with some guy I barely know saying something like that?

I don't think it's normal to be this angry when someone tells you he loves you. I might just be seriously deranged.

39

"**Just give him one more chance,**" Amanda argued.

"Why?"

"Because I hate to break it to you, but it's not unheard of for a guy to want to cop a feel. Especially in the Mondo Head—it's notorious."

"But he knows I don't want that! And what's with the whole love thing?"

Amanda ate another bite of zucchini muffin. She had come over for the Sunday report and also to sample whatever I'd made my family for breakfast.

"This is excellent, by the way," she said. "Okay, the love thing."

"He can't possibly really feel that way," I said.

"Why not? You're lovable."

"Right."

"Kit Cat, why is it so hard to believe that a guy could fall in love with you?"

"After two weeks?"

"After two minutes," Amanda said. "Remember me and Jordan."

"That's because the two of you are incredible. Who wouldn't fall in love with either one of you?"

"You're incredible, too," Amanda answered. "Can I have another one?"

I waved her toward the muffins. "So what am I supposed to do?"

"Let's go on another double," Amanda suggested. "That way I can evaluate him in action. Has he asked you to Vince's party yet?"

"Yes. I said no." It's an end-of-swim-season/pre-Halloween party one of the guys from the swim team is throwing next weekend.

"Well, change your mind," Amanda said. "Let's do this together. It'll be fine."

I sighed. Heavily.

"Kitty Cat, I'm only thinking of you. You just need to get a certain someone out of your system. What better way than to replace him with someone who thinks he loves you?"

I groaned. "Fine. But I'm not wearing a costume."

"Of course you are."

40

Day 66, Saturday, October 25

Halloween party: This was the first time I've been exposed to so much junk food since I started the project. And none of it mattered to me anymore. Chips and dip, chips and salsa, Chex Mix, M&M's—I didn't crave any of it. Unbelievable.

Of course Amanda stared me down about the whole costume thing. There's really no denying her once she sets her mind on something.

So she found the costume for me. Or more accurately, she created it. We went to the thrift store this morning, and she started gathering items here and there. She has an eye for that, so I knew I just had to trust her, even though the clothes she picked out made no sense.

But when she was done with me, it wasn't half bad. In fact, the costume was pretty hilarious, once you understood what I was supposed to be.

I wore high heels of my own, but everything else was from the thrift store: a short black-and-white-checked skirt, a pink sweater (a little too tight, if you ask me, but Amanda said to leave it), a long purple bead necklace, big hoop earrings, and a faded black suit jacket.

We dropped by Wal-Mart on our way home (I know, I was in the car again—but Amanda claimed this was the Halloween shopping exception, known to hominins everywhere. I'm not putting that in the research notebook). She picked up a few more items there: some Velcro, some glue, and a map of the United States. She also managed to sweet-talk one of the workers into giving us a large cardboard box from out of the storeroom.

Then we went back to my house to concoct her creation.

She cut a big section from the cardboard box and glued the map to one side. Then she attached a few strips of Velcro to the middle of the map and sewed their matching halves to the back of the jacket.

"Try it on."

I pulled on the jacket and practiced walking around my room with this big cardboard obstruction stuck to the back of me, learning where my corners were so I wouldn't keep scraping against the walls.

She had me detach the map again so she could add a few construction paper clouds and lightning bolts and some random numbers like 71 and 45 written across certain states.

The last step before we left for the party was me consenting to wear makeup. ("Halloween exception," Amanda explained. Whatever.) Amanda worked her particular makeup magic, so I have to admit I looked pretty nice, for me. And since I'd already violated that part of my hominin rule book, I let her go ahead and style my hair, too, until it was very large and stiff with hair spray.

"Perfect," Amanda said, and I had to agree.

Greg didn't get it, of course. No one did.

Well, not no one.

Matt stared at me from across the room. At first I thought he was glaring, but then I realized he was just concentrating. Suddenly he burst into laughter.

I turned away before he could see me smile. He would think I was smiling at him, not at the fact that Amanda was so clever.

Every time Greg tried to get me to tell him what I was, I said he had to guess. Finally he couldn't take it anymore, so I told him.

"Weather girl."

He scrunched up his face and looked me over. "Huh?"

I pointed to the clouds over my shoulder and said in my girliest voice, "We expect a high-pressure system over Cincinnati and rain to the south. For those of you in San Diego, the high will be eighty-eight—"

"Oh," Greg said. He still looked confused.

That's when I got a tightness in my stomach and the usual wave of sleepiness.

There were a few decent costumes tonight, but most of them were pretty lame. None could match Amanda's creativity. Several of the girls dressed like Catwoman to show off their incredible figures. At least three different guys wore Hawaiian shirts and sunglasses, as if that made a costume. Matt wore sweats and a tuxedo jacket, whatever that was supposed to be. Greg dressed up like the Wolfman—fur pasted to his face, and fangs and everything. Jordan dressed exactly like he does every day, except tonight he wore glasses.

"Who are you?" I asked.

"Clark Kent."

"That's it?"

Jordan shrugged.

Amanda said, "I begged him."

She looked better than all of us—bikini top, long black skirt, beach sandals, and a cape she made out of black sheets she bought at Wal-Mart (who uses black sheets?). She completed the look with a long black wig and a sun visor.

Oh, and she carried a small jar of mayo.

Greg didn't get that one, either. But Matt did.

He came over to say hi to Jordan, completely ignoring me. He turned to Amanda and nailed it. "Sand witch."

Amanda had to give Matt his props. She smiled. "Very good."

"Sandwich?" Greg repeated.

Matt walked away without another word or even a glance at me.

And I knew in that moment there was no denying it: Greg Beecher is no Matt McKinney.

Which is good—*great*—in a lot of ways. In fact, it makes sense to consider only those guys who are the exact opposite of Matt.

But there's this one small matter that I just can't escape: I like the way Matt thinks. I like how smart he is. And he's clever, like Amanda—he sees things in a way other people don't. If only he weren't such a miserable excuse for a human being.

I watched him weave through the crowd. Watched the back of his stupid tuxedo jacket and the tousled hair that made him look like he had just woken up. I watched him turn to talk to a group of people, and smile and laugh with them, the way he used to around me.

I don't regret that we aren't friends anymore. What we had was obviously a lie anyway. But a part of me can't help wondering how things would be different if I hadn't overheard what he said at the science fair. Would we still be hanging out together? Still inventing things, still looking through his telescope at night, me still pretending that he liked me more than he obviously did?

See, that's the point. No matter what I think I'm missing, it was all just a fraud.

So then why do I let myself keep feeling this way?

41

The good thing about my costume was it really thwarted any of Greg's attempts to put his arm around me. Not that he stopped trying.

"Why don't you take the map off?" he kept saying. "Everyone's seen it by now." He'd long ago removed the Wolfman teeth—they made it too hard to stuff his face. But I insisted that the map was the most important part of Amanda's costume for me, and I wasn't going to ruin it.

Around eleven, I'd had enough of the party.

I pulled Amanda to the bathroom along with me.

"Whatever you do," I told her as we waited our turn in line, "please do *not* leave without me tonight. I can't ride home with that guy. I can barely take another minute of him."

"That bad, huh?" Amanda winced. "I'm so sorry. I shouldn't have talked you into this."

"It's okay. I needed to know once and for all. And believe me, I know."

"I do, too," Amanda said. "He's definitely not right for you."

"Yeah?"

"Yeah. I've been watching you two tonight—actually, watching him. And there's just something . . . wrong. I can't explain it."

"Good. Then you'll let me off the hook?"

"Totally," she said. "Just let him down easy—he is still a friend of Jordan's. You don't have to make a big deal about it. Just tell him it's not working out."

"Do you think I should do it here?" I asked. "At the party?"

"Depends. How badly do you want to get it over with?"

"I don't know," I said. "I don't suppose you'd like to do it for me?"

"Sorry, sweetie, goes with the territory. To each girl her own breakup."

We were next in line. And there was something more I had to say, even though I considered not saying it. But if you can't confess everything to your best friend—

"Besides, I think you may be right. About the other." I leaned closer to whisper it. "About Matt."

Amanda's eyes widened. "Oh. Okay. Wow."

One of the Catwomen came out of the bathroom just then, and Amanda pulled me inside. She locked the door behind us. "Let's hear it."

I didn't really want to say it out loud. I brushed my finger across my heart, brought both fists together, and snapped them apart.

"Heartbreak," Amanda said.

I nodded and sagged against the sink. My map crinkled against my back. "I just . . . miss him sometimes, you know? As stupid as that is. I really, really miss him. And seeing him here tonight, looking so . . . good."

"Although what is with that costume?" Amanda said.

"Yeah, I know." And then for some reason I could feel myself getting a little weepy.

"It's just that—" I cleared my throat and made myself wait a moment. "I think maybe you're right—what you said about me and guys. And about Matt. I think I really don't want to like anyone again. It's too much trouble. And no one is . . . like him anyway. I think maybe I'm always going to compare every other guy to him. He really was the perfect one for me." I smiled and swiped away the one tear that sneaked out. "So how incredibly stupid is that? Considering what a jerk he is?"

"It's not stupid at all," Amanda said. "I think it makes perfect sense. It's like those baby ducks who'll follow around a human, thinking it's their mother. It's early imprinting. You can't fight it."

Amanda detached my map and gave me a big, sisterly hug. "But we still hate him, right?"

"Yes," I said. "Deeply."

Before we left the bathroom, Amanda whipped out her makeup brushes and touched up my smears. Then she patted me on the back and sent me out. "Now go break up with your boyfriend."

We returned to the packed living room and saw the three of them standing there talking—Jordan, Greg, and Matt.

Greg was laughing at something, Jordan was giving him a weird look, and Matt seemed really angry. Matt said something I didn't hear, Jordan braced his hand against Matt's chest, and Greg just laughed again. Then Matt saw Amanda and me coming, and turned and stalked back into the crowd.

As we walked toward Jordan and Greg, I suddenly lost my nerve.

There was no way I was breaking up with him at that party. In fact, I might have to make an exception to the cell phone rule just so I could text-message him tomorrow. *we r ovr.*

I tugged on Jordan's sleeve. "I'm tired. Do you mind if we go home now?"

"Okay," Greg said, as if I were talking to him.

"I think I'll go home with these guys," I said.

Greg looked like he didn't understand. "It's no problem. Let's go."

"She's on our way," Amanda said. "We'll just drop her off."

Somehow I knew it wasn't going to be as easy as that.

"Can I talk to you?" Greg asked.

Amanda and I exchanged a look. She was right—it was best to just get it over with.

"Sure," I said.

I followed him through the kitchen, out to the backyard. A group sat around the fire pit, all of them drinking and some of them smoking. Greg drew me toward the privacy of the trees.

"What's going on?" he asked.

I took a deep breath. "Look, you're a really nice guy—"

"Wait—are you breaking up with me?"

So much for my delicate intro. "Um, yeah—"

"Why?"

I couldn't see much of his face. It was too dark. But I did feel his fingers around my arm.

"It's not just you," I said. "I don't want to go out with anyone right now."

"Why? What did I do?"

"Nothing." His fingers were digging in harder. I started to pry them off. "I just . . . this isn't what I want."

Some people came out from the kitchen, and Greg pulled me deeper into the darkness.

"Cat, I thought we had something here."

"I thought so, too," I lied. "It's just not the right time for me."

"It was the right time last week. And the week before. What's your problem?"

I didn't exactly like his tone.

He must have noticed that himself, because suddenly his voice softened. "Come on, Cat, what's going on? Did I do something wrong? Tell me."

He closed the distance between us, and I didn't realize until that moment I'd left my map back in the bathroom. He wrapped me in his giant arms and pulled me too close.

I didn't want to be hugged right then—not by him and especially not that hard. I wriggled out of his embrace. But I still tried to be nice about it.

"I'm sorry," I said. "I shouldn't have gone out with you. It was a bad idea—I knew I shouldn't have—"

And then he really blew it. Without any warning he put his hands on either side of my face and pulled me to him and kissed me—hard, rough—not at all like the other times. It actually hurt.

I pushed him away. "Stop it!" I wiped my mouth off with my sleeve. "Don't do that!"

"Cat—"

"Just leave me alone! I don't want to go out with you anymore."

I turned and fled back into the house. It only took me a few seconds to find Amanda. "Let's go. I really need to leave."

"I'll go grab Jordan."

While she went to retrieve him, I watched the door to the

kitchen, afraid that Greg was going to come back through. I wasn't sure what he would do.

I was so distracted I didn't notice Matt had come up behind me.

"Why are you with that jackass?" he asked.

I whirled around. It was exactly the wrong time to get on my last nerve. "You should talk," I snapped. "You're a bigger jackass than anyone."

"*Me?* What did I ever do?"

"Right," I said, turning away from him.

"I mean it, Cat, what do you think I did?"

I faced him again. "I *know* what you did. I was there."

Matt ran a hand through his hair. "You're insane. You're the one who's hardly talked to me since junior high—"

"As if I didn't have a reason!"

"Why? Just because you won the science fair?"

"What?" It was so crazy I didn't even know what to say. "You're the one who ruined everything—it had nothing to do with me."

"How?" he said. "How did I ruin everything?"

I couldn't believe we were having this conversation—or that he was going to act so innocent. Luckily, Amanda returned with Jordan. The three of us headed for the door.

Matt followed. "Come on, Cat, tell me—what's this horrible thing I'm supposed to have done? Because I honestly have no idea. If you think you're holding some grudge against me—"

"If I *think*—?"

A new, louder song started up. The bass thudded through the walls.

Matt shouted over the music. "I have been nothing but nice to you all this time. You're the one who completely dropped me. One day we're friends, the next day you decide we're not—"

"You think that's what happened?" I shouted. "You think *I*

decided?" The bass line was giving me a headache. Or maybe it was the whole night.

"All I know is I'm the one who keeps making all the effort," Matt said, "and I'm tired of it. I keep thinking if I hold on a little longer, you'll snap out of it one day and go back to being you. But I don't think that's going to happen anymore. I think this is the real you now. I think you're just a bitch."

I was too stunned to say anything.

Amanda didn't have that problem. She called him a pretty colorful name.

"Let's go," Jordan told her.

But Amanda wasn't through. "How could you say that to her? You're the one who betrayed her!"

"How?" Matt shouted back. "How did I betray her?"

It felt like my blood was going to boil right out of my skull. "Please, can we just go?" I grabbed Amanda's arm and pulled her toward the door.

"How?" Matt repeated. "Cat—"

"Let it go, bro," Jordan said.

"Why won't she tell me?"

"Just leave me alone!" I shouted for the second time tonight. Only this time my voice broke as I escaped through the door.

42

Amanda showed up around noon.

"Seriously," she said, doing a belly flop onto my bed. "What was all that?"

We'd already talked about it some on the ride home, but with Jordan in the car we couldn't really cover everything to our satisfaction. There's a lot of history he knows nothing about. And I'm happy to keep it that way.

Amanda lifted her head and looked at me. "You shouldn't sleep in your makeup—it's bad for your skin."

As if I cared about my skin. I felt like I'd been crushed in a trash compactor. My head hurt worse than in the early days of caffeine and sweetener withdrawal. My body felt exhausted and diseased. I don't really do well with confrontation.

We spent some time cataloging the night: my bathroom revelation about Matt, my breakup with Greg, my fight with Matt. It was an awful lot to digest. And even after an hour of analyzing everything, I still didn't feel any better.

"Can I just tell you something?" Amanda said. She looked at me so solemnly, I thought it was going to be really profound. Like something about Matt's and my relationship, or about true friendship, or about love or hope—

"You looked totally hot last night," she said. "That outfit was *ridiculous*."

What else could I do but crack up? I think I was slaphappy by that point. And starving.

We moved our meeting into the kitchen, where I could put together some sandwiches—turkey and avocado on grilled homemade rye. Yum.

Amanda also helped herself to some Oreos my dad insists on keeping around. So much for him giving up junk food.

"So what do we think about Matt?" Amanda asked. "Do we believe him? Is he really clueless?"

I let out a big sigh. "I don't know. Maybe."

"You think it's possible someone can just forget something so evil?"

"I suppose."

"Wow, that guy is totally without a conscience."

"Yep," I said.

Amanda unscrewed another Oreo and scraped off the frosting with her teeth. I had to satisfy myself with a carrot.

"Not to change the subject," Amanda said, "but I still say you looked totally hot. We'll just have to find you another boyfriend."

"I'd rather have dental surgery."

"We can probably arrange that, too."

43

Day 68, Monday, October 27

Time to rethink everything about this project.

I was eating in the cafeteria today with Amanda and Jordan, and had the brief fear that Greg would show up despite what happened at the party. But when ten minutes went by and he still wasn't there, I felt like I could relax. Hopefully he's gone back to his off-campus lunches. Hopefully he's gone back to his pre-me life. I'm certainly ready to get back to a life without dating. What a disaster that was.

I said something to Amanda about how at least now I could stay awake during lunch again, and Jordan asked me what that was about.

"It was weird," I said. "Every time I was around Greg, it's like someone hit me with the doze stick. I had this wave of sleep come over me."

"Hmm." Jordan took another bite of his sub, then told me to hold out my arm.

"My arm? Why?"

"I want to test something."

So I stuck my arm straight out in front of me, and Jordan laid two fingers gently on my wrist. "When I tell you to resist, I want you to try not to let me push your arm down, okay?"

"Okay . . ."

"Adolf Hitler," he said. "Resist."

He lightly pushed down on my wrist and my arm went with it.

"Okay, try again," he said. I straightened my arm and Jordan reset his fingers on my wrist.

"Mahatma Gandhi. Resist." He pushed down and this time my arm stayed strong.

"One more time," Jordan said, resetting my arm. "Greg Beecher." Once again my arm drooped all the way to the table.

"Hmm," Jordan said. "Interesting." Then he picked up his sandwich and resumed eating.

Amanda and I looked at each other. "Sweetie," she said, "want to tell us what that was about?"

"Applied kinesiology," Jordan answered with his mouth full. "Cat probably knows all about that."

"Um, no."

Jordan scarfed a pickle. "It's the theory that your body automatically goes weak in response to negative stimuli. It's not something you can control—your body just takes over."

"How do you know about that?" Amanda asked.

"Read about it in a skateboarding magazine," he said. "One of the guys who won the X Games last year has been using it to improve his ride. He stopped playing violent video games and watching violent movies and listening to gangsta rap. Now he's into meditation and harp music. Seems to work—he's completely dominated lately. I've started experimenting with it myself. See if I can improve my swim times by next year."

Amanda and I exchanged another glance.

"Sometimes I feel like I don't even know you," she told Jordan.

He flashed her a grin. "Keeps it interesting."

I tried to absorb what he'd just said. "So you mean my body had some automatic reaction to Greg? Without me even knowing about it?"

Jordan shrugged. "Just a theory. Maybe it picked up on something none of the rest of us did. I can tell you for sure the guy isn't what I thought he was. I'm glad you ditched him."

Amanda looked as surprised as I was. "Why do you say that?" she asked.

Jordan shrugged again. "Let's just say I misjudged him, okay? He's not as solid as I thought."

The bell rang, and Jordan got up to throw away his trash. Amanda watched him walk away. "Is it just me, or is that guy the coolest boyfriend ever invented?"

"It's not just you." And there was that same dull pain—the one I get sometimes when I see the two of them together and realize I'll never have that.

I gave Amanda a smile. "He's great. I'm really happy for you."

And that was a hundred percent true.

But it didn't make it hurt any less.

44

By the time the bell rang in **Mr. Fizer's,** Matt wasn't there. So far both of the guys I wanted to avoid today were helping me do it. I let myself relax.

But that lasted about five minutes.

"Miss Locke, may I speak to you?"

Mr. Fizer was holding the notebook I'd just turned in. I did not have a good feeling.

I went up to the front.

"Out in the hall," Mr. Fizer said.

Even worse.

I had no idea what I'd done wrong. As far as I knew I was meeting all the criteria—doing my research, keeping accurate records, turning in my notebook every Monday.

"I'm concerned, Miss Locke. Your project seems to have stalled."

"Sir?"

"While it's fascinating to learn that you have perfected a recipe for lentil and barley loaf, I fail to see the science in this anymore."

I swallowed hard. I seemed to be out of saliva.

"Miss Locke, what is your project really about?"

The truth? As if I could tell him that. *It's about me trying to be pretty, sir, and maybe someday fit into a size 8. And hopefully kick Matt McKinney's butt in science while I'm at it and finally get my revenge.*

"It's about . . . trying to conform our habits to the healthier lifestyle of our ancestors."

That didn't sound bad. I kept going.

"And you can see from my notes that I've been doing a lot of research into other native and primitive cultures, just like you suggested, and comparing how much healthier they were without all the processed foods and modern luxuries we have today."

Mr. Fizer studied me over the top of his half-glasses. I hate it when he does that. It's worse than when Amanda stares me down.

"Let me ask a different question," he said. "Do you feel that your project, as it stands right now, rises to the level of a superior science fair entry? One that might qualify to compete internationally?"

Well, if he was going to put it that way . . .

"I guess not," I admitted. "Not right now."

"Are you bored with your project, Miss Locke?"

"No! Not at all."

"It's not a crime," he said. "Some of your classmates have found it necessary to shift directions. As scientists we can't afford to become entrenched in our ideas. We always need to be able to approach our work with fresh and open minds. If you feel you've done all you can with your original premise, then it's time to step back and re-evaluate. There's no shame in that. In fact, it's the mark of a great scientist that he or she constantly asks new questions and pushes ahead toward new horizons. Do you understand?"

I slumped against the wall. "Yes, sir."

Mr. Fizer handed me back my notebook.

"Don't be discouraged, Miss Locke. We all have moments when even our finest ideas seem to have run their course. Remember what Einstein said: 'The important thing is not to stop questioning. Curiosity has its own reason for existing.'"

I attempted a smile. "Yes, sir."

"You're a bright young woman," Mr. Fizer said. "I was impressed by your analysis of whether early hominins used fire. If you bring that sort of curiosity to your project in its present form, I know you'll find your way."

He opened the classroom door. Apparently we were done.

I sat at my lab table the rest of class, flipping through my notebook, feeling totally depressed over the fact that I might have to start over. But I knew Mr. Fizer was right: it's not good enough. It might be good for me personally, but it's not going to blow the judges' minds. Not the way Matt's projects always do.

The problem was, I didn't have any new ideas. None at all. I've been so absorbed by what I've been cooking and what I've been eating and all the research I've done over these past few months, it never occurred to me it might not be enough.

But then I realized something: maybe what Jordan showed me at lunch would apply here, too. Maybe when I got a great idea, I'd know it. My body would automatically tell me.

And that's exactly what it did.

45

Eureka.

Sometimes your best ideas come to you when you're standing at the kitchen sink, elbow-deep in soapy water while you wash out the pots and pans.

It's when your brain isn't fully occupied that it can sort through all the random mishmash of facts and pieces of information you've crammed in there.

So I stood at the sink tonight replaying my conversation with Jordan—that whole cool thing about kinesiology and how our bodies automatically go weak if they're exposed to negative stimuli. That's such an amazing idea. I've never heard of it before.

And then my mind wandered over to my conversation with Mr. Fizer this afternoon, and then to some of the conversations we've had in the past about what was and wasn't working with my project.

And then strangely, Jordan and Mr. Fizer morphed together.

—you're a bright young woman—
—not something you can control—
—your body just takes over—
—astonishing amount of chemical adulteration in our food supply—
—leave that to you to research more fully—
—impressed by your analysis of whether early hominins used fire—
—your body automatically goes weak—
Stop. There.

My hand halted mid-scrub. A sort of buzzing went through me, like a low level of electrical shock. I felt alive and awake as my brain quickly worked through the formula.

What if—

What if the human anatomy reacts to stimuli in the environ-ment, whether it's positive or negative—

What if *Homo erectus* reacted to a positive stimulus—the exis-tence of fire—by undergoing a radical change in anatomy, improving and streamlining the body—

But what if—

The same thing is happening right now. Only in reverse. Modern humans are reacting to negative stimuli—bad food, junk food, chemically tainted food—by undergoing a new radical change. But this time instead of improving and streamlining, we're growing bod-ies that are fat and riddled with disease—

And what if—

My original premise was right, and we can fix ourselves by re-turning to the simple habits of our ancestors, back before ice cream and potato chips and microwave hot dogs—

I mean, what if this is much bigger than I thought? It's not just about me at all. It's about reversing a dangerous, destructive trend in human physiology before our species ends up worse than it is.

Oh my gosh.

It'll be like convincing people to stop throwing garbage into the sea.

Only I'm going to convince them to stop throwing it into themselves.

46

"**H**UGE crisis," Amanda announced.

She burst into my room before the ten p.m. cutoff my parents have set for all visiting friends, crisis or not. And even though I was right in the middle of my research, saving our species would have to wait.

"What's wrong?" I asked.

Amanda dove face-first onto my bed and groaned into the pillows.

"What's wrong?" I asked again. Amanda might be dramatic at times, but usually she has a good reason.

She rolled over onto her back. "Darlene just called me."

"Darlene . . . from the Karmic Café?"

"Yes. She thinks she has to shut it down."

"Why?"

"No one comes in there, she's not making the rent—"

"That's because her food is awful," I said. "I'm sure the only time people go there is for Poetry Night."

"I know. And she said this Saturday's Poetry Night is probably going to be the last. Can you believe it? What are we going to do?"

"What do you mean—what *can* we do?"

Amanda sat up and hugged one of my pillows to her chest. "You should have heard her—it was so sad. She was crying and blowing her nose and I could barely understand her half the time. She's really such a sweet woman. But I have no idea why she thought she could run a restaurant."

"It's been there awhile, hasn't it?"

"Almost two years, Darlene said. But her lease is up next month, and she doesn't think she can renew. She's been borrowing all this money from her elderly parents, and now they're having trouble—I got the whole story."

"Why did she call you?" I asked. "I mean, it's not like you're friends with her."

"No, but she knows how much Poetry Night means to me, and she wanted to let me know this was the last one, in case I wanted to write something special." Amanda buried her face in the pillow. I heard through the stuffing, "This sucks."

Then she sat up and took a breath. "We have to save it somehow. We can't just let her close it down."

"How? We don't have any money."

"Yeah, but we have friends, don't we? We could make Jordan start bringing the whole swim team there, we could put flyers all over school—"

"Nobody's going to come more than once," I said. "You know that. Darlene can't cook."

And then Amanda's eyes narrowed. She looked at me like I was dinner.

"You can cook," she said.

"No—"

"Yes you can. You can cook." Amanda was getting revved up. "And then you can teach Darlene to cook. And people will come there. And they will love it. And then more people will come, and you will save the café. You, Chef Cat, can come to her rescue."

"No—"

"And I'll go work for her. I'll be her hostess, or a waitress, or whatever she needs. And I'll redecorate the place. And make sure people actually know how to serve there—none of this attitude like some of those waitresses give us. I'll teach them how to be nice to the customers, and how to dress right, and what to say to keep people ordering more—"

Heaven help us when Amanda is on a roll.

"That's what I'll do," she said. "I'll quit my job at Olympus and get someone to cover this weekend's shifts so my boss won't hate me. Then I'll go work for Darlene right away. I won't even charge her for a month—I'll just work off of tips. And you, Kitty Cat, need to start cooking right away. Like tomorrow. Start figuring out some new recipes so we can bring in new customers by the weekend—"

"Can I please say something here?" I interrupted. "NO."

"Why?" Amanda said. "You know you'd love it! It would be like having our own café again, but this time for *real*. I'm sure Darlene would let us come in there and do whatever we want. You should have heard her tonight—she's desperate. Plus you and I can run that place a thousand times better than she can."

"No. I can't. I'm serious." It all sounded like a dream. But I had to be realistic. "Amanda, I have so much work to do. I already have a job, remember?"

"So quit it—"

"I'm not quitting. I like it there."

175

"So you could work at the café on the weekends," Amanda said.

"Except I have homework. And I have to cook for my own family, remember? I just don't have any more time."

"But this is *important*," Amanda said. "And I know you're very organized. You can figure out a way, can't you?"

This time when she stared me down, it was so much more pathetic. She wasn't demanding, she was pleading.

And I felt myself starting to give in.

"I don't know how to cook vegetarian," I tried.

"Of course you do. You cook it all the time—all those vegetable dishes, those soups, those fabulous zucchini muffins—come on, Kit Cat, don't you think the world deserves your muffins?"

If Amanda were a puppy at the animal shelter, she'd be adopted in a flash. There's no way anyone could resist that pitiful face.

"Besides," Amanda said, "I can guarantee that everyone would rather eat your absolute worst vegetarian meal than any of Darlene's best. You *know* that's true."

I closed my eyes and heaved out a sigh. And Amanda knew she had won.

She jumped off my bed and hugged me. "Thank you! Thank you! You won't regret it—I mean it. We can really do something good here. We can save Darlene from ruin and still make a home for poetry. It's the most noble thing you've ever done."

"You're a very sinister person," I told her.

"I know. I love you, too."

She left me to go back to my homework, as if I could concentrate on that anymore. Instead I immediately started looking up vegetarian recipes. If I'm really going to do this, I don't want to embarrass myself.

Am I really going to do this?

47

Day 71, Thursday, October 30

My audition at the Karmic Café.

It's absolutely amazing what Amanda can accomplish in just three short days.

When I walked into the Karmic Café tonight, it was like I'd never seen the place before. There were actual living plants in there, and clean tablecloths, and enough new lighting that everyone didn't look like they had hepatitis anymore.

And just like in the days of our own café, Amanda had decorated the walls with pictures and signs and handmade artwork.

And there was music.

"What do you think?" Amanda asked. As if my dropped jaw wasn't answer enough.

"Un. Believable."

Amanda grinned. "You think?"

"This is . . . gorgeous."

Amanda squeezed my arm. "Thank you!"

She took me on a tour. "I made all the tablecloths out of sheets I found on sale—I was up cutting and hemming until about midnight last night. I went through Darlene's house and brought in everything that I thought looked cool—like those jelly jars over there I'm using for vases."

A little of this, a little of that—that's Amanda's decorating style. Nothing ever needs to match—matching is boring. Somehow no matter how odd the combinations are, they always end up looking perfect together.

She drew my attention to the lists she'd posted on the walls. *Famous Vegetarian Poets. Famous Vegetarian Artists.* And singers, and actors, and writers, and athletes—

And *Famous Vegetarian Scientists.*

Amanda followed while I headed in that direction. "Thought you might be interested."

I stood in front of the list and read.

"No way—Albert Einstein was a vegetarian?"

"Yep. I even put his quote on the menu—I'll show it to you in a minute."

I continued scanning the list. "Leonardo da Vinci?"

"Yeah, he earned the double—he's over on the artists' wall, too."

Charles Darwin, Thomas Edison, Jane Goodall—

And then I saw the name that really made my heart flutter.

"Brian Greene? The physicist? The guy behind string theory?"

"That's the one. Didn't you tell me you have a little crush on him? I can understand why—I saw his picture and he is *cute.*"

It's true, I do have a crush. A *big* one. Ever since I watched Dr.

Greene's series on PBS about string theory and quantum physics and alternate universes, he's pretty much been at the top of my list of men I would love to marry one day. He's funny, brilliant, and *very* good-looking.

"I read an interview he did," Amanda told me, "and he said he's been a vegetarian since he was nine. Obviously it hasn't hurt his brainpower any."

"Uh, no."

"Hold on," Amanda said. "Let me go grab a menu."

While she was gone, I continued reading her list: Sir Isaac Newton, Pythagoras, the inventor Nikola Tesla—

"Here," Amanda said. "Take a look."

The menu was beautiful. Of course. It wasn't handmade like in our junior high days, but it definitely had Amanda's touch: bright colors, interesting graphics, fun fonts.

"Did you do this yourself?" I asked.

"Yeah, another midnight job. I kept a lot of Darlene's dishes on there, just because I didn't know what else to put, but as soon as you tell me what you'll be making, I'll whip out some new menus." Amanda pointed to one of the sections. "I thought I'd cover some of it now, though, with 'Soup of the Day,' 'Dessert of the Day'—that sort of thing."

I glanced up from the menu. "Amanda, this is all absolutely amazing. You're just so . . . talented."

She bounced onto the tips of her toes. "Thank you!" Then she flipped the menu over and pointed to the bottom of the page. "Now check it out. There's your boy."

"Nothing will benefit human health and increase chances of survival for life on earth as much as the evolution to a vegetarian diet."—*Albert Einstein.*

Amanda elbowed me in the ribs. "Pretty good, huh?"

"Seriously?" I asked. "I've never heard about Einstein being vegetarian before." Of course, until I met Mr. Fizer, Albert Einstein wasn't exactly a big part of my life. These past few months I feel like he's always in my head.

"Come on," Amanda said. "Let me introduce you to Dave."

Dave is the part-time cook Amanda talked Darlene into hiring. She freaked out about the money, of course, but Amanda convinced her it was a temporary investment in what will turn out to be a long-term solution. "That way," Amanda told Darlene, "you can be out in front greeting the customers and making them feel welcome. You can handle more of the business side."

A very diplomatic way of not saying, "Your cooking is killing your crowd."

Amanda was obviously right about Darlene basically letting her take over. Right now Darlene was out on some errands Amanda had suggested, picking up a few more items to decorate the place for Halloween tomorrow.

"Dave, this is Cat."

"All right—the famous Cat." Dave smiled and shook my hand. "I hear you've come to save the day."

"Oh. I don't know about that—"

Amanda rolled her eyes. "Don't bother acting modest—there's no time. I'm going to leave you guys here. I have to get back to work. Dave, please do whatever she says."

"No, really," I said as soon as she was gone. "I'm just learning."

"Don't worry about it," Dave said. "I'm just going to be here a few hours a week. I don't want to be in charge. I've got enough stress with school."

He's a junior in environmental engineering at the university. He said he and his girlfriend come to the café for lunch a few times a week, and when he saw the Help Wanted sign yesterday he decided to apply.

Dave looked around to make sure we were still alone. "I couldn't do any worse than the food already is, right?"

I nodded.

He said he learned to cook vegetarian from his girlfriend. "She told me she wouldn't go out with me unless I gave up meat."

"Wow," I said. "Harsh."

"But worth it," he said. "You should see her. And you?"

"What," I said, "vegetarian? No."

"That's okay—as long as you can cook it."

"I think I can," I said.

Amanda popped her head through the doorway. "Hey, less chitchat, more action."

Dave and I sprang to work.

"Bossy," he muttered.

"You have no idea," I said.

While he chopped vegetables and prepped salads and filled the orders that came trickling in, I started experimenting with a few of the recipes I'd downloaded from the Internet. I'd already made some handwritten adjustments at home. I had no idea if they would work.

Eventually Darlene showed up. She flitted in and out of the kitchen a few times just to see how things were going. "Do you need any help?" she asked me, and I told her no. She actually seemed relieved.

When I pulled my first vegetarian creation out of the oven, Dave and I both took a whiff.

"Smells incredible," he said.

"Will you taste one?" I asked. "I don't want to send them out there if they suck."

We waited a few minutes for them to cool, then Dave set out two plates.

"Oh, no, I can't. I'm not supposed to have chocolate or sugar for another"—I did a quick calculation—"hundred and thirty-six days."

"Why?" Dave asked. "What'd you do?"

"It's a science experiment."

"Talk about harsh."

He took a bite of my very first try at a dairy-free, egg-free dessert—deep-dish double-chocolate espresso brownies. Dave smiled and took another bite.

"Phenomenal." He held up his palm for me to slap. "Looks like we're in business."

48

Day 72, Friday, October 31

My first Halloween without candy—I think in
my whole life.

It's weird how much things have changed. And in such a short period of time.

Ever since I got too old to trick-or-treat, I've been the one who's volunteered to answer our door on Halloween night. It's been my sneaky little trick: one mini-Snickers for you, one mini-Snickers for me. One Reese's cup for you . . .

By the end of the night I've always crammed as much into my mouth as into the little kids' bags.

But not this time. This time I don't even care. I'm going to be working at the café tonight, but even if I were at home I wouldn't get involved with the candy. I feel like I've lost my taste for manufactured food. I like the things I make with my own hands.

Which is why I was so tempted to try my own brownies last night. And the cupcakes and the pie I made after that. But I've already come this far, and I wouldn't have taken the job at the Karmic Café if I thought it would mean I'd have to give up my whole experiment. I'll just have to be satisfied with the fact that other people seem to like my desserts. It's just for another 135 days. A long 135 days.

But meanwhile I have the feeling that Halloween will never be the same for me again. It's possible I've kicked my candy bar habit forever.

It was pretty cute walking with Peter to school this morning. He was dressed as a vampire (I almost told him how cliché that is but decided I shouldn't give him a hard time). The whole way to school we kept seeing all these other little kids dressed up—witches, ninjas, pirates, even a mermaid tottering along.

"That's Trina," Peter whispered.

"Who? The mermaid?"

He nodded and kept walking.

"She looks mean," I said. "Look at that pinched-up, prissy face."

Peter shrugged.

"I hate her costume," I said, really getting into my role as protectress. "She looks stupid."

"No, she's not," he said.

And then I got the picture. "Do you like her or something?"

He shrugged. His main form of communication, it seems.

"You shouldn't like mean girls, Peter. That's a really bad idea."

"She's not mean."

"You said she told you that you were fat. That's pretty mean."

"She didn't tell *me*," he said. "She told Savanna and Savanna told me."

How well I remember the circuit. "So what did you tell Savanna to tell Trina back?"

"Nothing."

I made him stop and look at me. "Peter, you're a great boy. You're fun, you're smart, you're good-looking—"

He shrugged my hand off his shoulder and kept walking.

"Are you listening to me?" I asked.

"Yeah."

"Mean girls are . . . they're just bad. Stay away from them. If someone's saying behind your back that you're fat, that's a mean girl. Understand?"

Peter's voice was so quiet I barely heard it. "I *am* fat."

"No, you're not, you're just a little . . . filled out. But if we keep walking to school every day, that'll probably change, okay?"

He nodded.

"And maybe if you ate fewer hot dogs. Whatever. What I'm saying is, in the meantime, you're still a great kid and anyone should like you. Exactly as you are—understand?"

We were close enough to school that he started seeing some of his friends. Before he took off I made him look at me one more time.

"You're very handsome, Peter. I wouldn't say that if it weren't true."

He sort of smiled.

"No mean girls." I stuck out my hand. "Shake on it."

He smiled and looked off to the side as he shook my hand. He's a shy one, even with me.

I slapped him on his backpack. "Go suck some blood. And take it easy on the candy, okay?"

He nodded and ran off.

I remember being that age.

I'm sure I looked just like him.

49

A few people dressed up at my school—your standard zombies and slashers and again with the Catwomen. Lots of skintight outfits. Skinny girls just love showing off their bodies.

Greg dressed up, too. I saw him in between classes, wearing that same Wolfman outfit from the party. I caught his eye, and he gave me a sullen look and kept moving. Thank you.

I've been getting those same looks from Matt all week, ever since our big blowup last weekend. Fine. Guys everywhere should avoid me—spread the word.

"Your preliminary research papers are due next week," Mr. Fizer told us this afternoon. "Make them sharp—I will be grading them."

Next week. I have a lot to do before then. But at least I know what my project is about now—mostly. I need to take all the ideas that are colliding around in my head and somehow make them all work together. No problem. I'll just have to give up sleep for the next seven days.

Matt was back in class again today. Terrific. Like I really needed to see him. I accidentally caught his eye once, and we both immediately looked away. I didn't think it was possible, but things are even more uncomfortable between us now than they were before. It's like ever since the party, we're both afraid of what the other one might say.

When I left class, he looked like he was sort of lingering near the door. I gave him the coldest look I could muster.

That's my costume: Freezer Girl. Completely impervious to emotion.

I think he might have said my name.

But I kept right on walking.

50

Day 73, Saturday, November 1

Dinner at the Karmic Café. Poetry Night.

"Whoa." Jordan stepped into the bright, beautiful café and took a look around.

"I know, huh?" Amanda answered. "Darlene told me she was going to redecorate the place."

"Not bad," Jordan said, which was high praise, coming from him.

Amanda and I shared a secret smile. We had decided to surprise him. About all of it.

We sat at our usual table, and even though there were two servers on duty, neither of them waited on us. Amanda had told them not to. She got up to grab us some glasses of water, then I excused myself to go to the restroom.

But really I sneaked into the kitchen.

As soon as I'd done my part, I sat back down, and at a signal from Dave in the kitchen, Amanda took her turn. She left for a moment and came back with our food. But Jordan still didn't seem to notice.

He kept talking to us while he doctored up his burgers with ketchup and slapped his pickles and onions on top. Then he took his first bite. And creased his forehead.

"What's wrong?" I asked innocently.

Jordan opened the bun again to inspect what he was eating. "This actually tastes—"

"Fantastic?" Amanda finished for him. "Delicious? Superb? Gourmet? Like perhaps our own Kit Cat, that mistress of all things delectable, made it especially for you?" She held out her palms as if presenting me to royalty. "I give you . . . your chef. Tell him what's in it, Cat."

"Black beans, onions, garlic, cumin—"

Jordan held up his hand. "Huh-uh. Never explain what's behind a magic trick." He took another huge bite and smiled. "Thank you, Cat."

"You're welcome."

Okay, so it did take some magic to make room for everything I have to do. I dropped Friday afternoons at the Poison Control Center. Renegotiated with my mother so I only have to cook at home three nights instead of four. Agreed with Darlene that I'll work Friday and Saturday nights but only until nine so I can get home to do my homework, and I'll also give her recipes as I figure them out so she and Dave can cook some of this stuff on their own.

What did I used to do with my time? Watch TV? Bah—what a waste. Surf the Net? Talk on the phone? Go to movies with Amanda and Jordan? Oh, yeah, and work and study and go to school and sleep—

And eat. Let's not forget eating.

Either this is all going to work out—everything timed precisely to the second—or it's all going to catch up with me and come tumbling down.

But I'm betting on precision. It's true that I'm very organized. And it's actually kind of fun to be this busy.

We were Amanda's only table tonight. Darlene gave her the night off to be a poet. And even though Amanda brought out our food and bused our empty plates and kept refilling our glasses, it took Jordan a while to notice.

Finally he gave Amanda an odd look. "Should I know something?"

"Not bad," Amanda said, checking her watch. "That only took you thirty-two minutes."

"I was distracted by the food."

"Understandable," she said. "Yes, I'm working here now. I'll expect to see you in often—and please bring five friends with you every time."

Jordan smiled. "Done."

"And now comes my favorite part of the job," Amanda said. "Bringing out your dessert."

She disappeared into the kitchen and returned with what looked like a double portion.

"Chocolate peanut butter pie," Amanda announced, setting the plate down with a flourish. "With chocolate cookie crust and chocolate shavings on top and extra chocolate in the center."

Jordan dug in. A sort of blissful look came over his face.

"Don't you dare ask her to marry you," Amanda warned.

"Greg was an ass," Jordan said as he shoveled in another bite. "He should have treated you like a queen."

I wasn't expecting that. But at least I had an answer. "It wasn't

Greg's fault, it was mine. I never should have gone out with him in the first place—that whole thing was a huge mistake. I'm done trying to date. No more guys. Except platonic ones, like you."

Jordan's fork scraped his empty plate. "Can I have another piece?" I don't think he'd even been listening to me.

Amanda scooped up his dish. "Nope, no more pie. You're going to try the lemon cupcake with non-butter frosting next. And then you're going to clap for your girlfriend, who's about to go be a poet."

Jordan kissed Amanda on the cheek and then sat back and patted his stomach. "I have obviously died and gone to sugar and poetry heaven."

"Good," Amanda said. "Remember to tip your waitress."

51

Day 79, Friday, November 7

Preliminary research paper due today. At this
point I feel like I could do a separate report
on sleep deprivation.

"Here," Amanda said, "put this on." She met me at my locker before
school this morning and handed me a T-shirt that matched the one
she was wearing.

Veg Head, it said on the front, and on the back was this gorgeous purple logo saying *Karmic Café* with green vines twisting all
around it.

"Did you make these?" I asked, already knowing the answer.

"These and about twenty others. We're starting a T-shirt promo-
tion at the café tonight. Ten giveaways every Friday and Saturday
night."

"Ten? But that might be everybody who comes in there."

"I know," Amanda said, "but hopefully that will change. I figure the more people walking around wearing our T-shirts, the more they're doing our advertising for us."

"Oh, smart."

"Yeah. Then I also redid Darlene's website, and I've started some viral marketing, but I know you won't be involved in that, Cave Girl. That's why I want you to wear the shirt—very low-tech."

"I can do that."

"Good. You can alternate between the white tee and the black so it won't look like you're wearing the same shirt all the time. I want people to know you do your laundry. It'd be bad for business if they think our chef's a slob."

"When have you been doing all this?" I asked.

"Same hours you've been working on your research paper. See you in English. Wear the shirt."

This afternoon I turned in my big fat preliminary research paper along with everyone else's. Matt and the other people who've been gone a lot lately made brief appearances at the start of class to add their papers to the pile, then headed out again.

Matt didn't even look at me once. Which is good. I think he's finally gotten the message.

I think maybe I'm actually free of him.

52

Day 82, Monday, November 10

Third appointment with Jackie.

WOW. Wow, wow, wow. I mean, I knew I lost weight—it's obvious from how even my new clothes have been fitting and how my whole body feels these days—but I really didn't know what the number would be. My body mass index is a lot better, too—gained some muscle, lost some fat.

"Things will probably start leveling off soon," Jackie said. "A lot of that initial weight loss was from changing your diet so drastically and from starting to exercise after all those years of inactivity. Now your body is more used to it. So I expect to see less weight loss, but still a lot more improvement in your muscle mass. Remember, muscle weighs more than fat, but it looks much, much better."

Fine. Whatever. All I kept thinking about was the numbers. Yahoo!

"How much exercise do you think you're getting these days?" Jackie asked.

"I don't know, between walking to school and walking to work, it's probably about one and a half to two hours a day. It used to be more, but I can't walk home from work anymore—it gets dark too early. But I've started jogging a little on the weekends." With my anti-nuclear bra.

"You might want to add some upper-body strengthening," Jackie said. "Even push-ups while you're on your knees would be good. Or do you swim?"

"No," I answered quickly. "We, uh, don't have a pool."

"Too bad. Swimming is great for the arms. You know hospital staff has access to the rehab department's pool, right?"

No, I didn't know that.

"It's heated," she said. "You could swim there all winter."

I didn't want to hear that. It brought up too many things. I needed to change the subject.

"Can I ask you something?" I said.

"Sure."

"What do you think about . . . being a vegetarian?"

"I think it's great," she said. "I've been one for eighteen years."

"What? Why didn't you say anything?"

"It's not my business to say it," Jackie answered. "People need to make their own choices. I'm just here to give them nutritional support."

"So you think it's okay? I mean, obviously you think it's okay. . . ."

"Why are you considering it?" Jackie asked.

"Well, for one thing, I just started working at the Karmic Café—"

"Ech," Jackie said. "The food there is terrible."

"Um, I think it's getting better. Anyway, so that's part of it. I've been eating a lot of vegetarian food for the last week or so, and I actually really like it."

"It can be very good."

"Yeah. And then last week I had to do some new research for my project, and I found out a bunch of stuff about all the drugs and hormones and chemicals that get pumped into cattle and chickens and pigs—and even fish—and then we end up eating all of that in our meat. And a lot of scientists think that's what's causing a lot of the health problems people have right now."

"I think so, too," Jackie said.

"And it's not just the drugs," I said. "Did you know they sometimes put sawdust and other things into the animals' food, just to fatten them up? And then we're eating that, too. That can't be good for us."

"Those sound like some good reasons."

"And there's one more," I said. "At least for me." It was time to confess my string theory crush.

"I found out this one scientist I really admire"—*love, adore*—"is a vegetarian. Actually, a lot of scientists have been. And I think if *they* decided that was the smart thing to do . . ."

Jackie smiled. "Peer pressure—always the clincher. But I understand what you mean. Like I said, it's a very individual choice. I can't tell you whether I think it's right or wrong—I'll just help you to take care of yourself based on whatever you decide."

Sometimes you just want people to make your decisions for you. But Jackie was right—I'm sure no one else told Albert Einstein or Brian Greene or Sir Isaac Newton what to eat. They made that decision themselves, based on their own personal and scientific judgment.

"I think I want to try it," I told her. "At least for the rest of my project. I'm working on this new theory about how our bodies go weak in response to the negative stimuli of bad food. So I should probably try not eating sawdust and growth hormones for a while and see how I feel."

"Sounds like a plan," Jackie said.

She talked me through some of the principles, like making sure I still eat plenty of whole, natural foods like I am right now.

"There are some junk food vegetarians out there," she said. "They think they can live off of chips and soda because there aren't any animal products in those. They've forgotten the vegetable part of vegetarian.

"But I'm not worried about you, Cat. You've been eating extraordinarily well."

That was nice to hear.

She told me I need to take vitamin B_{12} every day, since that's the only nutrient we can't get from plants. Other than that, I should be fine.

"And I'll get enough protein and everything?"

"There's plenty of protein in plant foods," Jackie said. "Fruits, vegetables, grains, seeds, nuts, beans—even a box of raisins has a little."

"Really?"

"Read the label."

Jackie's next client knocked on the door.

"Can I ask you just one more thing?"

"Sure," Jackie said, standing up to let the person in.

"I saw this quote from Einstein about how the best thing we can do for human health and survival is to switch to a vegetarian diet. Do you think that's true?"

Jackie smiled. "Are you asking me personally or professionally?"

"Either."

Jackie thought about it for a moment. "You know, Cat, one of the things I love about your project is that you're letting yourself experience the answers to those kinds of questions. I think that's better than me telling you what I believe. I'd rather watch you do your science."

I think I actually really appreciate that.

I had a lot to think about this afternoon, and it wasn't just about going veg. It was something else that Jackie said.

"Hey, Mom," I said on the ride home, "did you know you're allowed to use the rehab pool?"

"Hmm, I guess I did know that," she said. "But I've never been much of a swimmer—not like you."

"So it's . . . for staff, right?"

"And patients."

"Oh, sure . . ." I hesitated. "I'm staff, right?"

My mother smiled. "Yes, you are. Are you thinking of swimming again? You used to love that."

"Thinking about it . . . But nobody else goes there, right? I mean, other than people from the hospital."

"No, I'm pretty sure it's restricted."

"Oh. Okay. Great." I couldn't believe what I was about to ask. "Could I maybe borrow the car tonight?"

53

I suppose I could have called Amanda. Picking out a bathing suit? She would have *loved* to get in on that action—but this was even more private than shopping for a new bra.

I haven't worn a swimsuit since the summer between sixth and seventh grade. That's when my boobs started coming in. And everything else—the stomach, the butt, the whole Fat Cat package.

I used to be able to live off of Doritos and Snickers and other fine food products all summer long, and just get back in the pool and work it all off. But somehow that summer my fat outpaced my exercise, and I was one roly-poly swimmer. It didn't really matter because I was still the strongest girl in my age group on the team, but I did start feeling a little self-conscious standing around in my bathing suit without the team T-shirt to cover it up.

The first time I heard "Fat Cat" was at the Monroe Heights meet. That scumbag Willie Martin—my own teammate—shouted it while I crouched on the blocks, waiting for my start. I heard him, the pistol went off, and I was so stunned I didn't dive in until everyone else was already two body lengths out.

I swam hard—mainly out of anger and humiliation—and managed to make up the time and still get second place. Then I climbed out of the pool, pulled my cap off, and went to the bathroom to cry.

It was mostly Willie Martin and Andy Pister saying it all summer long, and everyone heard it. Including Matt.

"Shut up," he told them a few times, but then he just started ignoring them the way I did. I tried to stay out of their way. And wear a T-shirt anytime I was out of the water.

I cut back on all the junk food, but it didn't seem to matter. My body was popping out all over, obeying some hormonal signal that said it was time to look like I'd be a great child-bearer someday.

I had some small hope tonight when I dug out that old swimsuit from the bottom of my drawer that it might still possibly fit. But of course that was a fantasy. I only wish I still weighed what I used to back when I first started thinking I was fat. Those were the days.

So I just got it over with. Grabbed my mom's keys, got in the car. It's been eighty-two days since I drove—can't say that didn't feel weird. For a moment I wasn't sure my foot would know the difference between the gas pedal and the brake.

When I got to the mall, I parked near the biggest department store and walked straight inside. I tried not to think too hard about what I was doing.

I sort of forgot it was November. Not exactly swim season. But there were still a few suits on the sale rack, and I wasn't in the mood to be picky. It just had to fit.

I found a black and green tankini that will do the job. It covers my stomach, it fits my chest—good enough. I was in and out of the store in less than half an hour. Amanda would have been impressed.

But I don't think I'm going to tell her. I'm not going to tell anyone. Is that wrong? Why wouldn't I tell my best friend I'm going to start swimming? It's not like it's anything to be ashamed of.

Except for the fact that I'm about to make a total fool of myself. All I can hope is that all the rehab patients are old and arthritic and out of shape and look even worse than I do.

I wish they sold full face masks for this sort of thing. It's one thing to expose my body to ridicule, but does everyone really have to know it's me?

What am I doing? Am I really going to do this?

54

Day 84, Wednesday, November 12

Dinner: Homemade corn tortillas with beans, homemade salsa, avocado, lettuce, tomatoes, rice. Family didn't seem to miss the meat—too full to notice.

Waited an hour after eating, because that's what our coach always said to do.

Standing at the edge of the pool in my bathing suit tonight may have been the hardest thing I've ever done in my life.

I felt naked. And ugly. And huge.

There were only two other people in the pool: a woman who looked like she was about a hundred, wearing a bathing suit with these big ugly red and orange flowers on it and a matching swim cap, and a guy who was maybe in his forties, doing really slow laps with a kickboard.

And I stood there feeling fat and ugly and exposed, thinking, *There was a time—*

There was a time when I would have thought I was better than those people. I would have laughed at them—and not just for the silly bathing suit and cap, or for resting on a kickboard, but for not being me. Because there was a time in my life, before Willie Martin pointed out how fat I was, that I would have known I could beat those two people and anyone else in the pool. Maybe not an Olympic swimmer or someone twice my age with longer arms and legs, but definitely someone my own size, Willie Bleeping Martin included.

Because I was good. Really good. I was a strong girl, and I loved my sport. I loved competing. I loved getting in the water and showing what I could do, shaping my hands just right to create the minimum amount of drag, angling my arms and shoulders and legs perfectly so that my movement through the water looked almost effortless, so that I sped along, so much power and speed and—I guess this is the word for it—beauty. I think I really was beautiful in the water. Because no one was looking at my face or my stomach or anything else—they were just watching me swim.

And so when Willie and Matt and the rest of them took that away—or really, when my bulging body took that away—I think maybe I lost something. Something more than just an activity that was fun to do every summer and that gave me an excuse to be with Matt all day, every day. I think I actually lost a part of my personality, like someone might wake up one morning and realize their thumbs had fallen off.

It wasn't just that I was embarrassed about being fat. It was that I was angry that part of my life was over. I'd never get to feel that strong again. I'd never get to dive into the water and forget everything but how it felt to push and pull and kick and propel myself through the pool and know I was as good as or maybe better than everybody else.

So when I stood at the edge of the pool tonight, sizing up my competition—the slow guy and the ancient granny—I knew what I'd lost. I didn't feel superior. I didn't feel like I could beat them. I didn't even know if I could keep up.

And, it must be said, standing anywhere in public wearing nothing but a swimsuit is a humbling experience anyway. But I think that might have been okay if I had known I could lap the granny.

I didn't dive in. I didn't even trust myself to do that. I took the steps, gently lowering myself into the pool like an egg about to be poached.

But here's the thing: from that moment on it was practically magic.

There are these tiny shrimp that live in potholes in the rocks of the desert, and whenever it's dry, they go dormant. You don't even know they're there. But as soon as it rains, you see them darting around in the water, as if they fell from the sky in droplets instead of just waiting around for the first sign of moisture to revive them.

Tonight I was a desert shrimp.

Something happened to me on a cellular level. I felt it as soon as the water reached my thighs. It's like some dormant portion of me moistened itself back to life, and as I glided forward into the pool and took my first few strokes, I didn't care anymore what I looked like or what people might say about me or whether they thought it was hilarious that a chubby girl was out there doing freestyle. I didn't care about anyone or anything. I just swam.

I think tonight I might have made the biggest scientific discovery of my life.

I think I was born an amphibian.

55

Day 99, Thursday, November 27

Thanksgiving!! Tofu turkey, stuffing (made
from homemade bread), mashed potatoes
(with vegetable stock instead of milk and
butter), corn, green beans, and pumpkin pie!

Okay, so my dad wasn't thrilled with the tofu turkey. Maybe it's an
acquired taste. And he said he won't be acquiring it. But the rest of
the meal was awesome, if I do say so myself.

My family's being really good about my vegetarian meals. My dad
still slaps a few steaks on the grill when he can't take it anymore, but
other than that they're letting me cook whatever I want on the
nights when I'm their chef. I've been testing out new recipes on them
before I try them at the Karmic Café. I can always trust my little
brother to make a face if I haven't gotten the taste just right.

Normally on Thanksgiving I love to eat my way into a food

coma, then spend the rest of the evening just digesting. Tonight I wish I could swim.

But the pool is closed. What's up with that? Like people don't need rehabilitation on holidays? What about that 500-pound guy who's recovering from a heart attack and does his jumping jacks in the shallow end? Or that old lady in the ugly flower suit who I found out is getting over a hip replacement? Or that guy who just started last weekend, who's recovering from a motorcycle accident? Doesn't the hospital care about them? And what about me?

Ever since I started again two weeks ago, it's like my whole body is this giant Rubik's Cube, and every time I swim, another row finds its right place. Blue, red, green—one by one I'm putting myself back together. I can't believe how whole I feel again.

On the downside, I'm a full-on swimming junkie again. If I don't get my nightly fix, I might have to start stealing cars or something.

Amanda finally busted me last night. Now I know how people feel when they're trying to hide the fact that they smoke. They brush their teeth right afterward, they wash their faces, they chew gum. But all it takes is someone with a good nose.

I wasn't expecting her to show up. Even though it was the night before a day off from school, we didn't exactly have plans to hang out. I thought she'd be with Jordan.

But there she was, sitting in my living room watching TV with Peter, when I came back home from the pool.

My swim cap keeps my hair dry, and I'd changed into dry clothes, so there wasn't any visual evidence of where I'd been. And Peter didn't know—I certainly haven't been sharing my whereabouts with him. But it still didn't matter. Amanda can smell fresh cookies baking a block away. So I really didn't stand a chance.

She followed me into the kitchen for a snack and leaned into me almost right away. She gave me a big sniff. Then she stepped back and pointed at me. "Ooooh . . ."

Before I could say anything, she smiled. "Good for you. But shame on you for not telling me."

It was such a relief for her to find out. I hate keeping secrets from Amanda. It felt good to tell her at that Halloween party what I really thought about Matt, and now my secret life as a swimmer is finally out in the open. It's been a hard two weeks keeping that from her.

"Why didn't you tell me?" she asked. "What did you think I was going to say?"

"I don't know, I was just kind of embarrassed."

"Why?"

I gave her the kind of answer Peter would and simply shrugged.

"Kit Cat, you should never be embarrassed to tell me something. I've told you some of the most embarrassing things on the planet. You have enough blackmail material on me to make you a billionaire."

She helped herself to a giant slice of pumpkin bread, and we retreated to my room.

"So," she said, settling herself and her plate onto my bed. "What's the plan?"

"With what?"

"Your swimming, obviously. Going out for the school team?"

I snorted. "The season's over, for one thing," I said, "and absolutely not. I'm still huge."

"Cat, you're not huge! Are you crazy? You look fantastic!"

"You haven't seen me in a bathing suit."

"Show me," she said, waving her hand. "Right now."

"No!"

"Then don't complain," she said. "I know what I see, and I know you look like as much of a swimmer as those Amazon girls on Jordan's team. Have you seen their backs? They're as wide as truck beds."

"I am never swimming in public again," I said. "I mean, other than the rehab pool. This is just for me."

Amanda rolled her eyes. "I'm not going to try to force you, but I really think you have a distorted picture of yourself. You're like one of those anorexic girls who looks in the mirror and sees a blimp. You're not a blimp, Cat. Do I need to do an intervention here? I'm serious."

"No. I know I've lost weight, thank you. I know I'm not such a blimp anymore. But there's a big difference between that and wanting to parade around in Lycra."

Amanda shook her head and ate another bite of bread. "Chef, scholar, champion athlete—what *can't* she do, ladies and gentlemen?"

"Um, sew a purse?"

"Oh, yeah. You really sucked at that."

56

Day 103, Monday, December 1

HALFWAY MARK!!!!!

"So," I asked Peter on our walk this morning, "how's it all going?"

"Fine."

"How's school?"

"Fine."

Some days we're pretty silent. Even after all the time we've been spending together lately in the kitchen and on the walks, I still feel like I don't really know my little brother all that well. Part of it is that he doesn't talk much, but part is also that I haven't really paid much attention to him since he was a baby. Back then he was like having a little live doll. But over the years I sort of got involved in my own life and forgot about him.

But I'm trying to change that.

"So what do you like in school?" I tried again. "I mean, to study?"

Peter shrugged. "Math. History."

"History? Uck. You wouldn't feel that way if you had my teacher Mr. Zombie."

Peter nodded and kept walking. He hasn't quite mastered the art of the follow-up question. Or maybe he just isn't all that interested in my life.

"So tell me the truth," I said. "What did you really think of Thanksgiving? I know you and Dad didn't really like the tofu thing, but was the stuffing okay?"

"Yeah."

"Really, really okay, or just kind of?"

"I like the way you cook," Peter said.

"Thank you! Do you have any requests? I mean, I sort of always make what I want, but I'd be willing to try something else."

"No," Peter said, "that's okay."

"Has the pizza been all right?" Because I've been sticking to our deal and faithfully making it for him once a week.

"Yeah, it's good."

Maybe this is why I haven't spent too much time talking to my brother. He doesn't really have much to say.

But maybe I wasn't hitting the right topic.

"Okay," I said, "if you want to talk about Trina, go ahead."

He walked along for another half a minute, not saying anything. Then he blurted out, "She hates me."

"Why would she hate you?"

"I told you. I'm fat."

"No," I said, "she told Savanna she thinks you're fat. That's not the same thing as *being* fat."

"Do you think I'm fat?"

"No, Peter, I don't."

"I think you used to be fat."

"Thanks a lot!"

"Well, you were."

It was hard to argue with him. "Yeah, I guess I was. Do you think I'm fat now?"

He laughed. "No."

"Do you think I'm pretty?"

He laughed again. "No."

I chucked him on the shoulder. "You're a brat. I knew I never liked you."

"Me neither."

I held out my hand and we shook on it. "We're even."

That was all the conversation we had in us until we got up to the corner. He was going straight ahead, I was going right.

Peter pretended to concentrate on the traffic as he asked the question. "Do you think a girl will ever like me?"

"Yes. I have no doubt."

He rocked back and forth on his heels. "Why? I mean, what do you think they would like?"

"Hmm. Can I only pick one thing?"

"Yeah."

I wrapped my arm around his shoulders. "Too bad. You're smart and you're thoughtful and you're kind, you're great at sports, you always get your homework done, you care about other people and animals, you have those beautiful green eyes, and the girls are going to go wild for you, but you should only go wild back for the very nicest ones. How's that?"

"Good." He didn't smile or act embarrassed or flattered. He simply took it in, as if I'd just told him I was done with the bathroom and it was his turn.

"Okay?" I said. He nodded. Then he crossed the street and went about his business, as if his big sister hadn't just given him some of the greatest compliments in the world.

Boys. I'm beginning to think they really should have been my research project.

57

Day 114, Friday, December 12

Still working on the applied kinesiology
portion of my project. Sometimes this whole
thing feels so huge I don't know how I'm
going to bring it all together into one
cohesive theory by next March. I guess I just
have to keep taking it one piece at a time.

"Hey," Nick Langan said in Mr. Fizer's class this afternoon. "How's it
going?"

I looked up from the chart I was making.

"Yeah?" I asked, because obviously he needed something, right?
Like to borrow a pencil or a sheet of paper. Because Nick never talks
to me. Nick lives in a world that doesn't involve talking to me. I

don't understand him, he doesn't care to understand me—we're both fine with that.

We've been fine with that since about third grade, when he announced to our teacher, Mrs. Tomarchio, that he wouldn't read any of the assigned books anymore because they were "irrelevant" (Mrs. Tomarchio used it as a teaching moment and had us all look up *irrelevant* in our dictionaries). Nick preferred to read "only the facts." So while the rest of us enjoyed stories about talking animals and ten-year-old private detectives, Nick read *Time* and *U.S. News & World Report,* and, if he really wanted to kick back, *Psychology Today.*

Which probably explains why Nick has never really had that many friends at school. Instead he stays in touch with kids he meets at the various brain camps he goes to every summer. I heard that last summer he hooked up with some Russian girl whose English was a little sketchy, and they'd have these incredibly loud arguments in the mess hall over their respective country's energy policies, then they'd both suddenly stop arguing and she'd jump on his lap and they'd make out right there in front of everybody.

Ewwww.

Nick is a major hound dog during the summers, total celibate monk during the school year. At least that's what everybody says. I'm not that surprised he can get girls when he wants them. He's not bad-looking—tallish, skinny but not geek-skinny, light blond hair he wears sort of long, decent enough face. If you can just get past the personality.

Turns out his, "Hey, how's it going," had a purpose behind it, but it wasn't to borrow a pencil.

"Winter Formal's next Friday," he said. "Want to go?"

"Huh?"

"We should go." And then he just walked away.

Okaaaayy . . .

For some reason Matt has been showing up in class again lately, and so he was there. And he overheard Nick asking me out, which was great. He looked thoroughly shocked. Yes, Matt, some boys might actually like me.

If I expected Nick to hang around after class, maybe discuss it a little further, I was wrong. He gathered his stuff and took off, as if we'd never even spoken.

Luckily I could talk to Amanda at work tonight.

We had a little time together in the kitchen while she helped me form more black bean burgers so Dave could keep grilling. Sometimes when we're really swamped in the kitchen I ask Amanda to scrub in and help.

It's amazing how much busier the café has gotten in the last month and a half. Amanda says it's because people found out they can finally get fantastic gourmet food there, but I know it's all really because of Amanda's hard work.

When you walk into the café now, it's so cozy and relaxing—the soft lighting, the music, the decorations. And Amanda improved the dress code of the servers—dark pants and a Karmic Café T-shirt. She's been cranking out new designs all the time, and now people have even started buying them. They're like individual works of art.

Plus she's been doing all these online promotions and specials, and so more and more new customers have started coming in. Business has improved so much, Darlene went ahead and renewed her lease. Yay! She's also started paying Amanda to manage the place, and she's giving her a portion of the T-shirt sales on top of it. Which only seems fair—she wouldn't have any of this if not for Amanda.

"So do you think that conversation with Nick was a real invitation?" I asked her as we continued molding burgers.

"Depends. Was he looking at you when he said it?" Amanda's

known him since junior high. "Because sometimes when I think he's talking to me, it's more like he's dictating a memo to himself and my face happened to be in his way."

"No, I'm pretty sure he meant me."

"Huh. So what do you think? Are you going to go?"

"No!"

"Could be interesting for a laugh," Amanda said. "Haven't you always wanted to know what he's like in real life?"

"No, seeing him in school is bizarre enough. Although I am curious what his project is—maybe I could worm it out of him. I overheard Mr. Fizer say something to him like 'cat's gill.' What do you think that could be?"

"Underwater genetic mutations in cats? Who knows. But I think you should go. Maybe talk a little Russian to him. Make him go wild."

"Thank you for your lack of help."

"My pleasure," Amanda said. She washed off her hands. "I've got to go check on my tables. Want to come over after work tonight? I think *Casablanca* is on."

"Haven't you already seen that like a hundred times already?"

"So? Love is timeless."

"Nah," I said, "not tonight. I just want to do some laps and go to bed."

"You Olympians are so boring."

"Yeah, well."

"Anyway," she said, "back to Nick. I think you should go. Could be a trip. What's the worst that can happen?"

"Being stuck on a date with Nick."

"Besides that."

"Why did he even ask me?"

"Kitty Cat, have you looked at yourself in the mirror lately?"

58

There's something about the monotony of swimming laps. Your mind can just wander. Stroke, stroke, *Nick, Winter Formal*, stroke, stroke, *Russian girl, Greg, Matt, Nick, Peter, can't figure guys out, should have been my research project*, stroke, stroke, *looked at yourself in the mirror lately*—

Eureka.

I stopped at the end of the pool and rested my arms on the ledge. My feet kept kicking, I was so excited.

Oh, it was wicked evil. But also kind of genius.

I needed a second opinion. I jumped out of the pool, quickly changed, and then drove to Amanda's house on my way home. She was in the middle of *Casablanca*, but she graciously turned it off.

"I have a new experiment," I said. "Listen." Then I told her my whole idea.

"Is it just too . . . wrong?" I asked when I was finished.

"Wrong how? I think it's funny. Besides, you said it yourself— you're just gathering information. It's all very clinical, very scientific."

"But, it's not like I'm tricking people?"

"How?" Amanda asked. "You're just finally accepting your powers—it's about time. There's nothing wrong with seeing how people react to that. And if it's Nick you're worried about," she added, "there's definitely no problem there. He asked you out, you're going to say yes, and then you'll just observe the night as it unfolds, right? In fact, since it's Nick, you could probably just tell him straight-out what you're up to. Superbrain can take it."

She had a point. And that really would make me feel better.

Amanda smiled and cocked her eyebrows. "And you know this means shopping."

59

Day 117, Monday, December 15

Research Project, Phase II: Effects on
male population of changes in female
appearance. Experiment #1.

I'm not really sure if I'm going to make this an official portion of my project—I think it might just be for me. But I'm keeping track of it in a separate notebook, just in case I think it's science fair worthy.

Today was my first experiment.

When I walked into Mr. Fizer's this afternoon, Matt noticed. I saw him notice. It was one of the greatest moments of my life.

The clothes were perfect: these soft black pants that flared at the bottom in a way Amanda said made me look taller and skinnier. A tight white knit top beneath a royal blue sweater that crisscrossed over my chest. Pearl stud earrings, my hair long and curly and unfrizzed (okay, some product in there), and a better makeup job than I've ever done in my life. Amanda made me practice with her this weekend until she was sure I had it right.

It felt weird to wear makeup again. In the past 117 days I've only worn it once, for the Halloween party. But even though it felt wrong in a hominin sense to wear it, I know it's all part of the new experiment. Besides, it's just temporary. I just want to satisfy my curiosity. Isn't that what experiments are for?

I walked up to Nick, very aware that both he and Matt were staring at me.

"I've decided to go with you to the formal," I told Nick. "You can pick me up at six."

He sort of acted surprised that I even needed to say that—as if there were no question I had already said yes. I guess in Nick's world, no one can resist him.

I sneaked a peek at Matt, who quickly looked away. Good.

I spent the class period on the computer, pretending that I didn't notice Matt and Nick taking turns staring at me. What a weird and yet satisfying feeling.

The question is, can I do this right? There are so many variables when you start involving other people. It isn't like working with fig wasps. I can't just crush boys into a petri dish and extract their DNA. Or really, in this case, their whole psychological makeup.

But it's like what Einstein said: "If we knew what we were doing, it wouldn't be called research, would it?"

60

Day 121, Friday, December 19

Phase II, Experiment #2: Winter Formal.

As soon as school was out I walked home, grabbed a shower, then waited in my robe for Amanda to show up at four-thirty to do my hair and makeup before she had to get to the café. I'm taking the night off, obviously. Some things are more important than crafting the perfect vegetarian pizza.

I told Amanda I thought I could handle the primping myself. "Didn't you think I did a pretty good job with my makeup all week?"

"Yes, but this is no time for amateurs. Step aside and let me do my job."

She set up all the tools of her trade, then before getting to work she planted herself in the center of my bedroom and whipped out a sheet of paper.

She cleared her throat. "A poem, in honor of your night:
Beautiful Catherine, her spirit afire
Nick the unwary, consumed with desire
How love finds us sleeping
It ensnares and infects us
As true today
As with *Homo erectus*."

I gave her a standing ovation and Amanda took a bow. "Can I have that for my research files?" I asked.

She handed the paper over. "Be my guest. Now, enough chitchat. Time to do some major construction."

By the time she was done, I looked like . . . not me.

I could see some of the basic parts—my chin, my cheeks, a few limbs here and there—but the whole girl was unrecognizable.

And a big part of it was the dress. *Amazing.* Amanda found it at a thrift store and surprised me with it. It smelled a little musty, but nothing a little perfume couldn't cover, she said.

She thinks it was from the 1940s or 1950s. It looked liked something Marilyn Monroe could have worn: ivory satin, about calf length, full skirt (the kind that puffs out if you twirl around—we tested that a few times), and a top half that made the most of what I have without being totally slutty about it. Topped off with some fake pearls, smoky eyes, and red, red lipstick, and I looked like I belonged in an old movie. Plus Amanda overrode my complaints and used both a blow-dryer and hot curlers to make my hair look like nothing it's ever been.

A pair of black velvet pumps Amanda lent me, and the look was complete. I was no longer Catherine Locke, Science Wonk. I was Sex Goddess Glamour Queen.

At least that's what Amanda called me. And I don't think it's conceited to agree, since it's not like that was the real me at all tonight. Amanda completely invented me out of satin and lipstick and hair.

Nick showed up at the door two minutes early, and his eyes nearly popped out of his head. He looked pretty amazing himself. There's something about a guy in a tux—it's like some fantasy of your wedding day or something. Nick isn't bad-looking anyway, but when I first caught sight of him tonight he sort of took my breath away. I had the passing thought that if not for the circumstances, I might actually be attracted to him. That came as a total shock, since I've known Nick so long and never ever felt that way.

But I put it out of my mind. This wasn't a playdate, it was research. I was on duty.

Still, nothing wrong with being polite. "You look very handsome tonight."

"You too. Wow, Cat." His eyes immediately snapped to the cleavage. But I was ready for that. I knew full well that no part of an actual breast was out there for the world to see—I had checked that in the mirror from several different angles. So even though my inclination was to stand there with my arms folded across my chest, I forced myself to keep them at my sides. I could be a little exposed for one night—this was for science, after all.

Nick was a great multitasker, able to negotiate traffic while at the same time sneaking endless peeks at my chest. I made myself sit on my hands.

"So, where are we going for dinner?" I asked.

"Karmic Café. Amanda told me you're a vegetarian now and that's the only place you'll eat."

Oh, she's good. Not only did Amanda look out for my dietary

needs, but this way she ensured she'd get a front-row seat to my date. Clever.

"Mr. Langan," Amanda said regally as we walked in, "so nice to see you this evening. And Miss Locke, aren't you stunning?"

She crisply removed two menus from the stack and escorted us to our table, over in the Famous Vegetarian Scientists section, of course. I started to sit down in the first seat Amanda offered, but she stopped me. "Oh, no, Miss Locke. You should face the room so that everyone can drink in your beauty."

I thought she was pouring it on a little thick—and gave her a look that said so—but she merely smiled in her most professional hostess manner and returned to her station.

I understood right away why Amanda had made me sit there—it was so she could sign to me from across the room. *"You look great!"*

Pretending I was covering my mouth to cough, I brought my hand to my chin, then forward and down. *"Thank you."*

"Nick looks hot!"

I glanced at my menu while casually nodding my fist twice.

Then more customers arrived, and we both got back to work.

"So," I said, "have you ever been here before?"

"No, I heard the food sucks."

I choked on my water. "I think it's gotten a lot better."

That was about all the small talk I was up for. My parents set my curfew at midnight, but I planned on being home much earlier—this wouldn't take the whole night. But it meant I had only a few hours for observation, and I didn't intend to waste any more of them.

"Look, Nick, we've known each other a long time, right?"

He chomped on a bread stick. "Yeah."

"Since first grade, right? And just because we haven't exactly . . . hung out before, we're technically old friends, right?"

"Okay."

"Great." I leaned forward, and his eyes snapped right where I expected. I cleared my throat to regain his attention. "So look, here's the deal. I don't want to play any games tonight—we've known each other too long for that. I want us to be able to relax and be honest with each other—no pressure, you know?"

He gave me a curious look.

"So I'll start," I said. "Do you want to know why I agreed to go out with you tonight? I could say it's because I admire you, I think you're so smart, you're so good-looking, blah, blah, blah. But the truth is, it's because you took me by surprise and I was flattered that you asked me. There—I said it. That's me being honest. Can you take it?"

Nick crunched. "Sure."

"So now it's your turn," I said. "Please be completely honest with me—why did you ask me out?"

He smiled and reached for another bread stick.

"I mean it, Nick. You can tell me. Is it my sparkling personality? My impressive GPA?"

He chuckled.

"So what is it?"

Nick lounged back in his chair. "You really want to know the truth?"

"I really do."

Little did he know I had a research notebook going in my head, and right then it was like I had a pencil poised to write down everything he said.

Because what I decided in the pool a week ago was that maybe Amanda's right. Maybe I've actually achieved that secret result I was aiming for when I first embarked on this whole hominin project.

Maybe in some small way I've actually made myself . . . pretty. Or at least better-looking than I was before.

I was starting to feel a little of that when Greg asked me out, but that was almost two and a half months ago, and I've lost a lot of weight since then. I know I look a lot different.

And since I've never really gotten attention for my looks before—except bad attention for being fat—is it so wrong to want to spend a little time here and see what it's like? It's all just for research purposes—sort of a social experiment to see what it's like to be a girl that guys notice. It's like the opposite of what Amanda does. She fools people at school into thinking she's plain. For a little while I'd like to see what it's like not to be.

"I'm serious, Nick. You can tell me the truth—I'm not going to get all weird. Just tell me as a friend—why'd you ask me out?"

Nick took another bite of bread stick, then leaned forward onto his elbows. "Okay, Cat, I'll tell you the truth. It's because I can't believe how incredibly hot you've gotten all of a sudden." His eyes strayed to my chest for about the eightieth time. I was beginning to feel at this point like my breasts should do some kind of trick.

"What happened to you?" Nick asked. "How'd you end up like this? You used to be so large."

Steady . . .

"Well, thanks for noticing, Nick. You've always been so observant—that's what makes you such a great scientist."

"So what happened?" he repeated. "Did you have surgery or something?"

Is that really what people think?

"No, nothing like that," I said, smiling politely. "Just good healthy living."

"Very healthy," Nick said appreciatively.

And this time I smiled for real. Because right then I was glad it was Nick who asked me out. Amanda was right—Superbrain could take it. He could deal with some honest conversation and not make it feel weird.

And I realized I could handle it, too. I didn't feel awkward or uncomfortable—or sleepy—around Nick the way I did with Greg. There really is something to be said for hanging out with someone you've known practically all of your life. Even if he keeps staring at your chest.

And once the ice was broken and we'd gotten all that beginning honesty out of the way, I felt like I could relax. I just sat back and let Nick entertain me with his stories. And believe me, they were plenty entertaining.

At first they were just about his various awards and accomplishments—from being first-chair cellist in the city youth orchestra to winning honors at the various international science camps his parents have sent him to over the years—but then he moved on to some of the more juicy details of his life.

Like all the girls he's dated since junior high. I had no idea Nick was so . . . successful. And since I'd already declared the theme of the evening to be honesty, Nick felt free to tell me everything I wanted to know.

That Russian chick we all heard about wasn't even the most exotic of the bunch. There was the South African ambassador's daughter, the visiting French physicist's daughter, and the Nobel Prize winner for chemistry's niece. Not to mention the odd high school science genius here and there. From the sound of it, he's been juggling multiple girls every summer since we were thirteen.

But never during the school year—once fall hits, it's always back to work.

Amanda kept coming over and refilling our water glasses all during dinner, even though that wasn't technically her job. Then she'd stand behind Nick and mouth what he was saying, a mere split second after he said it—another one of her talents. *Very* hard for me to keep a straight face for that.

By the time dessert came around (my apple and peach cobbler, thank you very much), I had said very little besides, "Uh-huh," and "Wow," and, "Then what happened?" And yet it was still a thousand times more interesting than any of my conversations with Greg had been.

"It's funny," Nick said as he dug into his cobbler. "You're not at all what I expected."

"What do you mean?"

"Even McKinney warned me about you."

I narrowed my eyes. "Excuse me?"

"Yeah, he told me to watch out for you."

Amanda happened to be pouring more water for me right at that moment, and she nearly spilled the pitcher on my lap. I didn't dare look at her.

"What, exactly, did he say?" I asked.

Nick took another bite of dessert. "Just that ever since you've lost weight, you've been seeing a lot of guys."

"A lot of guys!"

Amanda moved close enough to step on my foot. Unfortunately she didn't get to hear the rest because people were waiting up front to be seated.

I tried my best to seem nonchalant. "So, what else did Matt say?"

"Just that you seem pretty conceited lately, and I should watch out."

I could barely speak, I was so angry. "Watch out for what?"

Nick grinned. "Apparently you're quite the heartbreaker. Love 'em and leave 'em, you know?"

So that's what Matt thinks happened with Greg? Please. And what about Greg being the bad guy—the "jackass"? Now he's the victim and I'm the cruel one?

"Well," I said, smiling as best I could, "I'm afraid as usual, Matt McKinney is completely wrong. I hope you didn't listen to him."

"I like to find out things for myself."

"You're very smart," I said, and of course Nick agreed.

I was running out of time. I knew once we got to the dance, the music would be so loud we couldn't really talk anymore. I had to shake off my anger at Matt and instead focus on my task.

"So," I said, "I'm really curious about something."

Nick looked at his watch. "We should probably go." He signaled our waitress for the check.

I persevered. Because hearing all about Nick's history, I knew he had a few things to teach me. It wasn't like talking to a girl about her particular strategy with guys, but humans are humans. And sometimes a scientist has to broaden her research base.

"I hope you don't mind me saying so," I said, "but it sounds like you've been really successful with girls over the years."

Nick smiled. "What can I say?"

"Well, that's just it—I'd like to know what you do have to say about it. Obviously you're a smart guy, so you must know what your secret is. I mean, beyond just the good looks—a lot of guys have those."

Every time I mentioned how good-looking he is, Nick just ate it up. And the truth is, the longer the evening wore on, the better-looking he seemed to me.

"So what do you think your secret weapon is?" I asked. "I mean, if some random girl is out there looking over the vast array of guys in any particular place, why do you think she'd pick you instead of somebody else?"

People are funny. You just never know what they'll say in a given situation. I guess that's why there's a whole discipline of psychology to try to anticipate what people are thinking and how they're going to react.

So I thought Nick would say something about girls loving how smart he is, how he's going to Harvard, how he's going to win the Nobel, yada, yada, yada—who knows? He could have said anything.

But what he did say was this: "Because I know how to appreciate a beautiful woman, Cat. And tonight I'm appreciating you."

61

I **didn't mean to dance that close.** Really—it's totally against my nature. But something came over me—something chemical, something I couldn't control. I am shocked and horrified to admit that Nick Langan and I actually sort of made out on the dance floor, right there in front of everybody, the two of us mashed together, not really dancing but clutching and kissing for the entire duration of two back-to-back slow songs. Finally the DJ showed some mercy and switched to a loud, obnoxious dance track, so I could finally pry myself off of Nick and catch my breath.

"Oh," I gasped, "this is bad."

Nick grinned. His teeth flickered in the strobe light. He kissed my neck, then whispered, "I think it's pretty great. Come on—let's get out of here."

More than happy to, thank you. Because that whole room was like a giant centrifuge, spinning us around like test tubes, separating out my good sense from the rest of me. Then by some bizarre chemical process, this new me fell completely under Nick's spell, and when he went for it at the start of the first song, I went with him. I didn't care who saw us or what I did—it's like it wasn't even me inside my body anymore. I had become this creature, this animal, this girl in the movie star dress making out with a guy in a tux. Completely unreal.

But also scientifically instructive. Some part of my brain understood I'd have a lot of new data to analyze. Later. When the rest of my brain came back.

That was another interesting thing to notice: my brain. It wasn't like with Greg. I might have been dazed with Nick—out of my mind is more like it—but I wasn't sleepy. Feature that.

We stepped outside the hotel ballroom into the cold night air. Some kids were out there smoking. All I wanted to do was breathe.

"Nick—"

But before I could say something intelligent or even coherent, he grabbed me around the waist and pulled me to him. And there we were, kissing again.

I swear, my mind just abandoned me. I was nothing but brainless lips and hands. What a disgusting image. But it felt good while it was going on.

Finally I heard some people laughing at us, and it broke the spell enough that I could push away and gain some space. Nick stood there practically panting, his mouth smeared with my dark red lipstick like he was a wild animal that had just come back from a kill.

"Nick, this is such a bad idea."

"Then let's go somewhere," he murmured, as if my problem were that we were making out in public.

Believe me, that was a big part of the problem. I'm just not like that.

But the bigger problem was this uncontrollable urge to keep

doing it. How did I end up sharing tongues with a guy I never even liked before?

I adjusted my dress. Somehow there was more cleavage showing than when I started out the night. I did my best to rearrange it.

Nick kept me close. Even his breath—his garlicky, spinachy, appley-peachy breath—did something to me. I stepped a little more to the side so I could think.

"What time is it?" I asked. I forced myself to turn over his wrist and look at his watch. It was past eleven.

"I have to go," I said. "I'm on curfew."

"Come on," Nick whispered, pulling me to him and kissing my neck again. "We're just getting started."

"No, really. My parents are incredibly strict." Which was a lie, but I had to say something. It was hard enough to get those lines out, with his hands on my back and his lips on my throat. I could have stayed there like that all night.

"You really are a heartbreaker," Nick murmured. "McKinney was right."

And that did it.

What was I doing? Who was this creature I'd become? I am *not* that kind of girl, and especially not with a guy I've never even liked. I swear, it really was this freakish chemical reaction, somehow activated by a dark dance floor and the faint smell of Nick's breath and sweat.

I clasped both his hands in mine and removed them from my hips. Then I forced myself to create some distance between us. "I'm serious, Nick. I have to go. Really. I'm sorry."

"Mm." He pulled me back and murmured into my hair, "I'm sorry, too."

We walked to his car, arms interlaced, pausing every few steps to kiss again. It was starting to make me sick—not because I didn't like it, but because I knew once I was out of his presence, I'd regret absolutely everything about tonight. So much for scientific detachment. So much for my grand experiment. For all I know, Nick was doing an experiment on me, trying to see if he could overcome all my natural inclinations and somehow bring me to this helpless state.

But I wasn't helpless, was I? If that crack about what Matt had said brought me back to my senses once, it could do it again.

For the rest of the walk to the car and then the entire ride home, every time Nick reached for me or whispered something seductive or just emanated whatever those bizarre chemicals were that had me so entranced, I thought about Matt McKinney. Thought about how smug he'd be when we got back from winter break and everyone was talking about my slutty behavior. Thought about what Matt would say to Nick and to everyone else about me.

That worked better than if someone had slapped me.

When we got to my house, Nick turned off the ignition and the lights. He pulled me toward him, almost onto his lap.

"My parents are probably watching."

"Let them," he whispered, then he went for a breast.

I jerked away.

It's a lot different when a guy is pressing himself against you on a dance floor and feeling your breasts that way. Somehow I could handle that. But an actual hand cupped over an actual boob? No way. I still wasn't ready for that, whether it was Greg in the Mondo Head or Nick in front of my house. And my fear turned out to be an even greater deterrent than just thinking about Matt's smug face.

"I can't. I have to go." I flung open the car door.

"Cat, wait!"

I turned and waved, but kept on running. I felt like Cinderella escaping from the ball. Only the thing I almost lost control of wasn't a slipper, but a breast—I quickly tried to stuff it back in. I can't believe I let things go so far—no outsider except Joyce my lingerie guru has ever had access to my naked breasts.

I was barely in the house thirty seconds when I heard a soft knock on the front door. I opened it before my parents could hear.

Nick leaned against the doorjamb, his white shirt looking rumpled from all our exertion. "Cat. I think you're amazing."

I maintained my distance. "Thanks. I have to go. Good night."

I tried to close the door, but he blocked it. "Just one more kiss."

I took a deep breath. "This was a mistake."

Softly he gripped the side of my waist and started to pull me toward him. I stiffened my arms and held him off.

I had to tell him the truth. "I don't really . . . like you, Nick. I mean, not that way—not as a boyfriend."

He chuckled softly and pulled me toward him again. "That's okay." His mouth moved in for the kiss.

"And you don't really . . . like me that way, do you?" I asked.

He nibbled the lobe of my ear.

I don't know why I had to keep asking him questions when I already knew the answers. "This is just physical, right?"

"Mm," he whispered, "hope so."

Well, at least he was honest.

I removed his hands again. Nick leaned against the doorway and smiled in this incredibly seductive way. "Cat . . ."

I shook my head. "Huge mistake."

"When can I see you again?" he asked.

"At school. After the break. I have to go." I gently pushed him back so I could close the door. Again he blocked it.

"Besides school," he said. "I do like you, Cat—a lot."

"I thought you didn't date during the school year," I said, grasping at any technicality.

"I would for you," Nick said.

"This was a mistake."

Nick smiled. "It was no mistake, and you know it."

62

Amanda came over around noon. I don't know how people survive without best friends to share all their shock and dismay and horror at their behavior, and yet still tell them they're okay.

"So what are you going to do?" she asked.

"Stay far, far away."

"What are you going to say when you see him again?"

"'Stay far, far away.'"

Amanda stole a couple of pillows off my bed and settled beside me on the floor. "I just can't believe my innocent little Cat—"

"Stop. It's bad enough."

"Actually, I think it's almost good. You learned a lot last night. Apparently you're not as immune as we thought."

"Apparently I'm a slut is what you mean." I groaned and buried my face in a pillow. "What was I thinking?"

"I thought the whole point was you weren't. Lighten up, Kit Cat.

It's not the worst thing in the world. So you let loose for one night in your life—big deal. It's not like you slept with him."

"Yeah, but if it had gone on like that, who knows? I'm telling you, he had some kind of power."

"I know you'd never do that unless we went to the clinic first," Amanda said. "And by then I'd have talked you out of it."

I wasn't in the mood for logic. "Everybody's going to know."

"Know what? People don't care."

"Of course they care!" I said. "I'll tell you one person who for sure is going to care, and that's Matt McKinney. 'You should watch out for her,'" I mocked. "'Love 'em and leave 'em.'"

"Who cares what Matt thinks? You're a free woman. You can do whatever you want. And if that includes shoving your tongue down Nick Langan's throat, then so be it."

"Please stop."

"And look at it this way," Amanda said. "It serves Matt right. Nick was right about you being amazing. I'm glad to hear someone appreciates you—they all should. Let Matt say whatever he wants. The truth is, you know he's jealous."

"No, he's not."

"Then why would he go to the trouble of warning Nick about you? It's not like they're friends, are they?"

"No," I admitted.

"Then ask yourself why Matt did that. I say he was trying to keep away his rival—write that down in your notebook."

"I say you have a very active imagination," I told Amanda. "Let's try a different story: Matt McKinney hates my guts, and so he will do whatever he can to make my life miserable. Including telling guys not to go out with me. The end."

"Matt is a tortured soul," Amanda insisted. "He's Heathcliff and you're Cathy. He's Rochester and you're Jane Eyre. He's—"

"Darcy and I'm Elizabeth. I get it. And you're wrong."

"We'll see-ee," Amanda sang. "As far as I'm concerned, the experiment lives on."

63

Day 126, Wednesday, December 24

Christmas Eve feast of some sort. I still haven't figured out what to make yet. My dad just asks that it not involve tofu.

Nick showed up this afternoon.

Bearing gifts.

One being a beautiful pink fleece scarf that will be perfect for walking to school on cold winter mornings, the other being Nick's random collection of chemicals that once again pulled me under his spell.

I am so disgusting. And weak.

My whole family was hanging around, of course, so I had to introduce Nick to them (actually re-introduce in my parents' case, since they'd met him at a few science fairs, whether they remembered him or not). Then my parents, for some bizarre reason, showing no parental judgment whatsoever, let Nick come with me to my room for a while, where the minute the door was closed Nick and I went right back to it, mashing ourselves against each other and kissing and panting and—

I am so disgusting.

But once again, the hand went to the breast, and once again, the hand was forcibly removed.

"It's not happening," I told Nick. "Ever. So you might as well forget it right now."

"It's happening," he assured me.

I pulled both his hands away this time. "No, seriously. I've already decided I'm never going any further with you. So if that's what you're expecting—"

He looped my new pink scarf around the back of my neck and held me to him while he kissed all the sense out of me.

"I didn't get you anything," I said quite lamely during one of the few times I could catch my breath.

"Yes, you did," Nick said, and back we went.

After about ten minutes of that, I couldn't take it anymore. "You have to leave. Now."

"I don't think so."

I took a few steps back just to make the room stop spinning. "I'm serious—this is not what I want."

"Could have fooled me," Nick said, and I could see his point.

What had happened to all my scientific objectivity? This wasn't the way it was supposed to go. The experiment was supposed to be about how guys react to me, not how I completely lose my mind around them.

When did the whole thing get out of hand? One minute I was

interviewing Nick about why he thought he was so successful with girls, and the next minute I was demonstrating the answer for myself. I can't help that the guy is just incredibly sexy. Who knew that was hiding under all that intellectual arrogance all these years?

But I knew it was wrong. WRONG. Even aside from the fact that my experiment had turned into a total free-for-all, it was wrong because it's not what I want. A guy might have all the sexual magnetism in the world, but I want more than that. I don't want to be treated like a piece of meat. And I don't want to treat someone else that way, either.

No matter how exciting it might be in the moment.

I sat him down on the edge of my bed. Big mistake. He had me on my back in no time.

So I stood up. Held my hands out in front of me to ward him off.

"Go. Shoo. Bad. Go away. Thank you for the scarf. Now go."

Nick smiled and patted the spot next to him on my bed. I sat down but did not recline.

"Look," I said, "I'm incredibly old-fashioned this way. Believe me, if I weren't, you'd be the one." It was hard to think with him stroking my arm like that. "But I need to be in love. And I'm clearly in deep lust here, but I'm sorry, I don't feel love."

"That's okay," Nick answered. "We're friends. That's enough."

"Not for me. I need"—I circled my arms in the air—"big love. Big huge committed love. Maybe that sounds ridiculous, but it's what I've always wanted. And I know if I settled for anything less, I'd really, really hate myself. And you."

"Well, I don't want you to hate me."

"Thank you."

"But I do think you're being shortsighted," Nick said, still stroking my arm. "This could be really great, the two of us. You know it as well as I do."

"Yeah, great at the physical level, but I still need more. Sorry. Maybe someday I'll accidentally fall in love with you after all, and we'll be right back here."

"Will you let me know?" Nick said. "All it takes is a word."

"Really? Like 'now' or something?"

"'Now' would work. Or, 'Here, Nick,' or just whistle for me. You're hot, Cat. Anytime you're ready—"

I patted his leg. "Thank you." And then I shook his hand. Very businesslike. "Okay, then, I think we're through here for now."

"You sure?"

I wasn't, but I had to say yes. "Do you want your scarf back?" I asked.

"No, just the girl who goes with it."

Oh my gosh, that guy knows his lines. I tried to be cool, but my voice gave me away by cracking. "I'll let you know."

He kissed me once. "You do that."

And then he left. Just like I'd asked him to.

I fell back on my bed, my lips still throbbing from all the attention he'd been giving them, and I actually felt a little tear form in the corner of my eye. Not because I loved Nick Langan so much and I had just lost him, but because I didn't love him and had let him go.

I thought guys were complicated. Maybe they are. But maybe they're easy and it's really me who's complicated.

Ho, ho, ho, merry Christmas.

Now pull yourself together.

64

Day 138, Monday, January 5

A new year and only 69 days to go.
Phase II officially over. What was I thinking?

I felt like everyone was staring at me today—like everyone was talking about what happened at the formal. I even caught Greg Beecher
giving me a dirty look. As if I care what he thinks.

I'm back to looking like I did at the start of this project—no
makeup, no special clothes, uncontrollable hair. I'm done trying to
see what effect I can have on guys if I really put in the effort. If I have
some sort of powers, like Amanda said, I'd rather not use them, thank
you very much.

It was a stupid idea—and way too much trouble. Plus I've already
had enough effect with just two guys to last me until the end of high

school. I know Amanda is disappointed, but honestly, I can't take the pressure of trying to be pretty all the time. I don't know how girls do it.

So I walked into Mr. Fizer's today wearing just jeans (girl jeans) and a sweater and (I have to confess) Nick's pink scarf. I don't know why I did it, but I just did. Maybe I wanted to show him there were no hard feelings. I don't know, maybe I wanted him to still like me just a little.

He looked up and smiled when I walked in. Then he went right back to serious consideration of whatever it was he was working on. Scientist first, seducer second.

It looked like everything was back to normal, but then I saw Matt. Or more specifically, I saw Matt see me see Nick. And I must have blushed or something, because suddenly Matt's expression darkened, and for the first time in my life I saw him look at me so hatefully it made me want to turn around and run.

He quickly averted his gaze back to his notebook, but it was too late—I'd already seen.

And it really made me mad.

What does he have to be angry at me about? I wouldn't be surprised if he heard about Nick and me at the dance, but that's none of his business. And if it's for some other reason, then I can't imagine what. I've never been anything but nice to that guy, up until the time I realized he was a traitor. I admit I've been cold since then, but it's justified. And besides, I've certainly never set out to harm him in any way, other than beating him at grades or science awards. It's not personal—mostly—it's just business. So he has no reason that I can see for giving me that nasty look today. No reason at all.

I ignored him the rest of class. I had too much on my mind already to worry about why Matt McKinney might hate me. It's obviously been brewing for a while, since he made those rude comments about me to Nick.

Anyway, there's plenty to worry about with school. We're moving on to integration in Calculus, we're going to be doing twice as many labs in Chemistry, Ms. Sweeney has assigned us some ten-pound novel to read for English Lit, I have to prepare a piece for my spring recital in Piano, Mr. Zombie is heading into the Civil Rights Movement and the glorious sixties, which I just know he wants to re-live, and Mr. Fizer told us today that he wants our project prototypes by the end of the month so he can look them over before we head into the final few weeks of preparation—oh, and there's this little matter of all my AP exams. So yes, I'll be a bit busy this semester. The only thing that isn't going to kill me is Sign Language. We all have to perform a song or poem in front of the class, but I'm sure Amanda will help me with that.

So Matt McKinney can just save his surly attitude for someday when I actually have time to deal with it. Until then, I'm too busy to care.

As I was leaving class, Nick came up behind me and gave my upper arm a squeeze on his way out. My heart involuntarily sped up. Boy, that guy really has it.

Then he walked on without even looking at me, which was just what I wanted. I don't need to draw any more attention to us than I already have.

I was still standing there, dealing with my racing heart, when I heard Matt mutter under his breath, "What are you doing?" Then he, too, walked on without looking at me.

I liked it better when things were simple.

65

Day 151, Sunday, January 18

Breakfast: Oatmeal, walnuts, banana. That's all I ever have anymore because it's all I want. Simplify. I think from now on I'll just write "the usual."

Lunch: Spinach, garlic, and potato soup; homemade multigrain bread; apple with peanut butter.

"I think the problem," Amanda said, "is that you're a good girl. And when you went out with Nick, you were pretending to be bad. It just wasn't going to work."

Amanda can't stop analyzing my love life—now that I've finally given her something to analyze. It must have been hard for her before, with nothing to go on.

We were taking a break this afternoon from our Sign Language project, mainly because smoke was starting to come out of my ears from having to concentrate so hard. We're the first team who has to perform this semester, and I know if I don't start learning it now I'll never get it in time.

We've decided to keep it simple for my sake and just sign "Row, Row, Row Your Boat" in a round, even though Amanda could probably sign an entire opera. In Italian. So far I haven't made it past "gently down the stream."

Amanda settled onto the floor of my room with her bowl of soup and a hunk of bread. "So," she said, still grilling me about Nick, "anything lately?"

"The usual brush against me on his way past. Which, of course, drives me insane. A guy like that should walk around in protective glass."

"I admire your stubbornness," Amanda said. "I don't know if I'd be able to resist if I were you."

Which was just the opening I needed. Because I've been wanting to talk to her about it for a while lately.

"Can I ask you something?" I said.

"Sure."

"You guys . . . still haven't, right?"

"What, had sex? Don't you think I'd tell you?"

"So you're still sticking with the plan?"

"Of course," Amanda said. "For now."

Amanda developed her virginity policy back in junior high. Both her older sisters were in high school then, both of them were sleeping with their boyfriends, and each of them told Amanda separately how much they wished they had waited until they were older. That made an impression. So Amanda decided to take their advice and wait until college or even later, depending on how she felt at the time. Their point was, there's no hurry.

"But you still love Jordan, right?"

"Of course. Right now I'm hoping he'll be the one. But it's just too soon. He knows I'm not ready."

"And he doesn't get . . . frustrated with you for that?"

"Probably, but he keeps it to himself. He's the most patient guy I've ever known. That's one of the reasons I love him." Amanda smiled. "And one of the reasons I'd like to reward him, eventually, if you know what I mean. But let's talk about you and Nick—what's your plan?"

"I don't know. Sometimes it's so tempting, you know? Just give in and have a good time. But I keep thinking it would be nicer to have the whole package—not just the physical, but the love part, too. I want a real boyfriend who I know really loves me."

"I think you need that, too."

I groaned. "Why can't I just fall in love with Nick? Then everything would be so much easier."

"Because we're back to that 'should' thing," Amanda said. "You think you should love him because you're so hot for him, but it just doesn't work that way. It's either there or it isn't. And obviously it isn't.

"And," she felt it necessary to point out, "it's not like he's declaring his undying love for you, either. Right?"

Big sigh on that one. "I'm going to die a dried-up old hag, just like you said."

"Probably," Amanda answered. "Or maybe you're going to meet the love of your life within the next two hours. Could be either."

"I'm serious. Maybe you've been right all along, and I'm going to end up alone with only a bunch of science trophies for company."

"I doubt it," Amanda said, sopping up the last of her soup with the bread. "Now that we know what wild passion you're capable of, I have confidence it's only a matter of time."

"You really think so?"

"Kit Cat, you are primed. Some lucky guy out there is going to be very happy if he can only make you fall in love with him."

"I'm not picky."

"Ha! I'm surprised your nose didn't just grow."

66

What is with Matt? I have never seen him act more surly—and I've seen plenty of surl from that guy. But it's like he's refined it into a whole new art form.

He glares at me. He shakes his head at me. He mutters *constantly* whenever I'm close enough to hear. I'll catch little snippets like, "What a waste," and, "So wrong," and the inexplicable, "Done with it."

I even saw him talking to Nick again, and I wouldn't have thought anything of it except Nick looked up when I walked into class, and they both quickly shut up and shifted apart.

Which is why I've decided to just deal with this thing once and for all. Because I do not appreciate being made the object of discussion or observation by those two. I don't know what they're up to, but I can beat them at it, whatever it is.

So today I took affirmative steps to bring this situation back under control. I handed Nick a note on our way out of class asking him to call me tonight (phone exception—still part of my Phase II research). And in my boldest move of all, I decided to just confront Matt straight-out and tell him to stop all this stupid behavior.

What do I have to lose? A few minutes of discomfort from having to talk to him on the phone tonight, sure, but I stand to gain much more. I'll be proving to Matt McKinney that he can't intimidate me.

So right after I handed my note to Nick, I handed a separate one to Matt. Boy, was he surprised. He glanced up at me for a split second, then quickly kept on walking.

I told Nick to call me at seven, Matt to call me at eight. I doubt Matt will have the guts to do it, but that's okay, too. It still gives me the upper hand. It means I was the bigger, stronger person, and he was nothing but a coward.

Can't wait for the phone to ring. This whole stupid drama has to end.

67

"**W**hat were you and Matt talking about?" I began.

"When?" Nick asked.

"Today. Right when I walked in. I know you were talking about me."

"Guy talk," Nick said.

"Bull. Out with it."

Nick chuckled softly. Even his voice over the phone can do it for me these days.

"Why don't you ask him?" Nick said.

"Because Matt and I aren't exactly friends. And I thought maybe you and I were, considering."

"And here I thought you were going to tell me 'now' tonight. I'm seriously devastated."

"Will you just tell me?" I said.

"Nope. Sorry. Some things are just between men."

Hate him.

We hung up, and I waited. And waited. Past eight. Past nine.

Finally, a little before ten (my parents' traditional cutoff time for any calls to the house), the phone rang. I let it ring six times before I answered, all the while yelling to everyone else, "Don't get it!"

I acted bored, casual. "Hello?"

"Yeah, Cat, what do you want?"

He outbored me. I got flustered. "Um, I just needed to ask you something."

He didn't say anything. I guess I was just supposed to ask.

"Why have you been acting like that?"

"Like what?" he said, still dead-voiced.

"Like I ran over your dog and killed your parents?" I hadn't planned on being so flip, but this wasn't going the way I expected.

"You tell me," he said.

I took a breath and tried again. "Do you admit you've been really rude to me lately?"

And that made him laugh. Which I didn't care for one bit.

"Can't we just stay out of each other's way?" I said. "I'm not bothering you, and I'd appreciate it if you didn't go out of your way all the time to give me nasty looks and say things behind my back to other people and try to make me feel uncomfortable."

"Okay, Cat, whatever."

It sounded like he was about to hang up.

"Wait."

"What," he said, sounding like he was going to fall asleep any second.

I hadn't planned it out this far. He wasn't following the script. I hadn't accomplished anything—other than sounding like I was begging him to be nice to me.

"You're a real jerk, you know that?"

"Good night, Cat. Thanks for calling." And then he did hang up.

I didn't even get the chance to say, "You called me."

I hate that guy. This isn't going well at all.

68

Day 156, Friday, January 23

Phase II. Back on.

I dressed up again today: the royal blue sweater with a lacy white camisole underneath, black pants, black boots. And makeup.

Because this is war.

And if there's one thing I learned during my brief experiment with trying to look pretty, it's that what I wear and how I look actually does have an effect—on me. It makes me act differently. It gives me a kind of confidence I don't have when I'm feeling schlubby or fat or however I've been used to feeling. Maybe that's what Amanda really meant about my hidden powers—they're powers over myself.

Nick gave me a very appreciative smile when I walked into Mr. Fizer's. Thank you, Nick. Matt had already seen me in English Lit, and I could see I had an effect on him, too.

Good.

I thought about it a lot after Matt hung up on me—about how I've been letting him call the shots the entire time I've known him. When we were little, he was the one who picked what we were doing. He was the one I followed around—to the space museum, to the planetarium, to the movies he wanted to see. Granted, I liked most of those things once I was doing them, but the fact was I didn't have a voice.

Then when I caught him that night at the science fair, I thought I was going to break free and live my own life. But I realized the other night that was a lie. I was still following his lead. He had betrayed me, and rather than confront him, I had run away and hated myself and hated him. If I had only gone up to him that night and told him I heard what he said and forced him to admit it to my face, I think I would be a different person right now. Stronger. Fearless.

Instead I've spent the past three and a half years—no, almost four now—doing everything to stay out of his way. I can't help that we've been thrown into so many of the same classes over the years—it's the nature of our program—but I've always sat as far away from him as I could, and I've never willingly talked to him, except in response to whatever smug, sarcastic comments he felt like making.

Instead I should have been on the offensive all along. I shouldn't have hidden. I should have gone forth with my head held high and let everyone else see what an evil, backstabbing person he is. Instead I've cowered away from the whole incident, mostly because I was so embarrassed. But now I don't have to be embarrassed—I don't look the way I used to anymore.

So today I made sure I looked as great as I possibly could (Amanda approved my makeup), and at the start of Mr. Fizer's class—after Nick had thrown me that sly little smile (sigh)—I went right up to Matt and said, "I'd like to talk to you after class."

I didn't add, "If you don't mind," or, "If you have time," or anything weak like that. I just stood up tall and asked for what I wanted.

Matt didn't even look up at me. "Why."

Based on our conversation the other night, I expected that. "Because I'd like to clear the air, once and for all."

That made him look at me. He squinted, like we were standing in a sandstorm, and he ran a hand through his already-messy hair. "Cat, leave it alone."

"No. I think this has gone on long enough."

Matt looked down at the table again and shook his head like it was all making him so tired. I stood my ground. "I'll wait for you. It will only take a few minutes. I think you can spare that."

Then I turned away and walked to my seat and didn't give him a chance to argue any further.

Score for Cat.

Of course I couldn't do a bit of work the whole period. I just kept planning what I was going to say. How I would stand. What I would do with my arms—crossed over my chest or loose at my sides? Which would make me look more formidable?

Mr. Fizer reminded us our project prototypes are due next Friday. As if I can think about schoolwork these days. I need to be free of all these distractions. Which means meeting with Matt this afternoon was essential.

I waited in the hallway. Nick came out first. He pressed his hip against mine as he leaned in to whisper, "How can you be so cruel, walking around looking like that?" I couldn't help but smile. I really wish I loved him.

Matt came out, backpack slung over one shoulder, surly face in place.

"Do you mind walking a little ways?" I realized the moment it was out of my mouth I shouldn't have asked his permission. I should have said, "Let's walk." But it was too late.

He didn't answer, but he did follow. So far, so good. My plan was to get him away from school grounds, across the street, and into the neighborhood a little where I knew we'd have some privacy. What I had to say wasn't going to make me particularly proud. I didn't want any bystanders to hear.

But Matt wasn't sticking to the plan. As soon as we hit open air, he stopped and faced me. "What."

"Just a little further." I pointed to the street. "It'll only take a minute."

I made sure to keep my back erect. The boots were perfect because they gave me a long, serious stride. I gazed straight ahead and let my arms swing loosely at my sides. I looked far more confident than I felt, but Matt didn't need to know that.

We waited at the light, which took forever. I kept expecting him to say, "Forget it," and leave. But he stuck it out, not saying a word, just waiting for me to lead on.

"It's just up here," I said, pointing to some vague destination. He trudged on without comment.

When we were finally a block from school, I turned to him. "Okay, this is good enough."

I was wearing my sunglasses, and I kept them on. Part of my strategy—he didn't need to see my eyes.

I couldn't really see his, either, since he wouldn't look at me straight on. I knew that must mean he was nervous. Good.

"Okay, here's what I wanted to say," I began. This was the part I had rehearsed. "We have a year and a half of school left together, and I really don't want to spend it like this. I think it's apparent to both of us that we don't like each other and that we haven't liked each other for a long time, but I don't see any reason why we can't behave civilly when we're around each other."

I paused to see if he had anything to say, but he didn't. He just stared off to the side, like he was bored and not even listening.

I continued with my speech. "So I have a few suggestions for how we can get through the rest of school—"

Suddenly he looked right at me. "Tell you what, Cat. Why don't you start by explaining why you've been such an unrelenting bitch to me?"

I can't say I wasn't expecting that. He'd asked me the same thing at the Halloween party. So far it was all going according to plan.

"I think you know."

"If I knew," Matt said, "I wouldn't bother asking, would I?" Matt always enunciates his words very carefully when he's angry. He enunciated.

I blew out a breath. This was the embarrassing part. But if I was going to stand up for myself, it had to start here.

"I heard what you said."

Matt just looked at me and waited. I realized he thought I meant I'd heard what he said just then, not what he said before.

"At the science fair," I added. "In seventh grade."

He squinted. "What?"

"What you said to Willie Martin."

I could tell he still had no idea what I was talking about, which made me even angrier. Obviously the single biggest betrayal of my life wasn't even important enough to him to remember.

"Amanda and I were coming toward your booth. You were standing there talking to Willie Martin—remember?" Evil Willie Martin from swim team.

"No, Cat, I have no idea whatsoever what you are talking about."

So this was how it was going to be. He was actually going to force me to say it out loud.

"It was after they announced the winners, remember? I had just won first place, you were second. I kept waiting for you to come over and congratulate me, because that's what friends do, Matt, but you were nowhere to be found. So finally Amanda and I went looking for you. Because I thought you had a great project and you deserved to win first place, too, and I was going to tell you so. Because that's what friends do."

"Does this have a point?" he asked.

I was slouching, I knew it. But I couldn't help myself. I was starting to feel as small as I did back then.

"The point is, I heard what you said. Do you really not remember?"

"Is this going to take much longer?"

The smugness finally got to me. I stood up straight and the words came spilling out. "I heard you! Okay? I heard every word. Willie said, 'I can't believe Fat Cat beat you.' And you said, 'Yeah.' And Willie said, 'That fat cow is so stupid you probably did her project for her.' And you didn't say *anything*. And Willie said, 'Why do you even hang out with her? Is she your girlfriend or something?' And you said, 'No.' And Willie said, 'Fat Cat's your girlfriend,' and he laughed, and he said it again and you said, 'Fat Cat is *not* my girlfriend.' And he said, 'Then why do you hang out with her?' And you said, 'Because she doesn't have any other friends.'"

My voice was shaking now. I'm not good with anger. I usually skip right on to crying.

"Remember that, *Matt*? And then you told him you didn't even think I should have won. And then you and Willie made fun of my

261

project. And the two of you were just so *happy* together, weren't you? And meanwhile Amanda and I were standing right there at the side of your booth and I thought I was going to throw up."

Matt's expression had changed. He wasn't so smug anymore. He stood there, arms crossed, still gazing off to the side.

"I thought you *liked* me, Matt. I thought we were friends—that you were my *best* friend. But it was all a lie. You were just a disgusting, worthless traitor."

I fought hard to control myself. I would not let him see me be weak.

Matt's voice was low and calm. "I was thirteen, Cat."

"So was I! And I *never* would have done that to you!" And now I couldn't help it—tears streamed down my face. "I trusted you! How could you do that to me?"

"I don't know," he said softly.

"But you don't deny it!"

"No."

Somehow that made me feel even worse. I didn't realize until then that I'd almost been hoping it was all in my imagination. I knew it wasn't, but hearing him admit it made the whole thing feel real and horrible again in a way I wasn't expecting.

"Why?" I asked. "Can you just tell me that?"

Matt started to say something, then stopped and shook his head. "I don't know. I was thirteen. Kids say things."

"I *never* would have said that about you! I *liked* you. A lot."

I was really crying now, much to my humiliation. This wasn't at all the way it was supposed to go. I was supposed to be strong, fierce, free. And Matt was supposed to apologize.

I noticed he still hadn't.

"Are you even sorry?" I asked.

"Yes."

The answer sort of surprised me. I didn't know what else to say.

"Are we done here?" Matt asked.

I couldn't believe he was so cold. I wiped my nose on my sleeve. "Yes," I snapped. "Sorry to take up so much of your valuable time."

I set off at the best pace my boots could carry me. I walked the full length of the street before looking back.

Matt was already gone.

69

There was a letter stuck to my front door this morning.

CAT—

I WILL BE AT THE FRONT ENTRANCE TO THE ZOO AT
1:00 THIS AFTERNOON. COME IF YOU WANT.

MM

"What do you think it means?" I asked Amanda (emergency call).

"It means he feels terribly, terribly guilty. You caught him off guard yesterday, and now that he's had time to prepare, he's ready to talk to you."

"And say what?"

"'You misunderstood,' or, 'I was on cold medication that day'—who knows? But aren't you dying to find out?"

"No."

"Cat, come on! This is finally your chance to force Matt McKinney to apologize to you after all these years. I'm telling you, I'd drive a thousand miles if I knew my enemy was about to fess up how he'd hurt me."

"I just don't know if I can go through it all again. Yesterday was really bad. I was a mess."

"So today you go there at one, looking like a total knockout, and you hold your head high and you say, 'I believe you have something to say to me?' and then you just stand there and listen. You don't have to speak another word. And when he's done, you can just turn and walk away. Very classy. I think I'm going to hide somewhere and watch."

"You are not," I said firmly. "I can't do this if I know you're around."

"Come on, Kit Cat, be strong. This may finally be the moment you've been waiting for—Matt McKinney contrite and begging."

"Somehow I don't see that."

"Okay," Amanda said, "then how about at least contrite?"

"That would be nice."

"I'm coming over to do your makeup."

70

I **purposely arrived late.** About ten minutes. I thought about making it longer, but I was afraid he would think I wasn't coming and he'd just leave.

Okay, I looked *remarkable*. Amanda made me try on more outfits than Barbie until she was satisfied I made the right "statement."

Here's my statement: hair down and straightened, black turtleneck we bought on our clothing spree at the start of my secret Phase II project, dark-wash jeans that fit me *perfectly*, my black boots. Amanda said with my dark hair and the black turtleneck and my dark glasses, I looked like a spy. No purse, she decided, because purses make you look weak and girly. I needed my arms free so I could stand tall and confident with my hands on my hips like a warrior or an assassin.

She made me practice that.

Matt was waiting near the entrance to the zoo. I walked within a few feet of him and struck my pose.

"What's this about?" I said.

He didn't answer, but turned to the ticket window and paid for two. Then he walked through the gates without even a glance back. I waited a few seconds, then followed.

To the right was the zoo café (kind of an unappetizing thought), where a bunch of parents and children and teenagers sat at the small tables eating ice cream (in January?) and nachos. Matt chose the path just to the left of the café and kept on walking. I followed.

As the path crooked around we came to a chain-link enclosure, bordered all around with tall bamboo stalks. Inside the enclosure were palm fronds and thick ropes and a plastic version of a tire swing.

Matt stopped before the cage. And still said nothing.

I stood a reasonable distance away from him and gazed at what he wanted me to see: three monkeys the size of toddlers, with dark sable coats and white faces. Their hands and feet were white, too, like they were wearing gloves.

"Yeah," I said, "so?"

Matt answered, "This is my project."

A few seconds ticked by. "I don't understand."

"I'm paying you back," he said.

I still didn't understand. "You brought me here to show me monkeys?"

"They're apes," he said, "but yes."

"And that's supposed to make up for everything?"

I stared at him for a moment, then realized this whole thing was just a big joke to him. I turned and started back toward the entrance.

Matt followed. "Cat, if you'd just let me explain—"

"I don't care about your stupid project, you idiot. You don't get it at all, do you?"

"I'm trying to—" Matt had to take a few extra steps to catch up with me. My boots are really awesome. It's like they give me an extra six inches of leg.

Matt tried again. "I thought if I shared with you the secret of my project, you'd realize—"

I spun to face him. "Realize what? That you're a scientific genius? Am I supposed to be impressed?"

"No," he said quietly, "realize that you can trust me again."

I was breathing hard by now, because no matter how awesome the boots were, it was still my body having to keep up with them. Plus I was pretty keyed up from the whole experience.

"I'm never going to trust you, Matt. You ruined that. You were supposed to be my best friend back then. Why should I ever trust you again? What's the point?"

"So you're really going to hold this against me the rest of my life?"

"You haven't even apologized!"

"I'm trying to," he said.

"Well, try harder. Because monkeys or apes aren't going to do it. You hurt me, Matt—deeply. Telling me what you're working on for the science fair isn't really going to make up for that, now is it?"

I turned and took off again, and this time Matt didn't follow. Fine. We'd said all we had to say—at least I had. It didn't surprise me that he couldn't come up with a decent apology. He had stepped over the line. You don't get to fix that.

I was almost to my car (yes, I drove. I wanted my hair and everything to look perfect. So sue me) when I heard Matt call my name. I thought about ignoring him, but then curiosity made me turn around and wait.

He did a semi-jog up to meet me. He stopped about four feet away. I glared at him with defiance.

"What, Matt? Did you come up with something? Some explanation for why you were such a piece of—"

"I'm sorry," he said. "Cat, I'm so, so sorry. I don't know why I said it. I honestly don't."

"I do. It's because you were embarrassed of me. I was so ugly you didn't even want people to think we were friends."

"No," he said, "that's not it at all."

"Then why?"

He sighed. "I don't know. I was just a stupid kid. Willie was getting in my face, and—I don't know. I just said it."

I chuffed out a breath and turned to put my key in the lock. When I looked up again, he was right beside me.

"Cat, you have to believe me—I really miss you. I've missed you for a long time."

"Well, then, your loss, huh?" I said bravely.

He clasped my arm. A charge went through me. Almost as serious as when Nick touched that same arm.

I shook off Matt's hand. "You don't get it, do you? What you did was unforgivable. It's the worst thing anyone has ever done to me in my entire life." I hadn't planned on confessing this, but my mouth was on a roll. "I really liked you, Matt. A *lot*. As in, a deep and serious crush. As in, I actually thought I was in love. Did you even know that?"

He looked sufficiently shocked. "No."

"What did you think I was doing, then? Hanging out with you all the time, following you wherever you wanted to go—did you think it was just because I wanted to be your pal? Like I was a boy?"

"I didn't—I was thirteen—"

"Stop saying that!" I said. "It's no excuse. If I was old enough to like you that much, the least you could have done was not say all those horrible things behind my back. Even if you didn't know I liked you that way, you were still supposed to be my friend. I'll never get over what you did."

"Is that true?" he asked. "Never?"

"It's too late. You ruined it." I got into my car.

Matt stood off to the side and let me back up. I half expected him to knock on the window or try to get my attention, but he just stood there. So I kept on pulling out, then turned the wheels and headed for the exit.

He just couldn't do it, could he? Couldn't find the words to make it right.

I don't think those words even exist.

71

Jordan showed up at the café tonight to sample some more of my desserts. Amanda and I joined him at the table as soon as our shift was over.

She and I had already talked about the zoo performance over the last couple of hours, so I didn't need to get into those details again in front of Jordan. But she and I still had plenty to discuss about Matt—from how self-centered he is to how he looks and dresses (Amanda's critique, mostly) to how it's no wonder we never see him with a girlfriend—who would have him?

Jordan just shook his head and tried to concentrate on my three-layer chocolate cake. Finally he felt the need to speak up. "I don't know why you two are so down on him. Especially you, Cat—after he stuck up for you with Beecher."

"What?" I said. "When?"

"At that Halloween party."

Amanda and I looked at each other. I could see she didn't have a clue, either. "What are you talking about?" I asked.

Jordan swallowed another bite. "I was hanging out talking to Greg, and Matt came up. And pretty soon Greg's bragging about you."

That didn't sound too bad. In fact, Greg bragging about me in front of Matt seemed like just what I wanted.

"What did he say?" Amanda asked.

"Oh, just how he'd upgraded his model—you know, from the old one. Who was that girl he used to go out with?"

"I don't know," Amanda said impatiently. "Just keep going."

I was glad she said it. Sometimes Jordan's stories stretch out a little too long. Amanda and I like to talk fast and listen fast.

"So anyway," Jordan said, "Greg's saying how he upgraded, and now he has a fully loaded unit—you know, like a car—his dad owns that car dealership—"

Amanda widened her eyes at me because he was taking so long.

Jordan cleared his throat. "Do you really want me to tell you what he said?"

"YES!" we both shouted.

"He said he had this fully loaded unit now—'big brains, big ti—'" He coughed. "—chest. And how now that he had someone to do all his homework for him, he could cruise through the rest of school, and . . . do you really want to hear this?"

"YES!"

"And how everyone knows if you tell a fat chick you love her, she'll do anything you want."

Amanda and I were speechless.

"Yeah," Jordan said. "So then Matt goes all road rage, and I thought I was going to have to hold him off Beecher. Instead he tells the guy that he's a complete jackass—that he doesn't deserve you and doesn't even know what he has—and right then we see you two coming back and Matt takes off, and there we all are."

This cold feeling came over me, like I'd just fallen through the ice. "He said that?" I asked.

"Yeah, sorry. I guess I should have told you before, but I didn't want to hurt your feelings. And then I figured it didn't matter anyway, since you guys broke up right after—"

"No," I said, "I mean Matt. He really said that?"

"Yeah," Jordan answered, downing another bite. "So you want to cut my man some slack?"

72

I do not understand guys. I think I'm smart in a lot of ways, but this is definitely not one of them.

Here I thought Greg was a nice—if kind of boring—guy, and I just wasn't feeling the heat, and then I go out with Nick and *definitely* feel the heat, but that's not enough, and now Matt.

Have I been wrong about him all this time?

No, I haven't. Because even he admits what he said to Willie. And he has no good excuse for it, other than to keep telling me he was thirteen. I know that. I need more than that.

And what was that bit at the zoo yesterday? What was his point? As if showing me those monkeys—excuse me, apes, as if I care—was supposed to make up for anything. What kind of twisted logic is that?

I slept in late this morning after my long interview with Jordan at the café last night. Amanda and I must have grilled him for another hour after he told us that story, but he never really gave us more to go on. Jordan is a skillful writer, but not so much a talker. He kept falling back on phrases like, "He's solid, I'm telling you," when what Amanda and I wanted was *details*.

So then she and I analyzed it between ourselves for another good long while at her house, and by the time I dragged home, I could barely pry my eyes open.

When I woke up this morning, I thought maybe I'd dreamed the whole thing—the zoo, Jordan, all of it. Because it's not the path my brain has been taking all this time. I'm predisposed to believing everything Matt does is to hurt me or make fun of me somehow. But sticking up for me with Greg doesn't fit that pattern.

So now what? That's the thing.

Amanda told me last night that I might have to do the unthinkable: go back to Matt and give him a chance to make up.

There are two major problems with that, as far as I can see: First, it means I have to go crawling back to him, which is exactly what I don't want to do. I think I've established a very strong persona with him lately, and it's taken me so long to get here I can't stand thinking I'll have to give it up.

Second, who's to say Matt would even be receptive at this point? I couldn't have been colder to him yesterday. I think I was pretty clear we wouldn't be reconciling anytime soon.

Oh, and I just thought of a third thing: what if I just don't want to? I know that sounds petty and immature, but why does it have to always be me? Is it wrong to like being in the position of power for once? To have someone make the effort with me? To have someone else be the one trying to get me to like him?

Okay, so I admit that both Greg and Nick kind of liked me—or at least pursued me—more than I did them. So in a way, I've already had a taste of that. But the fact that it's Matt, and I've built up all this justifiable anger toward him over the years, and now just because I find out maybe he's not so completely evil after all doesn't mean I'm ready to give up all my resentment and go back to being buddies.

Besides, I've moved on. Amanda was there to take over the role of best friend, and I have a very fulfilling life hanging out with her and Jordan. And I have plenty to fill my time otherwise, between school and work and my various chef duties and now swimming and all my homework—so why do I need to make friends with Matt again?

But the worst of it is the idea of having to go to him now and say I misjudged him or I'm sorry or anything like that. Because I'm not sorry. He was wrong, and he admits it.

But maybe there's more to this story than I've been willing to believe.

Maybe Amanda's right. Maybe I should at least let him try.

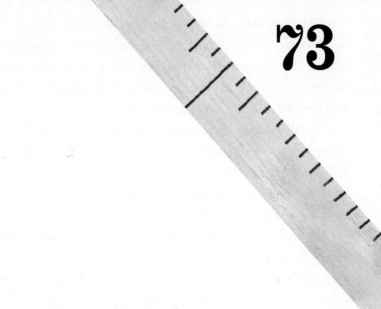

73

Day 159, Monday, January 26

Breakfast: The usual.

Lunch: My pride.

I wrote my note during lunch. Short and to the point: *Can we try that again?*

At the start of Mr. Fizer's class I walked right up to Matt and handed it to him. He didn't look at me, but he took it. He shoved it in his backpack without even reading it.

But he must have read it at some point when I wasn't looking, because by the end of class he had a note for me. One word: *Tomorrow.*

It's weird how my heart flipped a little at that. I think part of it was nerves, because now I have a whole night and day to think about what I'm going to say to him and what he might say back.

I'll have to take the afternoon off work at Poison Control, but it's worth it. If I could take time off from the café to go on some makeout date to the Winter Formal (not that I knew that at the time), I can take time off from poisonings to go look at primates with the guy who told Greg Beecher he didn't deserve me.

But that brings up an interesting point. Why did Matt say all those mean things about me to Nick Langan? About me loving and leaving. If Matt didn't think Greg deserved me, then why is he acting like I did something wrong by dumping him?

I guess I'll find out everything tomorrow.

Maybe I should make a list. This may be my last chance to ask Matt all the questions I've been wondering about for the past four years. Like why he continued to bother me and joke around with me when it was clear I hated him. And what sort of things he said to Nick behind my back. And why did he say them? Maybe Amanda is right and he was just jealous and wanted to interfere. But why not ask him? What do I have to lose? I'd also like to know why he thinks showing me a cage of apes is supposed to make up for stabbing me in the heart. Just a few questions, really.

There's the matter of what to wear, of course. I'm thinking Nick's pink scarf might come in handy. It looks good against my skin, and it would be my little secret about who gave it to me. I'll have to clear that with my dresser, of course. She's coming over after I swim tonight.

No wonder so many famous scientists have been loners. All this human interaction takes up *way* too much time.

74

Day 160, Tuesday, January 27

Breakfast: Forget it. Too nervous.

"Why are you so dressed up?" Peter asked when we set out this morning.

"I'm not *so* dressed up."

"Uh-huh. You never wear a dress to school."

"It's a skirt. I borrowed it from Amanda. Do you like it?"

"I don't know."

Stupid question to ask an eleven-year-old boy.

But Amanda and I agree it's the hottest thing I've worn all year. She loved the outfit so much when we finished putting it together last night, she made me let her take my picture.

Black boots, brown tights, a black-and-brown-checked skirt that falls just above my knee. Amanda's red turtleneck. Which means I couldn't wear the pink scarf because pink and red? Amanda says no. At least not this particular red and that particular pink.

I feel like I have a lot to learn. I never used to care about fashion— *at all*—but now that I'm actually starting to like the way I look in clothes, I can see getting into it a little more. Is that shallow? Probably. But as long as I stay at the top of my class, maybe people will overlook it.

"So what's going on with Trina?" I said her name just the way I think of her—unpleasantly. .

"I don't know," Peter said.

"Is she being nice to you at all?"

He shrugged.

"Let me rephrase that: has she stopped saying mean things about you to other people?"

"I don't know."

"Is that your answer for everything today?"

Peter grinned. "I don't know."

Maybe because I was about to meet with the guy who was once the eleven-year-old boy in my life, I felt like doling out a little more advice to my brother than usual.

"You know," I said, "the only people you can really trust in life are the ones who treat you the same no matter what you look like. Like Amanda—she's been my friend since seventh grade. And I was heavy for a long time, and she never once made fun of me or talked meanly about me behind my back. That's why we're still friends. Understand?"

"Yeah."

"My point is," I felt it necessary to say, "I don't think this Trina girl is worth even a moment of your time. Do you really want to be friends with someone who likes you only if you're skinny?"

Peter didn't answer. So I just kept going.

"And let's say one day you're my age, and you look really *hot*, and every girl in the school is drooling over you—"

Peter snorted at that.

"—and suddenly there's Trina saying, 'Oh, Petey, would you please go with me to the prom?' I hope you'll tell her that there are plenty of nice girls out there you'd rather take instead. Will you promise me that?"

Peter shrugged. Which told me he must have it bad for this girl.

I stopped and made him look at me. "It's not worth it. Trust me— I've been doing this a lot longer than you have. People who only like you when you look good are *worthless*. Understand?"

And suddenly I didn't care if he understood at all. Because *I did*.

How could I be so *stupid*? It was staring me right in the face. How could I have been so blind?

I cannot *wait* for this afternoon.

75

School got out at three, the zoo closes at four. I caught a ride from Amanda. The sky was charcoal gray, and the wind had picked up since lunch. Something was blowing in. "You can't walk home," Amanda said. "I'm going to wait."

"No, I'll be fine. Go home and take your nap."

"That's what backseats are for."

We pulled into the parking lot. Amanda turned off the car and then checked me over one more time to make sure everything looked perfect.

"I think you're wrong," she said as I was getting out, and I said, "I know I'm right," and that's where we left it.

I felt *so* good. Because as far as I was concerned, the mystery was solved, and I was going to get to relive my childhood betrayal and this time stand up for myself.

Matt was already waiting for me out front. I could tell he was checking me out as I walked toward him. Good. Perfect.

"Hi," I said pleasantly. I wasn't going to give away how I really felt. I wanted to set the trap. "Been waiting long?"

"No. Thanks . . . for your note."

"Well, I realized afterward I was a little too hard on you the other day. You were right—I should have given you a chance to make it up to me. So go ahead. Tell me all about your project." This was going to be easy. He had no idea what was coming.

I let him pay for me again, and we went back to the gibbon cage. Same three little guys—or maybe they were girls—climbing the chain link and swinging on the tire.

"Here's my picture," Matt said. He opened his research notebook and showed me.

I meant to be above it all and not really care in the least, but once he showed me that picture, there was no way. You'd have to be made of stone.

It was a little baby gorilla, frightened and shy, trying to hide herself inside the coat of her keeper. The caption said her parents had been killed by hunters, and she was found bleeding from multiple machete wounds. She'd been brought to this sanctuary where scientists nurse orphan gorillas back to health, then eventually return them to the wild.

"It was her eyes," Matt said. "The way she's looking straight into the camera. You can really see someone in there."

I saw what he meant. It was like staring into the eyes of a child. You wanted to protect her—to comfort her. To just reach into the picture and cuddle the baby close.

"Why did you smile?" I asked. "I saw you smile when you picked this."

"Because I knew," Matt answered. "This was exactly what I needed."

He gave me a little background on the internship he'd done at the university over the summer. He landed this great position in the astronomy department, working with one of the top research scientists in the nation.

"He thinks we'll make contact with other life-forms within the next twenty years," Matt said. "He's developing all sorts of software for communication—lights, sounds, images, pictographs—going at it multiple ways. He figures there are about 300 million potentially inhabitable planets in the Milky Way alone—maybe a billion if you count all the moons—so odds are there has to be at least some creature out there worth communicating with. At least that's the theory."

"Okay." It's been a long time since I've talked astronomy with Matt. He was always far more into it than I was. I didn't want this to turn into some hour-long lecture. "So what's that have to do with the picture?"

"Wait. So we're spending all this time and brainpower trying to figure out what creature X on planet 23 wants to be serenaded with—blues? Rap? Tibetan wind chimes? Right? And whether it would prefer the scent of vanilla or gas fumes. That's what this guy's been working on for *years*. And he looks it, too—he's all gray and hunched over, smells like he never takes a shower—"

"We don't have much time," I said, checking the nearby clock.

A gust of wind broadsided us, pushing my hair all over my face. Amanda's sweater wasn't nearly warm enough. Not to mention the short skirt and the tights. I may have looked killer, but it was totally impractical for the weather. I shifted from one leg to the other and hugged myself.

"You're cold." Matt started to take off his jacket.

"No, I'm fine. Finish." This would all be over soon. I had a speech to give, but there was still time. I was actually interested in hearing the rest of his story.

"Short version," Matt said, "I *hated* the guy."

"Oh."

"I went in thinking I'd landed the coolest internship out there, but by the end of the first week I wanted to quit. The guy's a psycho. A real megalomaniac. Don't get me wrong—smarter than anyone on the planet—but he won't let you forget it."

My teeth chattered.

"Cat, here." This time he took off his jacket and handed it to me.

Taking aid and comfort from the enemy seemed like a bad idea, but I really was absolutely freezing. I put the jacket on and gathered the collar around my face. Which turned out to be exactly the wrong thing to do.

Because it smelled like him. Exactly the way I remembered. Whatever chemicals and sweat and soap make up Matt, they were all trapped within the folds of his coat. And this wave of missing him hit me, even though the person himself was standing right in front of me.

Because the Matt I missed was the old one—the one I trusted, the one I wanted to spend all of my time with. Amanda's told me before how hard it was to get to be my friend back when she first met me in seventh-grade English, because I was always doing something with Matt. It wasn't until he was out of the picture that she and I got to be best friends.

Matt reached out and adjusted the coat around me. "Better?"

I nodded. I didn't trust myself to say anything.

I read somewhere that one of the ways torturers break down their victims is by first treating them kindly. The prisoner expects to be beaten, threatened, maybe burned with cigarettes, and instead the torturer offers him coffee and sugar cookies and a warm bed.

Then once the prisoner's defenses are down, BAM. I should have given him the coat back.

I felt the first spit of rain on top of my head.

"We should go," Matt said. "You're freezing."

I didn't want to go. I knew once I did, this moment would be gone. I needed to say a few things to him, and I wasn't sure if I'd ever get up the courage again.

"Just a few more minutes," I said.

"Cat—"

I looked up at the sky. "It's not so bad. Tell me the rest. What's all of that have to do with the picture?"

Matt turned to the gibbons, now huddling in one of the huts inside their cage. "This was as close as I could come to a gorilla," he explained. "I needed an ape. Do you realize we share over 97 percent of our DNA with those guys?"

I looked at their white faces, those gloved hands so politely folded on top of each other, like they were waiters ready to show us to our table.

"Same thing—look at their eyes," Matt said. "There's definitely someone in there."

He was right. I looked into the smallest one's eyes and saw it— not the same haunted, traumatized look of the baby gorilla in Matt's picture, but still something real and tender and almost . . . human.

"They're not that different from us," Matt said. "A few variables in the genetic structure, and they're in a cage, we're out here. Where you're freezing to death."

There was no denying it was raining. Cold, icy rain, coming down in dollops the size of spit wads.

Mothers raced their strollers toward the exit. Matt grabbed my hand. "Come on. Let's go."

We ran across the wet concrete, my boots seriously slowing us down. It made me laugh. Watching him pull me along like that, him in just his T-shirt getting totally soaked, me in my ridiculous skirt and boots and oversized coat, I didn't know who we were supposed to be.

I couldn't stop laughing. Because it was all so ridiculous. Matt McKinney was holding my hand, running with me like we were kids. And there in the parking lot was my co-conspirator and friend, just waking up from her nap, obviously confused by what she saw.

I waved her away with my free hand. Even if I could have worked out all the vocabulary, I didn't have time to sign, *"It's okay. This is weird. But I've got it all under control."*

Matt unlocked the passenger door of his car and I darted inside. He ran around to his side and hustled in. He started the car to blast the heater, then we both sat there for a minute, breathless, smiling, our hair and faces drenched.

Of course my hair had totally started to frizz. He reached out and gathered up a few strands at their ends. "I was so happy when you let it go back to being curly this year. It reminds me of when we were little."

My breath sort of caught at that.

And then Matt's smile started to fade, and his eyes took on a soft, almost sleepy look, and he gazed at me in a way he never has.

And there was a moment right then. I could have reached out and touched it like it was a thing separate from both of us. It was a moment when I knew if I had wanted him to, he would have kissed me. I don't know how I knew it, but I knew.

"I should go." I quickly checked to make sure Amanda was still there. Of course she was—she wouldn't have missed this show for anything. It must have been driving her crazy that she couldn't see us clearly through the rain and the fogged-up windows.

"Here." I started to take Matt's jacket off.

"What's the rush?" he asked. "Can't we just talk?"

The rush was the sickening sensation of my heart beating too fast. I knew the signs. I knew what could happen next if I let it—I'd seen it happen with Nick.

But this wasn't Nick. I couldn't just go with it and see what might happen for the fun of it. I had history to contend with, and my history with Matt is too complicated. Too full of heartache and pain.

And besides, I'd already accomplished most of what I came for. I'd confirmed for myself what I thought—that he does like me. That way. I've lost a bunch of weight, and now suddenly he's willing to give me a try.

I hadn't accomplished the second part—the part where I told him off—but somehow I didn't feel like it anymore. I just wanted to be done.

I handed him his coat and opened the door.

"Cat, wait—" His warm fingers closed around my wrist. "Don't go yet. I miss you."

"Then maybe you should have liked me when I was fat."

76

As soon as she saw me dart through the rain, Amanda started the car.

"Wrong outfit," she said, assessing the damage when I got in. "Sorry."

We all have our failures.

Mine was five minutes before, when I laughed as I ran to Matt's car. I let my defenses down. I let myself think it was all fine.

"Start at the beginning," Amanda told me as she drove past Matt's car on the way out of the parking lot. "Every word."

I needed the play-by-play myself.

Because when was the moment I decided it was okay to relax around him? How did I let things get to the point where he actually might have kissed me? And I might have let him?

"The Cat and Matt show," Amanda concluded. "Early imprinting. It might take a blow to the head for you to finally be free of it."

"I'm willing."

"So let me understand," Amanda said. The rain had turned into hail and was clunking against the roof. "As of yesterday, Matt was on your good side. Jordan told you what he said to Greg, and so maybe Matt was okay. Correct?"

"Maybe."

"Then this morning you have this epiphany that the only reason Matt is being nice to you now is you're so incredibly hot."

"I didn't say that."

"That's okay," Amanda said, "I did. So you go there this afternoon expecting . . . what?"

"To confront him about that. To get him to admit he only likes me because I lost weight."

"And how was that questioning going to go?" Amanda asked. "'Hi, Matt, do you like me now? Thanks a lot. And is it because I'm so gorgeous?'"

"I wasn't going to say that." She was starting to irritate me a little.

"No, you weren't. And do you know why?"

"No, Doctor Amanda. Why?"

"Because, my Kit Cat, Matt McKinney happens to be one of the reasons you lost weight in the first place."

"No, he's not. He has nothing to do with it."

Amanda turned onto my block. "Come on," she said. "You have been seriously in love with Matt since you were probably seven or eight years old. You can't deny that."

"Eight. But I'm not in love with him now."

"Early imprinting. You never forget your first love."

"I haven't forgotten him," I said. "Believe me. I'm well aware of where he's been the last four years."

She pulled up in front of my house and turned off the car. She unbuckled her seat belt and got comfortable, foot up on the seat, back propped against the door. I was wearing a cold, wet skirt, so I couldn't do the same.

"Here." She reached into the backseat and brought up a fleece blanket. No wonder she didn't mind napping in the car—she came prepared. She spread the blanket over both of us. I undid my seat belt and relaxed.

"Cat, whatever you say never leaves this car. You know that. You can tell me the absolute truth and I'm not going to criticize you or make fun of you. You know that."

I nodded.

"So tell me the absolute, hundred percent truth. Are you or are you not still in love with Matt McKinney?"

A drop of water rolled down my cheek. It must have come from my hair. "I am not. I was, but I'm not. I swear."

Amanda stared me down, but this time I wasn't budging.

She sighed. "Poor Matt. And he came so close."

77

Day 164, Saturday, January 31

Breakfast: Special brother-sister date at the Karmic Café. I made apple-walnut bread on my shift last night just so we could order some this morning.

"Okay," Peter said, pulling out his questionnaire. "Ready?"

He'd already interviewed both my parents over dinner last night. Now it was my turn. I told him I'd cooperate only if he walked with me to breakfast. My treat. Tough bargain.

The fifth and sixth graders at Peter's school are required to enter the science fair. A lot of them do it in groups. Peter came up with his project on his own. That's my boy.

On the way to the café I finally told him about my own project.

Because we were about to work on his. And because I thought it was time to stop keeping that secret from him. And because I've discovered I actually like my little brother a lot.

"Okay," he said once we had ordered and were ready to get to work, "can you roll your tongue?"

I demonstrated I could not. He demonstrated he could. "Mom and Dad can," he told me.

"Guess we're not really related."

Peter's project is about genetics. He's asking the same questions of all our relatives, as far out as cousins, aunts and uncles, and grandparents on both sides.

"Is your second toe longer or smaller than your big toe?"

I had to take off my shoe and sock to check.

Questions about eye color, hair color, fingers (which is longer—index or ring finger?), earlobes (hanging or attached?), right-handed or left-handed, preferences for salty or sweet.

"Those are good," I told him when we were done. "Did you think them all up by yourself?"

"Yep."

"What's *Trina's* project on?" I can't help myself—whenever I say that girl's name, it's like I revert to third grade.

"Flowers."

"Sounds stupid." As if I could tell from just that description. But I was going to say that anyway, no matter what he told me. Because I've got my boy's back.

We walked home, bellies full of bread and fresh fruit and an order of tofu scramble I convinced him to try. ("This isn't gross," he proclaimed. High praise.)

When we got back to the house, Peter took a few pictures—of

me not rolling my tongue ("Rub it in," I told him), of my eyes, of my toes. I think my little brother's project actually has a lot of potential. Who knows—maybe we have another scientist in the family. That would be pretty sweet.

"You are so going to beat Trina," I told him. "You're going to beat her so badly she'll cry."

Peter looked at me sort of surprised. I was a little surprised myself.

Settle down, Cat. This isn't your fight.

Your fight was over four years ago.

78

Day 178, Saturday, February 14

Valentine's Day. I admit it: I wouldn't mind
some chocolate right now. Like maybe a
truckload.

Amanda has Jordan. I accept that. I have no one. I can accept that,
too. Even on Valentine's Day. That's how it's always been.

Except the problem this year is that Nick came up to me after
class yesterday and asked if I wanted to go out to dinner tonight, and
I told him I was cooking at the café, and he asked if he could meet
me afterward, and I confess I was seriously tempted.

But I said no. Because nothing has changed. I still don't have any
real feelings for him besides lust, I still wouldn't be able to control
myself around him, and I'm math geek enough to know that equation
doesn't work out.

Amanda took the night off to be with Jordan. And Dave was with his girlfriend. So it was just me and Darlene in the kitchen tonight, filling order after order, while a bunch of happy couples sat out in the dining area gazing at each other with the googly eyes of love.

Whatever.

Even my parents are still out on a date right now. Disgusting. I mean, sweet. I don't know what I mean.

I didn't even used to care about Valentine's Day. Really, I didn't. Because it never seemed a possibility to me. I always knew I'd be home with my chocolate, and that was fine with me.

But this time I have been kissed by two different guys in the past few months, multiple times each, and a third one probably would have gone for it, too. So it's not so easy to ignore the possibilities anymore. It's like being certain you don't like chocolate truffles because you've never had one before.

I have to admit that if Nick Langan showed up at my front door right now, I'd find him very hard to resist. Greg Beecher? Not so much. Matt McKinney? Let's not go there.

Snap out of it. There are other things to think about besides love and romance. There's calculus. And history. And hominins.

I think I'll head into the kitchen and whip myself up a little Valentine's Night couscous, maybe go crazy and put a little parsley garnish on top, and then settle down and do some homework. I'd rather sit and enjoy a Valentine horror movie with my little brother, but it's still twenty-nine days until I can watch TV.

Yep, the life of a cave woman is nothing but glamour. That's why everybody's trying it.

79

I was already in my pajamas when the doorbell rang. It was just before ten, so even if my parents had been home, they technically couldn't have objected.

I knew it had to be Nick. And I'm pretty sure I didn't mind.

I yelled for Peter to get the door. Then I scrambled around, quickly throwing on the new bra Joyce recently fitted me with (36C!) and then pulling a sweatshirt over the whole thing.

I was just starting to leave my room when someone knocked on my door. Of course Nick knew the way—we'd spent some quality grope time in my bedroom already.

But it wasn't Nick.

And there was chocolate.

Matt looked really . . . good. He was wearing a gray sweater, and his hair was all mussed, and he had on jeans and sneakers, and I have no idea why that all seemed so attractive, but at the moment it did.

Maybe it was the chocolate.

He handed me the heart-shaped box.

"I . . . can't," I said, and it really hurt to say it.

"Cat—"

"It's not you," I hurried to tell him, although I don't know why. "I'm just off of chocolate."

"Oh. Okay."

We were both as awkward as if we'd only known each other thirty seconds. I stood there in my sweatshirt and pink flannel pajamas and felt really, really stupid.

I shook my brain to reset it. Then I sat on the edge of my bed and motioned for Matt to take the desk chair.

I still hadn't quite processed everything. Matt was there. He brought me chocolate. On Valentine's Day. I was wearing pajamas. And a bra.

I couldn't say anything. Didn't know what to say. So I hoped Matt had a speech planned, since I was just going to sit and wait for it.

He did.

"I've been thinking about what you said," he began. "In my car."

I nodded. My teeth felt like they might chatter. My body was having a flashback.

"About how I should have liked you when you were fat."

I nodded again. So far this was the weirdest conversation I'd ever had, and I wasn't even participating.

"I did," Matt said. "Really. But I was just . . . stupid about it."

"Yes." I said it as unemotionally as if he'd just asked me whether Wisconsin is known for its cheese.

"And said some really terrible things," he said.

"You were stupid," I repeated. It felt good to say that.

Matt must have felt he could do better standing up.

He paced a few steps in either direction, and moved on to the second part of his speech.

"Cat, I really like you."

I didn't answer. Because I was basically frozen.

"And it's not because you're not fat anymore, which is apparently what you think. Am I right?"

I nodded.

"But it's not," he said. "I've always liked you. Since we were kids. You know that."

"I thought I did. Until you betrayed me."

Matt tipped his head back and mumbled something to himself. Then he looked at me again. "Look, I can't keep going over that. I told you I don't know why I did it. I was stupid—let's just agree about that."

"You were stupid." I liked hearing it out loud. As often as possible.

"But can we just put that aside for a minute?" Matt asked. "Let's just agree that I was an ass, and I'll never say otherwise, and whether or not I was thirteen doesn't matter because it was just a really cruel thing to say."

My face relaxed a little. Because now he was getting somewhere.

"You admit it," I said, because you don't want to just leave a thing like that alone. "You admit that was a horrible, mean, ugly, unforgivable thing to say."

"Not unforgivable," Matt corrected. "But yes, everything else."

"So you're saying I should forgive you."

"Yes. And here's why."

For a minute I thought the thing he was pulling out of his back pocket was a list he was going to read from, but it turned out to be something else. A Valentine's Day card. A really old and rumpled one.

He handed it to me. I recognized the handwriting. Oh, no.

It was from when we were in fifth grade. Who knows what kind of sappy things I wrote back when I was eleven? If it was a poem, I was going to die. I'd never be able to show it to Amanda.

But it wasn't a poem. It was something that was probably even harder for me to write.

I like you because your smart.

Notice the misspelling.

"I feel the same way," Matt said. "I always have. I never cared how you looked. That's all I wanted to tell you."

And then he left. Just like that. And left me with the chocolate.

I sat there for a minute, then collapsed back onto my bed.

I DO NOT UNDERSTAND GUYS <u>AT ALL</u>.

80

"**H**e kept your valentine?" Amanda asked. "For six years?"

"Yeah. So what am I supposed to do?" I asked. "What does that mean?"

Amanda and Jordan sat on her couch, sampling the chocolates I had brought for show-and-tell.

Jordan was there having lunch when I showed up around noon, and I tried to wait him out, but it didn't look like he was leaving. Besides, I needed Amanda's advice more than I needed my privacy.

"These are excellent," Amanda said, biting into one with a caramel filling. "I say we give him another chance."

"You're reading it all wrong," Jordan said. "This wasn't an advance, it was debt."

Amanda and I gave him equal looks of, "Huh?"

"An advance," he said, taking another chocolate. "Like getting paid for something you write before they publish it. I'm saying he wasn't trying to buy some future right to you, he was trying to pay off a debt he already owed."

Amanda draped her hand over his wrist. "Sweetie, this is serious. If this girl doesn't have a strategy in the next five minutes, the world will stop spinning."

Jordan groaned. "It's obvious. If it was an advance, he would have stayed to get what was coming to him. If it was debt, he would have paid it and left. It was debt. He doesn't owe you anymore."

Amanda and I both paused to take in that bit of wisdom. And try to decide if it even was wisdom.

"So what you're saying," Amanda translated for us, "is that he brought her chocolate to buy her off?"

"No," Jordan said, "I'm saying he apologized. That's it. Everything about that was an apology. Why do you two have to make everything so complicated?"

Exactly what Matt had accused me of back at the beginning of the year.

"So what does he want?" Amanda asked. "What's the strategy here?"

"The strategy," Jordan said, "is you should both pull your heads out and stop overanalyzing everything. The guy's sorry. He wants to move on. It's up to Cat if she wants to."

Jordan crumpled his wrappers and left to go scrounge up something in the kitchen.

"He may be right," Amanda said. "Back to you, Kit Cat. What does the future hold for the Cat and Matt show?"

"I don't know," I said. "It's complicated."

81

Everything should be made as simple as possible, *but not simpler.*

I have been walking around for four years with this incredible burden on my heart. I have fed it, nursed it to health; made sure to keep the wound nice and fresh and open.

For what?

So that one day I could make Matt McKinney bring me chocolate and apologize to me? Or so maybe I could beat him so solidly at something someday that in addition to that triumph, I'd get to tell him I always hated him for what he said and so this was my revenge? I mean, what is it I've been doing all of this for? What is it I want?

I know what I want. I've always known what I want. I just didn't want to let myself know that I knew it. How's that for complicated?

I want a clean slate. Like the day back in August when I decided to start eating and living in a completely different way. If I could do that—and come on, that wasn't easy, no matter how great it's turned out—if I could do that, then why can't I change other parts of my life, just by deciding it's time?

I could pick a date, like saying I was going to start living like a hominin on that Thursday back in August. Fine. You just decide, and then you do it. Maybe you go on one last binge just to hold you over, but then you wake up the next day and start fresh.

So here's my binge: Matt, I hate you. Matt, you're a pig. Matt, you're stupid for not realizing I overheard you that night. Matt, you're an idiot for not realizing why I've been so mean to you for the past four years. Matt, your feet smell. Matt, why is it you haven't ever had a girlfriend all this time? Doesn't that tell you something about yourself? You're undatable. No girl is ever going to like you. You don't care how you dress, you don't care how your hair looks, you don't care what people think of you. You're going to lose to me in the science fair. You're going to graduate with a GPA lower than mine. Admit it, Matt: I'm better than you. I'm smarter, I'm better-looking, I'm nicer.

And I can cook, Matt. You can't even make grilled cheese.

And here's another thing: I have a really happy life now. I'm not sitting around waiting for you to make it good. I'm not sitting around thinking about how you made it bad.

Today's a perfect example. I did everything I wanted to do. I hung out with Amanda and Jordan, went swimming, cooked a gourmet meal for my family, caught up on all my homework. Normally on a three-day weekend like this—it's Presidents' Day tomorrow—I'd spread my homework out a little more and watch some TV or go to a movie or something. But I have just one more month of living like a hominin, and I'm going to see it through. Because now that I know what your project's about, I still think I can beat you. And I'm still going to try as hard as I can.

And here's the other thing, Matt: I know you're probably home today wondering what I'm thinking. You made that grand gesture last night, and today you haven't heard from me at all. You don't realize I can't use the phone, and I wouldn't use it anyway, because this isn't something you handle in a phone call. And so I caught up on all my homework today and cooked ahead, because I want tomorrow to be free. I have things to do, Matt, and you're part of that. So you go ahead and wonder what I'm thinking. Because I know something you don't know.

And I still know where you live.

82

Day 180, Monday, February 16

Breakfast: Nothing yet. We'll have to see how it goes.

It was only fair. He showed up when I was in my pajamas.

His sister, Gracie, answered the door. I wasn't sure she'd remember me—or recognize me the way I am.

She smiled. "No way."

It took a good ten minutes for her to look me over and question me. I told her all I had to do was give up chocolate, and the rest just melted away. She might have believed me. She's only twelve.

"Are you going to surprise him?" Gracie asked. "You should just go in there. Scare him."

That used to be one of Gracie's and my tricks. We'd hide in closets or behind shower curtains and try to scare each other. I was really good at that. The best was when I folded myself into the nook between their washing machine and the shelf above it. Gracie opened the laundry cabinet, screamed, and wet her pants.

She loved me.

"No, you should probably tell him I'm here," I said, being the mature one. Besides, I wasn't sure I wanted to know what Matt's room looks like these days. He always was a slob.

Gracie went off to scare her brother on her own, and I waited in the kitchen. No one else seemed to be around. His parents must not have had the day off from work.

I heard the water running in the hall bathroom and the sound of Matt brushing his teeth. A few minutes later he emerged.

Looking . . . it's hard to even describe it. Looking like a little boy, in a way. The little boy he used to be, except now he had the stubble of a beard. There's something about seeing people when they just wake up—before they have a chance to put on the face they show everyone else. There's like this last little hint of innocence.

He ran his hand through his serious bed-head hair. "Hey."

Not, "What are you doing here?" or any other obvious question. Just "hey," as if he expected me to show up one day out of the blue.

"Want to go out for coffee?" I asked.

"Sure."

It didn't take him long to get dressed. Why would it? Guys can just throw on shoes and they're ready.

Gracie grinned as we left. Kind of sweet.

"Can we walk?" I asked. No reason to call on one of my exceptions. It was beautiful out this morning—cold and sunny. I can take any temperature, as long as the sun is out.

The bagel place is about eight blocks from Matt's house. I didn't go at my usual race-walk pace. We both took our time.

"You never finished telling me your story," I said. "About what happened with your internship. And what your project's about."

Matt turned his head just slightly, then went back to looking ahead. "I think you should wait. Science fair's only a month away. I'll show you then."

"I'm not telling you my project," I said.

"I already know what it is."

"No, you don't."

"I saw your picture," he said.

"Don't even try."

We walked along in silence for a while, until it was time to make the turn.

"Hope you brought money," I said. "You're buying."

"This time," Matt agreed.

83

I think he understood. How fragile this morning was, and if he said the wrong thing, it was all going to fall apart.

If he'd asked me, "What gives? Why'd you come over?" or something else stupid like that, I would have bolted.

If he'd said, "So, are we square now? Everything okay?" I would have shaken my head in disgust and gotten up and left.

But Matt is smart. And Matt knows me. Knew me, at least, and I suppose I haven't really changed.

We sat in the bagel place drinking coffee (at least he did) and eating bagels (onion for him, with salmon cream cheese, gross; whole grain for me, nothing on it), and we didn't really say all that much. The conversation was in the fact that we were both there. My coming over this morning was a whole lengthy monologue, if he wanted to translate it, and his saying, "Sure," when I asked him to come with me was as good as a five-page speech.

I thought it might feel awkward, but it didn't. And I think the reason is I just let it all fall away. I think maybe it could always have been this way, no different at all from how we had been when we were thirteen, and the only thing that would have happened in the last four years is we would have become even more comfortable with each other, the way I've finally started feeling comfortable around my little brother. It takes the same boring dailiness of being around someone to really know him and feel all right about him knowing you. I think maybe if I'd never overheard Matt, we would have been right there at that bagel shop this morning, doing exactly what we were.

Except I probably would have still been fat.

Or maybe not. I've been thinking about it all weekend. Amanda made that comment about me losing the weight for Matt, but I strongly disagree. Because I know in my heart I didn't lose it for anyone but myself. I did it because I wanted to win the science fair, get an A in Mr. Fizer's, and finally look good for once in my life. For me. Not for anyone else. I'm a hundred percent certain of that.

Okay, and to beat Matt, too. But that's not the same as losing weight for him.

And I have to admit that my looking better changed things today—for me. Because maybe if I'd been sitting there in my old body, feeling fat and self-conscious, I might not have had the guts to imagine the possibilities. Even if what Matt said on Valentine's was true—that he never cared how I looked—I cared. I cared from the minute Willie Martin called me "Fat Cat," and I probably cared before then, too.

So what would my life have been like? If I hadn't lost the weight?

I'd still be Matt's fat friend. And I'd still be in love with him. I wouldn't tell him—I'd just suffer in silence. I'd watch while he dated other girls, and I'd let him tell me about them because I was his pal. His fat platonic friend.

But what if Matt really didn't care how I looked? Is it possible he might have learned to love me, exactly as I was? I suppose, although it's hard for me to imagine. Not because of Matt, but because of me.

I think I've really hated myself these last four years. I've finally started to see that. I've been blaming Matt for how miserable I've been, when really it's all on me. I'm the one who's doled out all these secret punishments over the years. I'm the one who's been mean.

I'm the one who deprived myself of swimming—no one else took that away. Even if I never went back to the team, I could have swum somewhere else. I could have given myself that gift.

I'm the one who fed myself all that garbage and junk food, then hated what my body had become. I could have stopped at any point—I didn't need a science project to force me.

I'm the one who swallowed my anger toward Matt and never just confronted him with what I'd heard. Maybe he would have apologized four years ago. Or three. Or anytime before now. Instead I guarded it like a treasure and hated him every day.

And yet I'm also the one who held on to the dream of the two of us—this fantasy of what could have been if only I'd been a skinny little thirteen-year-old. Then he would have loved me. Then he never would have said such horrible things about me. Then I'd be happy.

I was wrong. I could have been happy anyway. I just refused to let myself.

All this looking backward only hurts me. Jordan is right: I have to go forward. I can decide for myself right now what I want my relationship with Matt to be. He's paid his debt. Now it's up to me.

I can decide never to forgive him, never to enjoy his friendship again, or I can let it go. It doesn't mean it never happened or that it didn't hurt me or it wasn't wrong, it just means I get to decide right now, today, whether I want to carry this burden another mile. I'm not betraying myself if I just leave it on the side of the road. I'm doing myself the kindness of lightening my load. It's like taking your thumb off a bruise.

"Want to go?" I asked when we had both finished eating and Matt had downed the last of his coffee.

"Sure."

We took the long way home. Walked ten or more extra blocks. I could have walked twenty more. The morning was beautiful, and I was content.

"What are you doing tonight?" Matt asked me at some point.

"Homework."

"Want to go to a movie?"

"Can't." I saw no reason to say why. "Want to hang out?"

"Sure," he said.

I smiled and kept on walking.

When we got back to Matt's house, I told him I had some stuff to do. I left him in front of his house and kept walking back to mine. We didn't set a time, didn't talk about any of the details. Because this was us again, and there was no need for all that.

I did what I wanted to do. I swam, cooked myself lunch, put in some hours at Poison Control. And finally around five-thirty I strolled back to Matt's house.

As soon as I walked in, he asked me what I wanted to eat and I told him Ethiopian. Amanda turned me on to this great vegetarian platter they serve there. Matt ordered takeout and we drove over to get it.

When we got back his parents were home, and after a few obligatory, "How you been's," Matt and I retreated to his room. It wasn't so bad—he'd obviously picked up a little, since his clothes were piled in a corner instead of strewn all over the room. I noticed he'd also showered and shaved.

We settled onto the floor, takeout containers between us, and shoveled in a few bites. He clicked on his TV and I said, "No TV," and he clicked it back off.

And this time when our eyes met, I didn't look away. And when his gaze softened, I smiled. This time when I knew what was coming next, I let what could happen, happen.

He pushed aside the takeout and gathered me in his arms and gave me the kiss I've waited for for a lifetime. I wove my fingers into his hair and felt his smooth face against my chin and breathed in the smell of him that I remembered.

It wasn't like Nick. It wasn't like Greg. It wasn't like anything but what I've always hoped for. No, it was better than that. Because we were older, not kids. This was real in a way the little girl in me never could have imagined.

They say your muscles have memory. Once you've trained your arms to swing a tennis racket or your legs to ride a bike, you can quit for a while—for years, even—and all it takes is picking up a racket or jumping on a bike again and your muscles remember what to do. They snap right back to performing the way you taught them.

The heart is a muscle, too. And I've been training mine since I was a kid to fall in love with one particular person.

All it took was four years, a rainy day at the zoo, a box of choco-lates, a crumpled valentine, a sincere apology, and an order of spicy lentils, and my heart snapped right back into form. It knew just what to do.

I am still in love with Matt McKinney.

And Matt McKinney told me he loves me, too.

84

Day 207, Sunday, March 15

Done.

Everything should be made as simple as possible, but not simpler.

I simply want to win.

Not for the reasons I did before, but just because it's time. If you're going to keep competing at something every year, you need to bring home first place once in a while, just to keep your spirits up. People can only take disappointment for so long.

Tomorrow we'll set up our displays. I've got my abstract, my research notebook, my project board.

Amanda helped me with the board this weekend. I needed her artistic eye. The board is three-sided, just like the map I wore for Halloween. Bigger, though—enough to partition off my area so when you're standing in front of it, you can't see anyone's project but mine.

"I was thinking some before and after pictures," I said.

"Excellent," Amanda said. "We have to find one where you're really your heaviest. Then that one they took at the Winter Formal. Hot."

I winced a little to remember that night, but Amanda was right—the contrast was too great. She had made me look like a movie star for that, and even though I'm smaller now than I was then, she really did show me at my best.

We also used the picture she took of me in the skirt and boots— the outfit I wore to the zoo. That seems like so long ago.

Matt and I agreed not to see each other this weekend. We're both in last-minute mode, trying to get our displays as perfect as we can. We still haven't told each other what we're doing. I like it that way.

I thought it might feel weird to compete against him, after what's happened lately, but I realize it didn't make me uncomfortable when I was younger, and it still doesn't. What's made it so intense these past four years is that I wanted to beat him so bad. It's been my main goal—more so than even winning for its own sake. It's taken some of the joy out of it, I think.

I still want to win. Badly. But I don't think I care if I beat Matt. Obviously if I win other people won't, but I don't need one of those people to be Matt anymore. If that makes any sense.

We're competing in different categories—I'm in Behavioral & Social, he's in Physics & Astronomy—but besides winning our categories, we still have to win overall. There are just three slots to go to internationals—one for a team, two for individuals. I plan on winning one of those spots.

Amanda worked with me on my project board most of yesterday and today, and I have to say it shows. My best friend is the most artistic, talented person I know. She could make a clump of dirt look like a pile of gold.

"A poem," Amanda said when we were through. "From Kit Cat's project board."

I think she made it up on the fly.

"Tomorrow she will leave me in the cavernous hall
Among other, more pitiful boards.
The judges will see me, they will love me, they will need me
And shower me with all of their awards.
But Catherine will forget me, she will fold me away
And go on to more glorious pursuits.
But I will e'er remember, because it's pasted on my chest
How hot she looked in that wicked skirt and boots."

How could you not love a friend like that?

85

They let us start setting up our displays at noon. Mr. Fizer didn't hold class today, but told us to meet at the convention center instead. I caught a ride with Matt.

I kept my board carefully folded as I loaded it into his car. Matt's was folded up, too, so I couldn't read it. It's stupid how secretive we were, since we were going to see them anyway in about an hour, but somehow we both wanted to keep the mystery.

Once we got there we found our separate sections and both went off to work. It only took me about fifteen minutes to make everything look the way I wanted it to. Then there was nothing more to do until tomorrow.

Here's the schedule: Monday is setup, Tuesday is judging. The younger kids like Peter are judged just on their displays, but at the high school level we have to do presentations for the judges, too. Tomorrow. And then we won't find out who's won until Friday. So basically it's a whole week of agony.

Once people finished setting up, we all started cruising the place, snooping around each other's projects.

Nick's was a study of lichen and fungi. I still have no idea how "cat's gill" factors in. Alyssa studied some rare eye disease. Kiona did hers on aphids. Lindsay analyzed how climate change affects the caterpillar population. Lots of plants and insects this year. My fig wasps would have fit right in.

And then finally I saw Matt's.

COMMUNICATION BEGINS AT HOME

Why do we believe we will be able to communicate with alien species who share none of our DNA, when we can barely communicate with species who share over 97 percent of it?

Right beneath that was the picture of the baby gorilla. And on either side, pictures of other apes—gibbons, chimpanzees, orangutans.

And other pictures: Matt in front of the gibbon cage, doing some sort of hand signals to them. Matt at the back door of the enclosure, helping one of the zookeepers feed them. Matt standing right up against the chain link, one of the gibbons' fingers intertwined with his.

"You learned to communicate with them?" I asked.

"Not really. I'm still trying. It's not as easy as it looks."

I flipped through his research notebook—day after day spent at the zoo, trying this strategy and that. He included all sorts of clippings and scientific studies about the efforts made to bridge the human-ape gap. Matt was trying to take things another step beyond.

He also included graphs and other details about the amount of

money and manpower spent trying to communicate with alien creatures, including the project he'd interned for over the summer.

"I can't believe you did all this."

"You like it?" he asked.

"I love it, but . . ."

Matt smiled. "Say it."

"You entered this in Astronomy. Why? It could have been in Animal Sciences. Don't you think the Astronomy judges—"

"Are going to hate it?" he finished for me. "Yeah. I think they
will."

"Then why?"

"Because I'm done with all this."

"All what?" I asked.

He waved his hand around the conference hall. "This. The science fair. The competition. I just want to do science, Cat. I want to
investigate things I'm curious about without worrying whether I'm
impressing anyone. And I don't want to be stuck with astronomy
anymore. I'm tired of it."

This from someone who has been staring through telescopes
since he could focus his little eyes. This from the guy who could talk
about black holes and galaxies and quasars until even I, in my devoted girlish state, couldn't take listening to a word of it anymore.

"You don't really mean that."

"Yeah," he said, "I do."

"Why? Just because that one professor was a pig?"

"No, he proved to me what I already knew—that I'm not that interested in it anymore. It sort of ran its course."

It was as if Amanda had told me she was tired of words.

Matt smiled and wrapped his arms around my waist. "Don't look
so serious. It's fine. I worked on something this year that I thought

would be interesting, and it was. I know I'm not going to win any-thing for it, and I don't care."

"You might win," I said, knowing it probably wasn't true.

"It doesn't matter, Cat. Really. I wouldn't have even entered the science fair this year if Mr. Fizer didn't require it."

"But you knew that's the only thing his class was about—that's the whole point of it. Why did you even take it in the first place?"

Matt brought his lips against my ear. "Because I knew you'd be in there."

86

The group of judges finally reached me.

"Miss Locke?"

"Yes, ma'am." I cleared my throat and nervously began my presentation.

"My research project shows the potential evolutionary shift in modern human anatomy and biology as the result of dramatic changes in the quality of our food supply. As part of my research I conducted a thorough analysis of the various factors impacting the health of both modern humans and our ancestors, beginning with *Homo erectus*. I focused on the impact of environmental, nutritional, behavioral, and technological aspects of the differing lifestyles, and in addition used myself as a test subject to determine the effects of returning to some of the habits of our early ancestors. For 207 days . . ."

Amanda and I had shopped for today's outfit: slim black pants, my black boots, a lavender V-necked sweater. And a bomb-proof, yet feminine bra—Joyce's finest work yet.

Makeup, of course, and hair straightened, then curled. With electric curlers. Hurray for modern times.

I gave just a short speech, highlighting some of the features of my project. Then the judges asked me questions: What did I feel I learned; do I think the current state of human health is an actual evolutionary shift or merely a temporary condition; what kinds of food did I conclude we should be eating; what was the hardest part of the project for me?

"I'd have to say giving up technology," I answered to the last one. "On the one hand, my life was a lot quieter and more peaceful without all that constant noise and distraction. And I had a lot more free time, since I couldn't watch TV or zone out on the computer. But there are definitely times when you want to be able to use a cell phone or drive your car someplace."

"Do you think this project has changed you?" the woman judge asked. "Beyond the obvious physical changes?"

I smiled. "You have no idea how much."

And then it was over. The judges thanked me and moved on to the next display. I leaned back against my table and tried to breathe normally again.

When I saw Jackie last week, I tried out my presentation on her. And when I was done, she asked me the same thing I had asked her before: whether I thought Einstein's theory about how to save the human race was true.

"I don't know," I said. "It might be."

I'm not sure if I can speak for the whole human race yet, but I know I can speak for me. And what's true for me is that eating like Einstein and da Vinci and Newton and Dr. Brian Greene feels like the right thing to do. I like walking the road they walked. And my body likes it, too.

Although I told Jackie when this project is over, I wouldn't mind being a junk food vegetarian for a while. Maybe just a couple of days every now and then.

Even Amanda said she's happy eating just vegetarian food.

"Kit Cat, if you told me from now on you're only making things out of Bermuda grass, I'd eat it because I know you'd make it delicious."

"Really?"

"Yeah. So only use your powers for good."

After a few minutes I wandered over to where I could see what was happening with Matt. The judges still hadn't reached him yet. I caught his eye and gave him a smile.

I still can't get over everything he told me yesterday—about not caring about the competition anymore. I thought I knew him.

What really struck me is how futile this whole thing would have been if I were still trying to win just to beat him. Where's the glory in that if your opponent doesn't even care? So much has changed in the last month, it's almost hard to remember how desperately I wanted to grind Matt into the dirt at the beginning of the school year. It's like he and I were both different people back then.

Okay, maybe it was just me.

I went over to the kids' area to look at Peter's project again. Amanda gave him a little bit of her magic, too, and his board turned out great. He did all the cutting and pasting, but it was Amanda's idea to use different fonts and colors and scalloped borders. Not the kind of thing an eleven-year-old boy thinks of.

I looked for Trina's project, too. And I really tried to hold myself back—for Peter's sake. If he likes her, despite all her obvious flaws, I guess I should try to be fair. And who knows? Maybe someday she'll confess what a huge crush she had on him when they were in fifth grade. Could happen, I suppose.

So there was her board, all girly and decorated: *What Makes Flowers Grow?* She and two other girls tested a bunch of different additives to water to see which kept cut flowers looking fresher longer—not a bad experiment, I guess, although technically the flowers weren't going to "grow" anymore, since they were already cut. But I decided to overlook that.

They tried aspirin, ibuprofen, 7UP, Gatorade, and Red Bull. And still nothing was as good as plain water. Kind of like the experiment I did on my own body, in a way.

I left the kid area and went back to the high school zone. The Astronomy judges were finally at Matt's table. I wished I could have gone over and eavesdropped. At least Matt looked like he was enjoying himself.

"What did they ask you?" I said afterward as we headed out to his car.

"It was weird," he said. "All they wanted to talk about was you."

"Shut up." I bumped him with my hip. He wrapped his arm around my waist to hold me there.

"I hope you win, Cat."

"I hope so, too."

87

I didn't win.

Margo, who put together a whole program for teaching autistic children to better understand the facial cues of people they were talking to, won first place.

And some guy who did his project on how people talk when they're on their cell phones, versus how they talk to each other in person, won second.

And I got nothing.

I went up to Margo after the ceremony and gave her a big hug. Because at least it was one of us.

"Let's go somewhere," Amanda said. She and I had both taken the night off of work. "Let's go somewhere where everything is completely mechanized—somewhere you're not even allowed to scratch your own nose. Reintroduce Cat to the world of technology."

"Sharpy's," Jordan suggested, and we went there instead.

Over the sound of people cheering the basketball game on TV, the four of us did our best to analyze the competition.

None of us could really deny that Margo deserved first place. But Amanda just couldn't accept the guy who won second place. "Were the judges on crack? Did somebody pay them off?"

We ate our veggie fajitas and let her rant away.

"That project was completely pedestrian! Totally lame! What did he do—sit around the mall all day listening in on people's conversations? Big deal! You gave up *cookies*! And caffeine! And bubble baths! And movies!"

"You gave up bubble baths?" Matt murmured. I squeezed his hand under the table.

"And what's with Petey only getting second?" Amanda continued. "That project was *golden*! He was robbed!"

And all I could think was, *This is nice*.

Nice to be a foursome, for once, instead of me always being the third wheel.

Nice to be holding my boyfriend's hand under the table while we listened to Amanda carry on. Nice that I had tortilla chips for the first time in seven months, along with Sharpy's extra-hot gut-incinerating jalapeño salsa, which I may regret in the morning. Nice that Matt and Jordan like each other, so it's comfortable for all of us to hang around. And nice that even though I didn't win this year, the sky didn't fall and I wasn't sitting there all depressed.

Nothing to be depressed about.

We split up in the parking lot, Amanda still fuming over the injustice of it all, and when Matt and I finally shut ourselves into his car, we both took a minute to breathe.

"Are you upset?" Matt asked.

"No," I answered truthfully, "are you?" His project, like mine, hadn't even placed.

"Nope." He started the car and turned up the heater.

I jumped at the sound of Amanda knocking on my window. I rolled it down.

"I forgot to tell you," she said. "You looked absolutely gorgeous tonight. Not everyone gets to be both smart *and* beautiful, you know. I mean, Margo's pretty and all, but YOU—" She looked to Matt for confirmation.

"Smart and beautiful," he agreed. "I'm a lucky guy."

"Okay, then. Don't forget it." Amanda pinched my cheek, then ran back to Jordan's car.

"Subtle," Matt said. I tried not to laugh.

Instead I leaned back against the headrest, closed my eyes, and let out a small groan. "I am so tired. Can we please just go back to your house for a while?"

"Watch some TV?" Matt asked.

I smiled and opened one eye. "No TV."

Which turns out to be our signal that Matt McKinney should kiss me again.

Acknowledgments

As if any of us can write our books alone.

I wouldn't have been able to write more than fifty words of this one without the valuable contributions of a variety of scientists, writers, teachers, editors, and other brilliant people. Turns out this story had a lot of moving parts, and I could only pound on a few of them to make them work all by myself.

So let me thank the following people for all their assistance, advice, and efforts on behalf of this book:

My glorious editor, Michelle Frey, for always pushing me to go deeper, higher, further, stronger, truer. Thank you for all your wonderful ideas for this book, and for giving me the freedom to fix what needed fixing in my own way and time. With every line, every scene, every story we work on together, you are making me a better writer. I couldn't be more grateful.

Associate editor Michele Burke, for your valuable insights into food, romance, and other vital elements of this book. Thank you for not letting me off the hook until you thought I got it right.

The rest of the Knopf/Random House team, including but not limited to fellow foodie and all-around VP of Fun Nancy Hinkel; publicists extraordinaire Noreen Marchisi and Meg O'Brien; the ever-classy Tracy Lerner; sharp-eyed, sharp-brained copy editors Karen Taschek and Alison Kolani and proofreader Diana Varvara; and the designer of this gorgeous cover, Stephanie Moss.

Carolyn Sweeney, who, besides my editor, was the single biggest influence on the creation, continuation, and completion of this book. Thank you a million times over for your encouragement and advice all the way through. You have no idea how instrumental you were in getting this story done.

Science teacher Margaret Wilch and her class of geniuses, specifically Joe Fisher, Lindsay Liebson, Margo Johnson, Kiona Brown, Alyssa Ashley, Alexandra Lombard, and Farah Chatila. Thank you all for letting me pick your brains!

My food and nutrition gurus, Jacalyn Elder, RD; Amy J. Lanou, PhD; and Amy Armstrong Wilke, JD. Needless to say (but I'll say it), any mistakes herein are mine, not theirs.

Authors Barbara Kingsolver, Michael Pollan, Dr. John A. McDougall, T. Colin Campbell and Thomas M. Campbell II, Annemarie Colbin, Brendan Brazier, and Colleen Patrick-Goudreau for making me *really* think about food. And for ultimately changing my ways as I worked through the writing of this book.

Emily Baade for patiently trying to teach me calculus. Thanks for the attempt, but I'm such an English major. (So are you, but we're not all so multitalented.)

Michele Meadows for keeping the writing equipment in top working order.

American Sign Language teacher Sarah Tomassetti and her students, especially Sara and Nancy, for helping me learn some of that beautiful language.

My author pal Barry Lyga for once again playing the role of first editor. Your wise advice always helps me sand off the rough edges.

My agent, Laura Rennert, for all her superb advice and hard work. Thank you always!

My niece, Amanda, and nephew, Matthew, for creating the at-home café that I totally stole for this book.

And last but never least, my husband, John, for support of every kind. Thank you for everything you are and everything you do. xxoo

For Further Reading

Campbell, T. Colin, and Thomas M. Campbell II. *The China Study*. Dallas: BenBella Books, 2006.

Colbin, Annemarie. *Food and Healing*. 10th anniversary ed. New York: Ballantine Books, 1986.

Kingsolver, Barbara. *Animal, Vegetable, Miracle: A Year of Food Life*. With Steven L. Hopp and Camille Kingsolver. New York: HarperCollins Publishers, 2007.

McDougall, John A. *The McDougall Program: 12 Days to Dynamic Health*. With recipes by Mary McDougall. New York: NAL Books, 1990.

Pollan, Michael. *In Defense of Food: An Eater's Manifesto*. New York: Penguin Press, 2008.

www.compassionatecooks.com

www.goveg.com

A CONVERSATION WITH ROBIN BRANDE

What inspired you to write *Fat Cat*?

Toward the end of high school and all through college, I was very overweight and very unhappy about it. Which only made me eat more because I was so depressed. Then I'd see some crazy diet in a magazine—"Eat Brussels sprouts and toast for a week! Lose 10 pounds!"—and I'd try that, but the diets were always horrible for you and never really worked. So after a few days of suffering, I'd run right back to my cookies and ice cream and Big Macs, and things went on like that for a long time.

Eventually I realized I could feel a whole lot better if I exercised and stopped eating everything in the world, and so things settled down over time. But I think once you've been overweight, there's always a part of your brain that's secretly still focused on food and eating and body image. At least that's how it's been for me.

So one day when I was doing research for my first novel, *Evolution, Me & Other Freaks of Nature*, I came across this illustration in *National Geographic* of a cavewoman and some cavemen, all of them naked and very fit-looking. And my first thought when I saw the woman was "Wow, look how strong and athletic she looks—that's so cool." And my second thought was "I wonder what she ate back then and how much exercise she got to look like that." Which, let's admit, is a weird thing to think about an illustration, but then I thought,

"What if I wrote a whole story about a girl who just had the same reaction I did?" And *ta-da*, a book was born. I love it when it happens like that.

How did you get the idea for the drawing on the first day of Mr. Fizer's class?

I love shows like *Project Runway* and *Top Chef*—anything where a bunch of creative people have to come up with ideas on the spot and then produce something in a very short time. Like having to make an evening gown out of wrapping paper or a gourmet meal out of ramen noodles and pie dough—that sort of thing.

So I thought it would be fun to have a science class like that, where people picked a picture at random and had to come up with a science fair project off the top of their heads. I hope some science teacher out there is trying it!

How much research did you have to do before you wrote the book?

A LOT. But I love the research phase of all of my books, so it was really just a fun excuse to read everything I could about food and nutrition and ancient diets and all of that. I've listed some of the books under the "For Further Reading" section, but I read many, many more. Research is one of my favorite parts of being a writer.

But I didn't just read about it, I lived it. I decided to put myself through the same seven-month experiment Cat went through so I'd know how to write about it realistically. Many of her diary entries are actually mine!

What was the hardest thing for you to give up?

Oh, definitely coffee. And sugar—my little friend sugar. Sigh. So sad when that had to go.

But once the initial withdrawals wore off, it was amazing how much better I felt eating just fresh, simple foods. I was also really surprised how easy it was to stop eating meat and dairy and eggs. My body really loved the whole switchover to a plant-based diet—just beans, greens, grains, and fruit. It was a good and healthy change for me, and I've made it permanent.

The other change was I went back to cooking—something I used to love, but sort of got lazy about and stopped doing so much. But if Cat had to cook everything from scratch, so did I. It turned out to be fun trying out new recipes all the time and even making up some of my own. Yes, it takes a little time to cook for yourself, but it's so worth it when you taste the results.

Do you still not drink coffee or eat any sugar?

Um, next question.

How did you come up with the character of Amanda, Cat's best friend?

Oh, how I loved writing Amanda. She's my favorite best friend EVER.

I based her in large part on my own best friend, whom I met my sophomore year in high school. She's still my best friend these many, many years later. And yes, she is exactly as loyal and funny and talented and exceptional as Amanda is.

The character is also based on my niece Amanda—especially the way she looks and the way she dresses. And the real Amanda is the one who gave me the idea for the at-home café Cat runs with her little brother. Because one summer my niece did exactly that with her own little brother, my nephew Matt.

Wait—Matt, Amanda—are there any other characters named after people you know?

Often. Frequently. Okay, usually.

Why would you be a writer if you couldn't do things like that?

When you write a book, do you know how it's going to end?

Hardly ever. I usually don't know what's going to happen in a story until I see it on the page—like watching a movie unfold in front of me. I love it when I'm surprised—when something I've just typed makes me laugh out loud or cry. I probably wouldn't have that experience if I knew everything that was coming.

What were some of the surprises for you with *Fat Cat*?

I had no idea Cat and Amanda would crack me up so much when they were together. Their scenes were always a delight to write. I also didn't know there'd be a Karmic Café, or that Cat would end up having such a sweet relationship with her little brother, Peter. And I had no idea that Nick would have such a big role or be such a hottie. He was a *lot* of fun to write.

But the biggest surprise—one that I kept waiting and waiting for—was how Matt was ever going to make up for what he'd done. I just didn't see what he could say or do that would ever make Cat forgive him.

She did hold that grudge for an awfully long time.

Dude, Cat is an amateur grudge-holder as far as I'm concerned. I could have held that grudge much, much longer. Well, maybe not if Matt had shown up like he did and said what he said. But if not for that, he'd still be getting the silent treatment when he was eighty.

So how did you finally come up with Matt's apology?

It took me forever. And then finally one day there it was, right in front of me, and it just felt like . . . yes, okay, that would do it. Not only would she want to forgive him, but she'd probably also have to fall in love with him. Again. Still. Siiiiigh.

Do you ever get crushes on the guys you write about in your books?

Every time. Always. Why—do you think that's weird?

Cough Next question. What are you working on now?

I'm having a great time writing a very complicated tale involving quantum physics, string theory, parallel universes, extra dimensions—and romance, of course.

Your books always seem to feature science. Did you love science when you were in school?

Um, no, I believe the word is *hated*. I never felt I was good at it, which in turn made me not interested in it. It was kind of one of those "You can't break up with me; I'm breaking up with you!" things.

But now that no one is grading me or telling me which science to learn and in which order, I *love* it. Can't get enough of it. The natural world is fascinating, and there's always so much more to understand about it. So as long as I keep writing books that involve science, I have the perfect excuse to spend hours and hours studying all the things I'm interested in.

But don't tell anybody. I like people to think I'm working.

VEGETABLE SWEET POTATO CHOWDER

(used with permission of Mary McDougall)

I make this soup at least once a month—it's like salad in my soup bowl!

3 cups frozen corn kernels
½ cup diced carrot
½ cup diced celery
½ cup diced onion
½ cup diced sweet potato
½ cup diced tomato
¼ cup diced green bell pepper
¼ cup diced red bell pepper
1½ quarts vegetable stock or water (that's 6 cups)
1 tablespoon soy sauce
½ teaspoon Tabasco (optional)
¼ teaspoon ground pepper
½ teaspoon dried thyme
2 bay leaves (be sure to take these out after cooking—
    choking hazard!)
¼ cup cornstarch mixed in ¼ cup cold water
1 cup chopped fresh kale

Place the vegetables and stock or water in a large soup pot. Add the soy sauce and other seasonings. Bring to a boil, reduce the heat, cover, and simmer for about 45 minutes. Add the cornstarch mixture (slowly, a little bit at a time so it dissolves rather than clumps up) while stirring. Add the kale, stir, and cook another 5 minutes.

SPICY BLACK-BEAN BURGERS

(from *The Vegan Table* by Colleen Patrick-Goudreau,
used with permission of Colleen Patrick-Goudreau)

Depending on how much heat you prefer, you can make these burg—
ers super-spicy or mild. Leave out the jalapeño if you prefer them on
the mild side. Warning: be very careful when dealing with jalapeños—
especially the interior ribs, which hold all the heat. Use gloves when you
slice them, or be sure to wash your hands thoroughly after handling,
and don't touch your eyes or mouth or anything sensitive until you do!
Your body will thank you.

¼ cup all-purpose, unbleached flour
¼ cup coarse cornmeal
Olive or canola oil, for sautéing
   (approximately 1 tablespoon)
1 yellow onion, diced
1 small jalapeño pepper, minced (seeds removed)
1 red bell pepper, diced
2 cloves garlic, minced
½ teaspoon dried oregano
2 cups cooked or canned black beans, drained and rinsed
½ cup canned or frozen corn kernels
½ cup bread crumbs
2 teaspoons chili powder
¼ teaspoon cumin
½ teaspoon salt
2 tablespoons fresh parsley, minced

On a shallow plate, combine the flour and cornmeal, and set aside for coating later.

In a saucepan over medium heat, heat the oil and sauté the onion, jalapeño (optional), red pepper, garlic, and oregano until the onion becomes translucent. Set aside.

In a large bowl, mash the black beans with a potato masher or fork. Stir in the onion/pepper mixture, along with the corn, bread crumbs, chili powder, cumin, salt, and parsley. Mix well.

Shape into patties. Coat each with the flour/cornmeal mixture.

Fry in a lightly oiled sauté pan over medium heat 5–10 minutes, or until browned on both sides. You need very little oil, if any at all, when using a nonstick pan.

SWEET POTATO AND/OR BUTTERNUT SQUASH FRIES

(used with permission of Mary McDougall)

You can use 2 sweet potatoes or 1 butternut squash, or any combination you like. (Hint: If you're making the Vegetable Sweet Potato Chowder on p. 337, you can use the leftover sweet potato for this.) These fries are beautiful to look at, and sweet and tasty to eat!

Preheat oven to 425 degrees.

Peel the sweet potatoes, or if using butternut squash, peel it and remove the seeds. Cut into French fry shapes. (They cook best if you make them fairly large, like home fries.) Place on a nonstick baking sheet in a single layer. Sprinkle with salt, if desired. Bake 15–20 minutes, then flip over and bake for another 15 minutes. The fries should get lightly brown and crispy but still be a bit soft in the center. Delicious!

HOMEMADE HUMMUS

(from *The Vegan Table* by Colleen Patrick-Goudreau,
used with permission of Colleen Patrick-Goudreau)

Okay, so if you made this the Cat way, you wouldn't use a food processor, which means you'd have really strong biceps by the end of all the mashing and stirring. But you can do it! Or we'll look the other way while you bust out the appliance. Remember, you're not actually competing in the science fair. Or are you?

2 cans (15 ounces each) chickpeas
    (also known as garbanzo beans), drained and rinsed
Juice from ½ lemon
    (or from a whole lemon, if you like that tangy taste)
2 tablespoons tahini (sesame seed butter)
2 or 3 whole garlic cloves, peeled
    (or more garlic, if you love *that* taste)
½ teaspoon cumin
Water for thinning out spread (about ¼ cup to start)
Salt, to taste
Paprika, for garnish (optional)

Place the chickpeas in a food processor or blender with the lemon juice, tahini, garlic, and cumin. Process until very smooth, 1–2 minutes. Add a little water to thin out, if desired. (Start with just a little, and add a bit at a time until you reach the consistency you like. Remember, it's easy to overdo the liquid, and hard to undo!) Add salt to taste. Scrape into a serving bowl and sprinkle with paprika if you'd like to fancy it up with some color.

Great on bagels or pitas, or as a dip for vegetables such as tomatoes, cucumbers, carrots, or celery. Also fantastic with tortilla chips.

You can build a great veggie sandwich by toasting a bagel ("everything"-flavored bagels are perfect for this), spreading hummus on both sides, then adding lettuce, sliced tomatoes, and sliced cucumbers. Slap the bagel halves together, cut in half—a huge, filling meal with so much goodness inside.

Or if you really want a treat, use the hummus for No-Queso Quesadillas on the next page.

NO-QUESO QUESADILLAS

(from *The Vegan Table* by Colleen Patrick-Goudreau,
used with permission of Colleen Patrick-Goudreau)

Great party food, great studying food, great to share with friends. This recipe makes 4 whole quesadillas, so if you just want one as a personal snack of your own, reduce all the ingredients accordingly.

about 2–3 cups—depending on how thick you want to
    slather it—Homemade Hummus (p. 341)
8 (10-inch) flour tortillas
    (corn are fine, too, but they're usually smaller)
½ cup chopped scallion (green onions)
½ to 1 cup salsa
pinto or black beans (optional)
avocado (optional)

Spread 3 heaping tablespoons hummus on a tortilla and place (hummus side up) in a large-size nonstick skillet over medium heat.

Sprinkle with chopped scallion and spread on a thin layer of salsa.

Top with a second tortilla, and cook until the bottom tortilla is warm and turning golden brown, 3–5 minutes. Turn over and cook the second side for another few minutes, until golden brown. (This process becomes a lot quicker once the pan is hot, so stay close to the stove! The first one always takes the longest because the pan isn't totally hot.) Either cut in half or into pizza-shaped triangles to serve as finger food. Repeat with the remaining tortillas.

Alternatively, spread hummus on half of a tortilla, place the tortilla in the pan, add other toppings to the hummus in a thin layer, and fold the empty half on top of the filled side. (Just be careful not to overload it, which makes it too difficult to flip.) Let the tortilla get golden brown on the bottom, then carefully turn over to brown the other side. Remove from the pan and serve hot.

To make the quesadilla extra fancy, spoon a little salsa on top and add some chopped avocado before serving. And if you want to make it a little heartier, add pinto or black beans inside with the hummus and salsa and scallion. Yum!

BANANA CHOCOLATE CHIP MUFFINS

(from *The Joy of Vegan Baking* by Colleen Patrick-Goudreau,
used with permission of Colleen Patrick-Goudreau)

These muffins are totally worthy of the Karmic Café! You can make them as muffins or as a loaf of Banana Chocolate Chip Bread. Perfect to bring to a party? You bet. Or just have your best friend over and use it as study fuel. So delish!

2 cups unbleached all-purpose flour
1½ teaspoons baking soda
½ teaspoon salt
1 cup granulated sugar
⅓ cup canola oil
4 ripe bananas, mashed with a fork or masher
½ cup water
1 teaspoon vanilla extract
1 cup nondairy semisweet chocolate chips
1 cup walnuts (optional)

Preheat the oven to 350 degrees. Lightly grease your muffin tins.

In a medium-size bowl, mix the flour, baking soda, and salt together.

In a large bowl, beat the sugar and oil together, then add the mashed bananas. Stir in the water and vanilla and mix thoroughly. Add the flour mixture, along with the chocolate chips and walnuts (optional), and stir to mix.

Fill each muffin tin halfway with the batter. Bake 20–30 minutes, until they are golden brown and a toothpick inserted into the center comes out clean.

Makes 12 muffins.

If you decide to make this as bread, lightly grease a loaf pan, then spoon in the batter. Bake 40–45 minutes. Check for doneness by inserting a toothpick into the center and looking to see whether it comes out clean.